FOOD FOR THOUGHT

Charlotte couldn't take her gaze from his firm body as he walked over to the glowing coals of last night's fire and laid several logs on them. That majestic body had given her more pleasure than she could ever imagine. She stretched beneath the covers. Her muscles were sore from the new task she had given them, but she felt so . . . She smiled and sighed. So satisfied.

Tyler returned to her. He picked up his clothes and sat on the edge of the couch as the fire licked at the fresh wood as if grateful for its meal.

"I know it is unromantic," he continued, "but I'm starved." He smiled. "For food." His smile widened. "For the body."

"Me, too." Charlotte smiled back.

"I'll give you first dibs on the bathroom." He brushed the hair from her forehead. "It's the least I can give you after the wonderful gift you gave me."

Charlotte hesitated in her shyness to let him see her body. He had traveled over it but he hadn't seen her. She took a deep breath and sat up clutching the quilt to her. She swallowed hard and opened her hands. The quilt formed a puddle around her hips as if she were a gemstone in a display case.

BOOK YOUR PLACE ON OUR WEBSITE AND MAKE THE ARABESQUE ROMANCE CONNECTION!

We've created a customized website just for our very special Arabesque readers, where you can get the inside scoop on everything that's going on with Arabesque romance novels.

When you come online, you'll have the exciting opportunity to:

- View covers of upcoming books

- Learn about our future publishing schedule (listed by publication month and author)

- Find out when your favorite authors will be visiting a city near you

- Search for and order backlist books

- Check out author bios and background information

- Send e-mail to your favorite authors

- Join us in weekly chats with authors, readers and other guests

- Get writing guidelines

- AND MUCH MORE!

Visit our website at
http://www.arabesquebooks.com

SNOWBOUND WITH LOVE

Alice Wootson

ARABESQUE
★BET
BOOKS

BET Publications, LLC
www.msbet.com
www.arabesquebooks.com

ARABESQUE BOOKS are published by

BET Publications, LLC
c/o BET BOOKS
One BET Plaza
1900 W Place NE
Washington, D.C. 20018-1211

First Printing: July, 2000
10 9 8 7 6 5 4 3 2 1

Printed in the United States of America

One

Charlotte shifted her weight from one foot to the other as she waited for the desk clerk to come over. She tightened her fingers around her room key to keep from tapping on the counter.

Finally, the clerk approached her. He frowned as he looked at the key she held out.

"Miss Thompson, are you sure you want to check out now? Maybe you want to wait until the snow stops?"

"They've predicted only three to four inches." Charlotte turned her head toward the picture window. She turned back and tried to match the clerk's smile with one of her own. But she failed as she had failed at so much lately. Too much. Instead, she pulled herself up to her full five-feet-one-inch height, hoping to give the impression that she was sure of what she was doing.

"Miss, it's almost that much snow already." The clerk glanced out the window and then back at her, obviously not impressed by her stance. "We never know how much snow we'll get up here in the Poconos until it's over."

"I think I can make it home all right." It was about two hundred miles, but mostly turnpike traveling. She'd have to drive slower so it would take longer than the three hours it took to come up here, but she could do this. This time, Charlotte didn't try to find another smile to spread across her honey-colored face. She knew she didn't have any more inside. She hadn't had any for a long time.

It wasn't a matter of not wanting to stay longer. She had to leave for home now. It was check-out time, and she couldn't afford another night in this or any other hotel. She breathed in deeply. "I think it's slowing down already, don't you?"

The clerk shrugged, took the key, and gave her a receipt. "Do you at least have a cell phone just in case?"

"I'll be all right."

Charlotte tucked the paper into the outside pocket of her purse. She had had a cell phone until it became a luxury like vacations and fancy restaurants and. . . .

Taking a deep breath, she went out to face the weather.

The wind threw swirling snow at her as if trying to make her change her mind and go back in. She pulled her collar closer around her face. Her boots scraped a path to her car through the already deep snow. She tried to ignore it. Tonight she'd be in her own home, though it would be after dark when she got back. Some might call it early tomorrow, but the time didn't matter to Charlotte, since no one was waiting for her. And she didn't have money to stay there.

She pulled her Geo onto the country road that would take her to the turnpike. The wind became more generous with the snow it was hurling. The middle of January was looking like it was going to be a longer, harder winter.

Hours later, Charlotte peered through the windshield. In normal weather, she'd be in Philadelphia by now and heading for I-476. But this wasn't normal weather.

The road looked like a white velvet blanket, carefully spread, and Charlotte was the only one who dared to disturb it. The rapidly moving wipers tried hard, but they were no match for the snow determined to thicken the cover. She urged her car on, but the snow was covering her trail faster than she could make it.

"I can't fool myself." Charlotte's words wobbled out. She took a deep breath to try to steady herself, and she found the courage to put into words what she was thinking. "It's not going to stop anytime soon." The flakes fell as though someone above still had too much snow and was getting rid of it with a bucket.

Moving at what would be a walking pace in clear weather, but was as fast as she could go now, she continued driving down the road but made a decision. *Forget trying to reach the turnpike and getting home tonight,* she thought to herself. There had to be a motel somewhere close by. She'd worry about what expenses she'd have to cut from next month's budget when she had to.

Charlotte approached a curve hoping to see something after she got around it, but was disappointed. All she could see through the thick covering was two branches in the road. She took a deep breath and followed one. Was this still the main road or had it veered off? She continued on because she didn't have a choice.

Feeling as if she were the only person in the world, Charlotte cut a path through the snow. When she saw a smooth place between cotton-looking bushes backing up to trees with the same covering, she turned off onto another hint of a road. No longer hoping to find a motel, she'd settle for any kind of shelter. There had to be houses along here. Her car crept along as if it were towing a car as big as itself.

Thirty minutes later, the tiny flakes still fell as if they hadn't been at it for hours. The wipers tried to help. They swished, but there was nothing to see beyond the white blanket ahead and covered trees and bushes on both sides.

Charlotte made yet another turn and her car skidded as if skis had replaced the wheels. Where were the houses along this narrow road? Why build a road if there were no houses?

She tried not to think of the horror stories that make the news after any major snowstorm. She tried not to remember

the tales of people stranded in their cars and not found until
it was too late.

Charlotte brushed back a heavy dark curl that had escaped
from the clip at the back of her head. She wiped her forehead, surprised at the sweat forming there.

"Stay calm, Charlotte," she muttered. "You know you've
been through worse than this." Pain painted a frown on her
face. "A lot worse," she whispered. "You can survive this,
too."

She urged the car on.

In the late afternoon, she saw something that let a slight
smile push away the frown that was acting as if it intended
to stay.

"At last." Her worry escaped with the sigh she released
as she eased her car into a turn off the road. A stretch of
clear white stared at her from between wooded sections on
both sides.

A flat surface—she prayed it was a driveway—wound its
way up to a sprawling stone house that blended into the
hills around it, as if nature had made it with rock not needed
for the mountains. The white curtain falling tried to hide
it, but the house was too massive to be hidden by anything.

Charlotte relaxed her fingers on the steering wheel, making
room for the color to find its way back into them. Suddenly,
the car lurched off the road and to the side, then stopped.

She unbuckled her seat belt and opened the door, but before she could step out, the car jerked as if a rope holding
it had snapped. Her head banged against the steering wheel
as the car slid into a gully and stopped against a clump.
Flakes began to claim the inside of the car through the open
door, turning it white like the rest of the world.

Charlotte shuddered and brushed at the flakes settling on
her. She swiped at her head and moaned. She had to get
out. As she tried to pull herself out, the car slid again.

This time it rammed into a tree, tore her hand from the door handle and flung her away as if she weighed no more than one of the snowflakes still swirling furiously down.

She landed against a bush. The snow tried to cover this new thing so it would fit in with everything else. And Charlotte was unaware of it all.

"What is it, Juno?" Tyler Fleming flexed his wide shoulders and pulled his attention from the flames in the fireplace in front of him. His dark green sweater molded to the solid chest underneath as he stretched his hands to the warmth. "What is it, girl?" The huge dog whined and ran to the front door and back to her master. "What do you hear? Some fool creature that doesn't know enough to wait for this mountain storm to stop?"

Juno whined again and put a paw on Tyler's knee. The gentle eyes staring at him seemed to be a mistake in the massive black and tan head of the rottweiler.

"Okay, let's see what has you so excited." Tyler pulled on his boots and jacket. He pulled the hood up over his thick black hair, and stretched leather gloves over his strong bronze hands. He opened the door and the dog dashed out as if set free from a small cage.

Juno leaped a short way through the tall drifts, then returned to Tyler and barked. She stared at him before charging off again, barking as if to make him follow her.

"Okay, okay. I'm coming." Tyler looked down his almost smooth driveway. Almost smooth. Where it met the road, shallow twin paths led off to the side and into the ditch. As he watched, the storm continued trying to finish filling in the paths.

"What the devil . . . ?"

Juno trotted back to him and pulled at his jacket edge.

"Okay, girl, I see it. I'm coming."

Tyler trudged down the driveway through the deep snow.

His boots wouldn't help at all. He was a few inches over six feet tall, and the snow was already up to his waist. Juno then bounded ahead, turned once more to look at him. Satisfied then that he was coming, she plodded a path to a bush in the gully. There she pawed at the almost entirely covered bundle that didn't belong there.

Tyler followed the dog's trenches. He took a quick look at the nearly covered car against a tree. The door was open like it was waiting for him. He pushed his way over, but the car was empty. He shoved the door closed and waded over to Juno. He shook his head and nudged her aside.

"Good girl." He patted her head. "Let's see what you've found."

He knelt in the snow and gently brushed the white cover from the heap. New snow tried to undo his work, but, using his body as a shield, Tyler managed to uncover his find. He brushed the last bit of snow away.

The nearly bloodless face of a young woman revealed itself. Thick, long lashes rested above pale cheeks. Drops of red trickled from the cuts above her thick eyebrows. A wrinkle formed in Tyler's broad forehead as he removed a glove and pressed his fingers to the side of the woman's neck. A weak, slow beat pulsed as if reluctant to show itself. He put his glove back on.

The sigh that escaped from his generous mouth was as heavy as the snowstorm. He had to move her. But she should be checked by paramedics before she was moved. He sighed again. He had no choice. To call the paramedics or anyone, he needed a working phone. If he had kept the cell phone he had when he wanted to talk to people, he could have used it now. He could use a lot of things he didn't have anymore.

He brushed new snow from the girl's face and stared at her. He rubbed his strong jaw. He didn't have any more choice in this than he did in a lot of things in his life. He hoped she didn't have any back or neck injuries. Even if he could call the paramedics, they couldn't get out here through this. Nobody could. He swallowed hard.

Tyler picked her up and prayed he wasn't causing more harm. She didn't weigh much more than a child, but he was glad for the morning runs that he forced himself to take with Juno. When he cradled her in his arms, a weak moan escaped from her pale lips. Then, except for the crunching of Tyler's boots and Juno's soft padding behind him, the muffled wind was alone in the air.

Late afternoon shadows led the way as Tyler waded along the new narrow path back up to the house. His hood slid down and the snow covered his hair. He slipped a couple of times, but he stayed on his feet and the woman remained safe in his arms. He was grateful for the trail he and Juno had made coming down. He was more than grateful when he finally got back up to the porch. He shouldered open the door and carried the woman into the house.

"Let's see what we have here."

Tyler laid Charlotte on the rug in front of the fireplace in the living room. Blood caked the ugly gashes on her forehead and the side of her head. He brushed snow from the thick, long curls framing her face and looked closely to see if the bleeding had stopped.

Satisfied that it had at least slowed to a trickle, Tyler probed with strong, sensitive fingers around the cuts marring the skin that looked frighteningly pale.

Carefully, he removed her coat and gloves. His hands swallowed up hers, they were so small Her hands felt as if the blood had left them to seek warmth someplace else. With her thick coat gone, she was even smaller than he'd thought. He leaned back on his heels. She hadn't moved since he had laid her down. He didn't want to think of what that could mean.

"Why were you out in this?" He didn't expect an answer

from her and would have been shocked if he had gotten one. He shook his head and stared. Then he hurried from the room.

He returned with the first aid kit he needed to clean her wounds. She still hadn't moved. She lay as if fastened in place. Tyler felt her arms and legs for broken bones. Her bones were small, but right for her frame. She was lucky she hadn't broken one of them. He let out a thankful breath when they seemed to be as they should. Then he reached for her boots.

She was quiet when he pulled off the first one, but when he removed the other, a hard breath pushed out from her.

He pulled off her socks and probed her ankle with sensitive fingers. No other sound escaped from her. Maybe a sprain, probably just twisted. Not a break. He hoped.

"You're lucky your coat and these thick boots cushioned you," he said, though he knew she couldn't hear him. He didn't know if he should think of it as luck. If she had been lucky, she wouldn't have gotten caught in the storm in the first place.

He washed her wounds and bandaged them. She'd have nasty bruises on her head, and probably a headache, but she should be all right. As if he were an expert. He sighed. He wouldn't know for sure what condition she was in until she came to. And what could he do then if she wasn't all right? What if she needed more care than he could give her?

"Cold," the woman mumbled. What little blood that had been in her face when Tyler found her seemed to have disappeared. He put his hands around her face. He would expect a thinner face to top such a small frame. He brushed his hand across her high cheekbones. Her face was almost as cold as it had been when he found her.

"Yes, you are," he answered, although he knew she didn't know he was there. She couldn't even know where she was.

He hesitated. Then he began to remove her damp sweater and jeans that were too baggy on her. He tried not to notice the curves that went in and out at the right places. He tried not to notice the twin hard points pressing against the lacy fabric under her sweater, fabric that molded itself to her fullness. He tried not to notice any of that. He swallowed hard and stood.

"You should be ashamed," he told himself. He looked away, but his gaze forced itself back to the woman. And, small though she was, she was most definitely a woman. He lifted her up onto the sofa and laid her down as if she were a piece of delicate, precious crystal.

He poked the fire and the flames leaped up as if they had been asleep before he nudged them awake.

The heat from the fireplace and the woodstove were all he had to warm her. He sighed. It was too bad the storm had knocked out the electricity. He knew she needed more heat than the two fires would throw off.

He pulled the quilt from the back of the sofa that had become his bed since the power had gone off the day before. He tucked the cover under her chin. His hand curved around her cold cheek as if it and his hand were made for each other. His other hand copied the first one and formed a frame around her face. Slowly, barely touching her, he moved his hands back and forth. A little color came back to her face as if to find out where the heat was coming from.

Next, Tyler tried to rub warmth back into her hands. Again, he noticed how his hands swallowed hers. His long, slow strokes tried to warm her hands enough so that her own body would send heat to help him.

Next, his hands moved to her feet, which felt as if a block of snow had replaced the flesh under her damp skin.

"Cold, so cold," she mumbled again and pulled into a ball. Her shivering grew stronger.

Tyler looked down at her. At least he knew she didn't have serious neck or back injuries. He hesitated. With a sigh, he tossed a pillow from the back of the deep sofa onto the floor. The others followed. He took off his boots and socks. His sweater, shirt and jeans soon joined them. Then, before he could change his mind, he got under the cover with her.

She snuggled closer to him, drawing heat from his body

as if he were a furnace. And he was feeling like one at that moment.

Her hands curled against the thick hair on his chest and searched around before they relaxed again over his heart. If she was getting warm as fast as he was, she'd be hot in no time, he thought. He wrapped his arms around her cold body, willing to share his heat.

It had been a long time since he had held a woman like this. It had been a long time since he had held a woman, period.

He thought of Tiffany. She'd understand.

The woman's shivers slowed, then stopped. She nestled her head against his chest as if she had found the place she had been looking for. Her legs, her long, full legs a pleasant surprise considering her size, tangled with his as if the two pairs belonged together. She sighed. He did, too. Her breathing found a rate it liked and stayed with it. Tyler's speeded up ahead of hers. He didn't mind at all.

He looked down into her face. More color dared to come back to her cheeks, coloring her high cheekbones better than any makeup could. He noticed the faint shadows under her deep-set eyes. The dark smudges looked like they had been there before she'd fought with the storm. What had put them there, he wondered?

He brushed her hair from the bandage. No blood seeped through.

He tried to ignore the soft curves molded to him, curves that were increasing his own body heat. Curves that fit him perfectly, as if made to order for him. Only for him. He sifted strands of her silky hair through his fingers. *Burnished mahogany.* He smiled as he tucked her head beneath his chin. *And soft as warm, rich velvet.*

Maybe later he'd eat supper. He should be hungry, but he wasn't. He'd eat after she was warm. Maybe then he'd leave her.

The scent of flowers, a field of glorious flowers, drifted up to greet him.

Two

The chill woke Tyler. He glanced at his watch. Eight o'clock. He looked out at the heavy curtain of still-falling snow. It looked to be much earlier. His breath made a cloud trail in the air. No electricity yet.

He blinked as the woman in his arms stirred. Her hands opened against his chest and brushed across it as if looking for the right spot. Then they stopped as if they had found it. Tyler felt his muscles tense as if someone had squeezed them into a too-tight bundle. Who needed electricity for heat?

He forgot that he had missed dinner. If he had been thinking about food, he'd realize it was time for breakfast. If his mind had been on food. The tightness inside him had nothing to do with hunger for food.

He looked down at her. How had he forgotten, even for a second, that she was here? He brushed her hair back to check the bandage. Were her eyes as rich and soft as her hair? He let his chin brush across the silky top of her head. Then he forced himself off the sofa.

Rubbing his arms briskly, he walked over to the wood box built beside the fireplace and pulled out a log. The coals scattered as the wood landed on the glowing ashes. After several pokes, blazing flames once again threw heat out into the room. Tyler put more wood onto the embers in the large stove at the side wall. He prodded and was rewarded with flames licking up to greet the wood as if they had been waiting for breakfast, as he should have been. He moved the kettle to the top.

He pulled on gray sweatpants over legs that would be more at home on an athlete instead of a composer. His gaze never moved from the woman on his couch.

As if she felt his eyes on her, she shifted to her side. The cover slipped and revealed the swell of her breasts.

Tyler should have been thinking about how the movement of her arms and legs showed that she had no back injury, and he knew it. That should have been on his mind instead of wondering how the bit of delicate lace and satin could contain such fullness without bursting. He tried to blink all of those thoughts away.

Tyler tucked the quilt back up under her chin. Out of sight, out of mind didn't work. Not at all. He grabbed a breath of the cold air, hoping it would cool him off.

Juno padded over and whined. He let her out and went to fix his coffee. After he spooned instant from the jar, he heard Juno scratch to get in. *It must be wicked out there for her to come back so soon,* he thought.

His gaze found the woman, who took up so little space on his couch. The chill that swirled into the house when he let Juno out and back in should have cooled him off enough so he could think clearly, but it didn't. Juno settled herself in front of the fire and Tyler filled his cup from the kettle. Then he went to stand beside the couch.

The woman's eyes finally fluttered open and he made himself concentrate on them. He smiled as the same dark, velvety brown of her hair greeted him.

"Who are you?" She sat up. "What happened?" She grimaced and touched the bandage on her head. "Where am I?" She looked down. Her eyes, already too wide for her face, widened even more. "What happened to my clothes?" She grabbed the quilt with both small tan hands and pulled it firmly under her chin.

One hand stole out and pushed back her hair. "I demand

to know who you are." Fire sparked in her eyes and color flooded her face, chasing away the pallor that had been at home there since Tyler had found her.

Finally, Tyler thought.

"Calm down." He put his arms into his sweater and pulled it down over his shirt. "Welcome to Thornhill Township and my humble abode. How are you feeling?" He pushed the wing-back chair over so it touched the edge of the sofa.

She shrank away from him. Her eyes got wider still as her back let her know that there was no more space on the sofa behind her. She molded herself there.

Tyler leaned back in his chair, giving her the space she was looking for. Her eyes let some of the wildness in them go.

"I'm not going to hurt you. I'm Tyler Fleming. Your car slipped off the edge of my driveway yesterday. What were you doing trying to travel in this mess?" He looked toward the window, where the white fury showed no signs of easing.

"I had to get home so I left . . . ? Where did you say this is?"

"Thornhill Township, but I doubt your business was here."

"I have to get home." Her soft chin tilted upward. "You haven't answered the rest of my questions." She pulled the cover closer around her. "How did I get here? What happened to my clothes?" She glared at him.

Tyler watched her color deepen and her eyes widen as she looked at the place on the sofa beside her.

"Why are there two pillows here? Why does it look like you just got out of bed?" Soft velvet eyes changed into brown glass. She freed one hand and picked up the second pillow. "You were in this bed with me." She threw the pillow to the floor. "Weren't you? Don't try to deny it." Both of her hands tightened on the quilt and pulled it even higher. Her chin disappeared behind it.

Tyler leaned forward and rested his elbows on his knees. Long bronze fingers clasped each other loosely.

"I'm not denying anything." His deep voice was patient, as

if he were speaking to a child. "As I said, it was my driveway you pulled into yesterday evening after you finally had the sense to get off the road. You must have missed the first curve and your car slid sideways into the gully. I assume that's how you got those nasty bumps on your head. And how's your ankle? It seemed to bother you when I took your boot off."

Charlotte's hand went to her ankle. Then she touched the bandage.

"I don't remember any of that."

"Unconscious people usually don't remember what happens when they are unconscious."

"My ankle is okay. A little stiff, but it's okay. You didn't answer me. What about my . . ."

"If you keep interrupting, I'm not going to answer the rest of your questions." His hazel eyes sparkled in his warm face. "And you just might find some of the answers interesting." He let his gaze focus on the swell of her breasts. The quilt was doing a poor job of hiding anything.

She snatched the slipping quilt up higher and her glare grew darker.

"Now, to continue. I found you almost covered with snow. You must have been thrown from the car when it slipped." He looked over at the dog stretched out in front of the fire. "I should say Juno found you."

At the sound of her name, the dog padded over. She sniffed at the woman and flopped down beside the couch.

Tyler continued. "I carried you up here. You don't weigh much, but still, it was not an easy task through snow that deep."

"That doesn't explain the rest. What about my clothes? What happened to them? How did I get undressed?" She frowned. "Are we here alone?"

"One question at a time. You were almost blue with cold. Your body felt as if you had spent some time in a freezer. Your clothes were wet. I had to remove them." Tyler moved his shoulders in what he hoped was a casual shrug. But he didn't feel casual, then or now. "When you still complained about being cold after I placed you in front of the fire, I got under the covers with you to use my body heat to help warm you."

"You did that for strictly noble reasons, right? You had to force yourself." The words were shoved out of her now rosy, full lips. A blush showed on her cheeks. Tyler was afraid the memory of her in his arms showed on his face.

"Listen, I'm not in the habit of assaulting unconscious females or any other kind. The storm knocked out the power as well as the phones. The heat is electric. This fireplace and stove are all we have." He crossed his legs. He folded his arms and leaned back in his chair. "Now it's your turn. What were you doing out there in this weather? The storm started the day before yesterday. You couldn't have been out there all that time. Why didn't you just stay where you were, Miss . . . ?" He frowned. "What is your name, anyway?"

"I'm . . ." She put a hand to her head. "My name is . . ." She grabbed her head with both hands as if to keep it in one piece. "I-I don't know. I don't know my name." Panic filled her eyes.

Tyler touched her hand.

"Hey, don't worry. It's probably the bumps on the head. From the way the one looks, you must have hit your head pretty hard."

"But my name. I should remember something as simple as my name." The panic grew and put a shake into her hands. "How could I forget who I am? How will I ever find out?"

"It will come back. I'm sure of it." Tyler held up a hand. "No one loses their memory forever." He hoped he was right. He continued before she could ask how he knew. "It's not like leaving an umbrella someplace and not missing it until it rains. Your memory is still inside your head. Besides, when the skies have decided we have had enough of this, the snow will stop. Then we can get to your car. You'll have identification in it. You were driving. At the least, you have to have a driver's license."

"Yes. I-I guess so."

Tyler touched the side of her head. He had a hard time pulling away.

"Your memory will come back when it's ready. Don't try to force it."

"I guess you're right." She stared down before she looked back at him. Her generous eyebrows lifted and she leaned forward. "I'm sure I had a good reason to be out in the storm. I don't do stupid things."

Tyler smiled as her chin tilted up. Daylight coming in the picture window, although weak, gave her hair a fiery halo as it bounced off the reddish highlights.

"How would you know?" Light danced in his eyes. "You don't even remember your name. Hey"—he patted her shoulder when tears filled her eyes—"don't do that." He brushed his thumb across the tears that had escaped and were making a path down her cheeks. He wiped away others that tried to follow. "It will be all right. I promise. Okay?" He let his hands cradle her face even after the tears stopped.

She sniffed and nodded. A slight smile softened her lips.

Tyler stared for a few seconds. Then he blinked. "I have to call you something . . ."

Her eyes started to fill again with panic.

"Just while we wait the short time it will take for your memory to return," he added. "What do you think of 'Venus'?"

"Venus?"

"Yes, Venus. A Roman Goddess."

"I know who Venus was." Her eyes flashed.

"Well, excuse me. I don't know how amnesia"—he stopped as her eyes widened—"temporary amnesia works. I don't know what gets remembered and what doesn't."

"I don't, either." She frowned. "I do know who Venus was. Why 'Venus'?"

Tyler forced his hand to stay away from her. He shook his head to free himself from the pull.

"Besides the obvious?" His gaze traveled from her full face, pausing at the wide, deep-set eyes, lingering on her full mouth before moving on. Then his eyes continued a slow path down her quilt-covered body before tracing a path back to her face again. "Venus rose from the sea. We might not have an ocean of water out there, but if that snow had been rain, we would have needed a sea-going boat. I think we can say that qualifies it as an ocean." Again he let his gaze wander over her face as if memorizing it before settling on her eyes. "Regardless of all that, you remind me of a goddess. I expect a queenly wave from you at any moment." He smiled as color flooded her face.

"I am not arrogant." She sat up taller, but the effect was spoiled by her frantic grabbing at the slipping cover.

Tyler chuckled.

"I need my clothes and I need them now." Fire in her eyes contrasted with the ice in her voice.

Tyler laughed again.

"Yes, your highness. They should be dry by now." He bowed low. "You know, maybe not Venus. I think that's the wrong name. 'Cleo' is better. After Cleopatra, Queen of the Nile. That will go better with that soft honey color that has decided to return to your face." He had to fight the pull her eyes had on him. He felt he was drowning in melted chocolate. "We have to call you after some queen. You have that air all queens have about them."

Dimples in Tyler's cheeks deepened and matched the one in his chin. He walked over, got her royal blue sweater and pants from the chair next to the stove, and took them back to her.

"Now you have to . . ." She waved her hand.

"I know, Cleo. I know even without the wave. I will leave your highness to get dressed in private." Tyler bowed again.

"I'm going to figure out what will be her royal highness's royal breakfast." A final bow, and he left the room.

Charlotte watched him disappear. The man looked like a football player, the one who carried the ball. He could handle anything. Nothing would phase him. He wouldn't have run off the road, like she had. He would have been in control.

She was stuck with a stranger and instead of being afraid, she felt safe. She thought of his black eyes and the worry she saw even though he tried to cover it with his light words. His hands on her face had been strong but tender. His rugged face had shown nothing but concern for her. Not quite a giant, but he was gentle.

The quilt fell from her numb fingers. Her hands acted as if the cold was still at home there. She took in a deep breath. Then another. When she let it out, her hands were able to do their job. She pulled her sweater over her head. Quickly, she pulled on her pants and stood to fasten them.

Dizziness washed over her and she sat back on the sofa. She took another deep breath and stood slowly as if to fool her body. It worked. Her ankle gave a slight twinge, but she ignored it. She pulled her sweater down. She sat back down and rubbed her ankle as she moved it around.

The shake tried to move back into her hands as she worked on her ankle. *"Stop,"* she shouted inside. She took in a breath to soothe herself. It didn't. *Who am I?*

She would not think of anything but now. She would not let her mind fill with the panic that was waiting for a chance to move back in again. If she let it in, she would never be able to chase it away.

She folded the quilt and tried to will away the panic that threatened to overcome her. *Go away.* She closed her eyes. *Please go away.* She had to believe . . . She frowned. 'Tyler,' he'd said his name was. She had to pray that Tyler was right about her memory.

Her hands were steadier when she placed the blanket on the back of the sofa. Another deep breath and her hands behaved as if they were sure of what they were doing now. That didn't let a smile out, though. She wasn't sure she had any more smiles inside.

She walked over to the window that spanned the entire wall. Her ankle took her there without much protesting.

A cotton-covered world greeted her. She frowned. If this is how it had been yesterday, what had she been doing out in it?

Sunlight sparkled off the snow as if gold dust had been sprinkled on the white surface that still hid everything. Beautiful. She sighed. Somewhere out in that beautiful world was her car, and something in it would tell her who she was. How could she forget her own name? How could she forget something as simple but as important as her name?

She stared out the window, but she may as well have been looking at a blank wall. She could almost remember. The answer: her name, who she was—it was all hiding just a little way down. She almost had it. If she only tried a little harder. . . .

A dull throbbing began behind her eyes and quickly filled her head. It pushed as if the space inside was too small— much too small to hold it in. Charlotte pressed both hands against her temples to keep her head from bursting.

"How's this for starters?" Tyler carried a tray into the room. But his smile was shoved aside as he looked at her face. It was almost as pale as it had been when he had brought her in.

He set the tray on the table at the side of the fireplace. "This is my special, no-electricity breakfast nook." His light words didn't match his frown, but she didn't notice. "Of course, I use it for lunch and dinner, too." He walked over to her. "What is it?" He saw the pain in her eyes. "A headache?"

She nodded and tightened her hold on her head as if that was the only thing keeping it from splitting open.

"Calling this just a headache is like calling that snow a light dusting." Her hands moved in a circular motion as if trying to push the pain back.

"Let's see if I can help. In some circles, I am known for the magic that lives in my hands. Come here." He held out his hand to her.

She hesitated. Then, still holding her head, she walked over to him and sat in the chair he had pulled out and placed in front of him.

Gently, Tyler pulled her hands away. He replaced them with his own. Slowly, his hands traced small circles over her temples before his fingers, barely touching the bandages, found their way to her forehead. Then they made their way, slowly, as if there was no need to hurry, down to the knotted muscles at the back of her neck. As if moving over a road they had traveled before, his fingers slid along first her head, then her neck and shoulders, pushing away the pain and letting peace settle in its place.

She closed her eyes and let his hands show her the magic he had promised her. Her headache pulled back and surrendered to a more powerful force. A sigh formed and floated out from her.

"There. Is that better?"

"Yes." 'Better' wasn't powerful enough to describe the difference between how she had felt before and how she felt now. She opened her eyes. She found she did have at least one smile left. She gave it to Tyler.

For a few long minutes, he looked at her.

"Is something the matter?" Charlotte frowned. Tyler blinked.

"No, nothing at all." He blinked again and took in a deep breath. "I wasn't sure what you drink, so I brought coffee and tea."

"I drink tea." She frowned. "I know I drink tea," she insisted as Tyler raised an eyebrow.

"Okay. Tea it is." He got the large kettle from the stove and filled the small white teapot on the tray. Then he took a frying pan from the tray and put it onto the stove. The other things, he set on the table.

The smell of sizzling bacon reminded Charlotte that it had been a long time since her last meal. Her mouth watered as Tyler lifted crisp strips from the pan onto a paper towel. She watched him pour beaten eggs into the pan and stir.

"Perfect." He divided the eggs onto two plates and placed the bacon strips on the side. "Today we eat as if cholesterol has never been discovered. Today we are back when this was considered a healthy breakfast." He smiled and sat across from her. "No matter how she stares," he said, pointing to Juno, who sat beside the table, "don't give her anything."

Juno lay down and rested her head on her paws.

Charlotte barely glanced at the dog. Her attention was on Tyler's smile. She knew, even if her memory was where it belonged, that she had never seen a smile like that before.

"Eat up, Cleo." His smile brightened even more, if that was possible. He poured water into their mugs.

She blinked as Tyler went on.

"Sorry there's no toast." He held out a small plate with hand-sliced bread. "I suppose we could put this on the stove, but it wouldn't be the same."

"You bake your own bread?" She took a slice.

"My machine makes the bread. I just dump in what it needs. Now eat up. Don't let your food get cold. I really did slave over a hot stove for this, you know. You saw me." He reached for a jar of jam with a handwritten label.

"You even make your own . . ."

"No, I do not make my own jam. I found someone who does that job better than I ever could. Mrs. Baxter has a small store in the village. She makes jams, jellies, relishes and other great tasting things."

"Village?" Charlotte took a sip of her tea.

"Yes, village. There is a village not too far from here. If you came from the main road, you must have passed it."

"I didn't see anything before I saw your driveway." She looked at him. "Don't say it. I don't know how I know, but I didn't see anything like a village. I didn't even see another house. If I had, wouldn't I have stopped before I got here?"

"Probably so." Tyler nodded. "Most houses in this area sit way back from the road. Many are on low hills or in valleys. Just about all have a lot of trees between them and the road. The way it was snowing yesterday, visibility had to be bad and everything had to be covered almost as it is now. If my house didn't sit high on a hill, you probably wouldn't have seen it, either."

Charlotte shuddered and Tyler covered her hand with his.

"Don't think of 'what ifs,' " he told her. "You're here and you're safe. How about more tea?"

"Yes, please." Charlotte felt calm settle back inside her. "Do you live here with your wife?"

"No." Tyler wrapped his hands around his cup as if he was afraid it would leave him. He picked it up and stared into it.

"You aren't married?"

"Not anymore. Not for three years." His mug should have split, the way it landed on the table. Charlotte blinked and sat back. Not a trace of a smile softened Tyler's face anymore. It looked as if it had never known one.

"What happened?"

"She died." He stood. "I don't talk about it." He didn't look at Charlotte.

He stacked the plates onto the tray and took them into the kitchen.

Charlotte sat a minute longer before she picked up the mugs and followed him into the kitchen.

The kitchen window gave Charlotte another wide view of the still, white world beyond it. Blond cabinets lined the walls from floor to ceiling, leaving just enough room at the top for baskets of all shapes and sizes.

The dining area floor was the same wood as the cabinets. What could he possibly find to store in all these cabinets?

A picture of another kitchen floated up into her mind. Her own kitchen with its dark cabinets along one short wall. Her white counter speckled with pink and gray under those cabinets. The clutter of the blender, toaster, mixer, and any other gadget she was lucky enough to nab during her weekly yard sale visits came next.

Charlotte frowned. Her hands went to her head as if to keep the memory there, but her memory drew back to where it had come from and left no trace behind.

Another odd memory. Twin lines creased her forehead as it faded. Somehow, she knew her kitchen was small but cozy. She also knew it was far from this dream kitchen she was standing in. Blue flecks in the black and gray granite counters and floor in the kitchen portion of the room provided the only bits of color.

"Beautiful." Charlotte stroked the polished smooth surface beside the double stainless steel sinks. The counter seemed to go on forever.

"Yes." Tyler stared at her as if his mind had never taken him away.

Charlotte stared back. Redness flooded her face.

"A queen does not blush," Tyler said. "It's bad for her image." He walked over to her. "Here, let me take those." He reached for the dishes in her hands.

"No, I'll do the dishes. It's only fair. After all, you cooked. You shouldn't do the dishes, too."

"If you insist. Washing dishes is not one of my favorite activities. That's why I have a dishwasher." He smiled. "And if we had electricity, we could run it."

Charlotte smiled back at him and for a moment she forgot her problems.

She put the dishes into the sink and ran the water. Tyler

got hot water from the kettle and added it. Then he took a towel from the hook and wiped as she put the clean dishes into the rack.

"I don't ever remember a storm as bad as this." Tyler put a plate into a cabinet. "We have had some bad ones, though. I remember a few years ago, we had four feet of it."

As they finished in the kitchen, Tyler told Charlotte about that storm and others almost as bad. His voice made the large room warm and cozy. Charlotte wished she had storms of her own to tell him about.

"I think we should get back to the warm room." Tyler filled the kettle that had been emptied into the sink. His other hand at her waist felt right to Charlotte, as if it belonged there.

"What are you doing way up here alone?" The fires made the room comfortable enough for her to let her question out.

"This is ideal for me. I'm a composer and I need the quiet." He smiled. "Although I have been told that when I'm working I don't hear anything, anyway."

"I'm sorry I didn't recognize your name. I'm sure you're well-known."

"You don't even know your own name," Tyler gently smoothed the crease between her eyebrows. "How can you expect to remember anyone else's? Now, if you don't recognize my name after your memory returns"—he brushed a finger down her cheek—"then my feelings might be hurt." He laughed.

"How did you get started? With your music, I mean?"

"It's not a very interesting story." He shrugged. "My third-grade class went to a rehearsal of the symphony orchestra. The musicians demonstrated each instrument separately. Then they finished by playing one of their numbers together. When I heard how they all fit together, I was hooked."

Tyler's voice sounded far away, as if he had found the way

back to that long-ago time. He blinked himself back to Charlotte and smiled. "It was fantastic. They created a world made up of beautiful music that painted pictures in my mind. I knew then that I had to try to paint the same kind of pictures for others." He glanced at her. "I don't know how I can explain it so you can understand the effect it had on me."

"You're doing okay." She nodded. "I understand." She leaned forward. "Go on. What happened after that?"

"I checked out every record from the library. Every last one of them. Mrs. Jones, the librarian, bent the rules and let me take out records from the adult department. My favorites went home over and over." He chuckled. "On some of the slips, mine was the only name." He looked at her. "Are you sure you want to hear this? It might bore you."

"It's not like I have somewhere else to go." She tucked a leg under her. "I do find it interesting, but I am having a hard time picturing you at eight years old." She looked up at the strong bronze face with its full features and strong jawline. Was he as impressive looking as a child?

As if he heard her unasked question, Tyler went on. "I was indeed eight years old. A skinny, too-tall, eight-year-old. 'Intense' was how my mother described me. I read everything I could find about music. I even struggled through the books from the adult section. Mom said I'd sit for hours with the book on my lap and the dictionary beside me for when I came across words I didn't know." Tyler continued. "The community center had a piano teacher. I begged my mother for lessons and she managed to cut expenses somewhere to pull out the fee each week. Mrs. Stanton, our neighbor, let me practice on her piano. She said it did her piano good to know it was loved and needed."

Charlotte could picture a serious little boy trying to feed his craving for music. She smiled. Tyler smiled back.

"Bless Mrs. Stanton's soul. She's gone, but I know she's a saint for putting up with my scales and other exercises, over and over, seven days a week." He laughed. "Mama kept her supplied with any goodies she made. I think she was trying to erase the guilt for letting me torture the poor lady with my playing." He laughed again.

He didn't notice the frown that flitted across Charlotte's face and then away at the word 'guilt.' Charlotte felt it, but she didn't understand it. It hadn't brought any explanation, and it left as quickly as it had come.

"Mrs. Stanton swore after each session that she heard improvement." He smiled and his voice softened. "I dedicated my first recording and then my first album to her." He stretched. "There you have it. The exciting early years of Tyler Fleming."

"It is exciting to hear how your passion for something stayed with you. Do you ever allow anyone into your studio?"

"There's nothing special about it. It's just a room. I used to let visitors in all the time. I don't much anymore. I guess it's because I don't get visitors." He blinked twice before he smiled. "To you, I will open the doors. Want to see it?"

"I'd love to." She stood and stretched, her sweater pulling tightly across her full breasts.

Tyler stared at her. He remembered the black lace underneath trying to contain and confine them. He remembered them pressed against his chest as she slept. What he forgot was why he had stood.

Charlotte's gaze caught his and the two held together for many heartbeats. Heartbeats that accelerated as if somebody held a string tying them together and was running with it.

Finally, Tyler broke the spell. He didn't want to feel this attraction. He knew where such feelings would lead. He couldn't take the pain if something happened afterward. Not again.

"Follow me." His voice was rougher than the words.

Charlotte blinked. "All right," she said weakly.

"Remember, it's going to be cold in here."

He wrapped the quilt around her shoulders. His hands stayed. He sighed before he led her to the studio and moved to the side so she could go in. Her body warmth reached him as she passed in front of him. Her legs were as unsteady as his felt. He'd have to have a talk—a long talk—with himself. Soon. Real soon.

Charlotte stepped inside and stopped. The room was cool, but the thick stone walls must have stored up enough heat to prevent the bone-chilling cold the huge room could have easily held.

She stood with her mouth slightly open. 'Awesome' was the only word to describe it.

Slowly, she scanned the room. A cathedral ceiling topped the walls built of fieldstone in shades of brown. A gleaming grand piano filled the center of the room, planted on gleaming wood floors. Floor-to-ceiling shelves lined the two opposite walls. Charlotte felt as if she was in a library. Or a music store. A ladder hung from the top of one shelf.

A built-in media center held a compact disc player, record player, and a dual tape player. Beside that, in matching wood, was a storage unit. One door was slightly open. Charlotte saw shelves of records, compact disc containers, and tapes. She shook her head. More than a music store.

An image of a stereo system flitted through her mind and was gone.

She turned around slowly. Two massive, matching black leather chairs flanked the low table with its slate slab top. The chairs seemed to be waiting for company.

No other furniture was in the room. None was needed.

"It's . . . breathtaking," She managed. She stepped farther into the room and nodded. "It suits you." She didn't realize she'd spoken the last part aloud until Tyler answered.

"It does?"

"What?" She blinked.

"How does it suit me?"

"It's . . . strong, no-nonsense." And beautiful, she didn't add. But she was tempted to.

"And that's how I come across to you?"

"Yes." She shrugged. "Is it true? Is that how you are?"

"I guess so." It was his turn to shrug. "At least I guess that's part of me." Pain flashed across his face and was gone.

"Would you play something for me? Maybe the song that became your first hit?"

"I don't play that first song anymore." His whole body tightened as if that was part of the answer.

Charlotte bit her lip to keep from asking why.

Then Tyler relaxed. "I'll play the very first song I recorded. The one I dedicated to Mrs. Stanton. Come. Sit here." He took her hand and led her to one of the chairs.

Charlotte felt sudden heat warm her hand. She wondered if he felt it too. When he released her, she felt alone.

Tyler sat at the piano. Soft, barely audible sweet notes drifted into the air, where they danced and swirled so vividly that Charlotte could almost see them. As the music swelled, it reached the high ceiling and pushed against the walls.

Charlotte closed her eyes to get closer to the song. In her mind, the other instruments of a symphony orchestra joined in at the perfect spots until all of them were in harmony, as if it was the only way they could fit together.

She felt the music lift her and take her along on a slow-moving roller coaster ride. Then she was lost in the music. Her feelings rose and fell with the pictures painted by the rich sounds. Pictures she became a part of. The sounds bathed her and pushed away the world and the troubles it was holding for her.

The final notes faded, taking their pictures with them and leaving Charlotte behind. She blinked back to the present.

"That was . . ." She swallowed and wiped her eyes. She shook her head. "I-I can't describe how I feel." She took in a big gulp of air. "I wish I could. I feel I should be able to.

I wish I could find the right words to say." She wiped her eyes again. "I don't think there are any words that could do that."

"I'm glad you enjoyed 'Suite Dreams.' " Tyler left the piano and sat in the other chair.

"Tell me how you wrote it. Where did the idea come from?"

"That's the hardest question for anyone who writes anything to answer: 'Where do you get your ideas?' I don't know where mine come from exactly." Tyler leaned back.

Charlotte noticed how his pants fabric molded to his thigh muscles as he crossed one leg over another. She tried to ignore it. She had enough to worry about without more complications. Especially a complication like Tyler Fleming.

"Dreams have always fascinated me. Often I wake up with pieces of music floating in my mind. Sometimes I'm fortunate enough to capture them before they fade away." He smiled. "Some of those bits were the beginning of this song. Other bits helped complete the album."

"Are you working on anything now?"

Tyler's mouth tightened. "I just started writing again."

"That's good. With such talent you shouldn't let it waste."

"There's a lot that's wasted in this world." Pain settled on his face. "A lot that doesn't have to be." He stared into space.

Charlotte waited for him to return to the present. He was staring at the wall as if it held the answers he needed for a question hidden deep inside him. One that could only be answered by him.

When he continued to sit so still, when he seemed to have gone and left only his body behind to keep her company, Charlotte stood and quietly left the room.

Three

Charlotte stared at the door she had just closed. Her own problems were pushed aside as her mind filled with concern over the pain Tyler carried inside him. His pain had found a rift and come to the surface to show itself to her. It was so strong, it was like a living thing growing on his face.

Does his hurt do this to him often? she wondered. *Does it come alive and tear at him very much? Did I do something to let it loose this time?*

Another question marched into her mind and then away to make room for the next. *How long will he be like this? How long will his hurt blanket him and block out everything else? What can I do to help him? What do I do now?*

She sighed and went back to the living room. No answers dropped down with the snow still falling, as if the clouds were cleaning house.

She faced the window as if watching would make the snow stop. Funny. She shook her head.

Tyler's memories were causing him such pain, it was like the things he was remembering were happening now. He probably wishes they would go away, or at least stay small enough so they won't hurt him so much. The pain was so real for him, Charlotte felt she could almost grab it and pull it away like a deep-rooted weed.

Tyler's memories are too real, yet I can't get to my own—

the ones that mean something—to show themselves at all, she thought to herself.

She stood again, as if that would help her decide what to do, and stared at the studio door. It still held in Tyler and his mind demons. Charlotte sighed again.

She went to another door and opened it. Shelves hugging the walls of the wide room and stretching to the ceiling were echoed in the shiny wood floors they rested upon. The only break the shelves allowed was for a window. And what a window. It matched the shelves in power as it touched the ceiling and the floor, and spread itself to meet the shelves at its corners.

Charlotte felt nonexistent as she stared out at the world outside stretching on and on as if never-ending.

Tyler didn't do anything on a small scale. Charlotte walked over to the massive fruitwood desk set at an angle facing the window. Again she looked at the endless view of the white world outside.

She could see the top sections of the posts marking the low deck along this side of the house. If they were showing their true height, she could step over them without brushing at the snow covering the top rail that ran along until it reached the sides of the house. She could easily go down the driveway to her car and get her purse. She could retrieve her identity. If only the snow wasn't covering the way.

Charlotte sighed and turned her back to the window as if that would make the world it was showing her disappear.

A butterscotch-colored leather sofa flanked by two matching chairs invited her to visit. Another time, she might be tempted to see if it was as soft as it looked, but not now. The cold surrounded her, to make sure she knew it was there.

She tried to rub her arms warm as she scanned the books. A wide variety was housed on the shelves, and she selected a poetry collection. She looked at the couch and the warm rug trying to lend heat to the room. The task was too much for them. As welcoming as this room was, it was too cold for her to stay. She shivered and went back to the living room.

Tyler still had not come out. The crackling of the fire did its best to greet her, but it was too soft. Too weak. Charlotte put another log on it and poked at the fire. Flames licked at the new wood as if they were a pet that hadn't been fed in a while. Juno padded over to her, sniffed, then went back to spread herself in front of the fire.

Book in hand, Charlotte sat on the couch and opened the book to the first page. At first her mind kept pulling her away from the book and to Tyler or to her own problems, but she shoved it back. Soon she won the battle and was lost in the worlds the poets had painted. Their worlds had more gentle faces than the one showing itself in the fury outside the house.

Tyler never heard the door closing, shutting out the real world and blocking out everything in the present. He let his mind draw him back among his memories, as it did too often. It dragged him over the path like new gravel: jagged and unforgiving. It took him back to that last happy day that lay at the path's end and made the trip worth the pain he suffered in getting there.

The sun had formed a halo behind Tiffany's hair that morning, catching the reddish highlights and dancing with them.

"You can throw better than that," she had told him. "You just wanted to see me chase after it." Her laughter twined through her words as if they were a climbing frame and her laughter was a vine.

"I did not. You're just jealous because you can't catch."

Tyler's deep laughter floated out and met Tiffany's. His gaze followed the Frisbee as she threw it. It curved toward him and he plucked it out of the air. He tossed it back as soon as it landed on his fingertips. Juno galloped back and forth between them as if she wasn't sure which side she should be on. She added her barks to the two notes of laughter, and the three sounds danced above them on that perfect early summer morning.

Perfect? If it had been so perfect, why hadn't he stayed outside with Tiffany? Why hadn't he stayed with that happiness?

The backyard edged then, as it did now, up to a stand of trees on three sides that quickly became the thick woods of state game lands. Oaks, maples, and other trees spread their arms over the couple as if to shield them and keep their happiness in, even though the joy surrounding them that day was too great to be contained even by the towering trees.

Why had he thought that something, anything, was more important than their time together? Why did he always end his time with Tiffany instead of treasuring it and letting it take its own time? Why, instead of holding on to it, had he tossed it away?

He remembered looking at his watch that morning right in the middle of their game. Something as trivial as looking at his watch, he remembered so clearly. Why had the sun chosen that moment to desert them and hide behind a cloud? Why had it decided right then to allow the gray to cover its light?

"Got to go," he had said to her. "I've got work to do." Tiffany smiled and nodded. It hadn't been disappointment that Tyler had seen hovering just behind her eyes when she nodded, was it?

Disappointment that Tyler hadn't noticed then, but was remembering now?

"I know." Her smile had been gentle. Tyler' s mind added

the next words now: "You always do." She hadn't said them,
but she could have. It was true. He was always pulling away
from her and going to his music.

"I want to finish that section I've been working on."
There was always something he was working on.

"I have things I should be doing anyway." She gave him
an out as she always did.

Never in the three years that they had been married had
she asked him to choose her over his work. Never in the
two years before that, when they had been college students
who had vowed to be together for life.

He left early the next morning. He had slipped his arms
from around Tiffany so as not to awaken her. He kissed
her, and though she was still asleep, a smile spread over
her face. He still saw that smile, even at times when his
eyes were open.

He had made himself leave her that sweet morning. He
had a plane to catch. Barbara, his agent, was expecting him
and they had a lot of work to cover.

He met with Barbara and they had thrashed out contracts,
and schedules for concerts and appearances. The new collection was discussed. Important things.

When they had finally finished, they had gone to dinner
to celebrate. He should have gone right home. Why hadn't
he? He could have caught a late flight if he hadn't gone
to dinner with Barbara. If he hadn't thought staying was
more important than going. If he hadn't thought that Tiffany
would be waiting no matter how long he took.

Tyler sighed and eased away from the past. He could have
stayed with her just a little longer that day they played in
the yard. If she had asked, he would have stayed with her.
He frowned. Wouldn't he have? Then his memories of that
day would have been longer and fuller, and maybe would

have taken some of the space used by those other memories. The ones that came later.

He shook his head. But no. There had been more important things to do with his time than spend it with his wife.

His sigh was heavy. He had been so busy when he returned. He remembered being so caught up in a mad rush to finish one more number for the new album that he hardly left his studio.

Every day, Tiffany had brought his lunch and dinner to the studio on a tray and eaten with him. If she hadn't, she never would have seen him during that time. And then he left her for an appearance on a talk show. He shouldn't have left. He had been so busy. Too busy. There wasn't enough time. Never enough time.

He hadn't known how little of it they had to spend together. He shook his head. Now he had too much of it.

He let his mind drag him back over the path that was no smoother leading to the present than it had been going to his past. He had to let it go. Tiffany would want him to let go and live. She would be sad to see his sadness. She would have said, "Enough, Tyler. You always did overdo things. Let it be. Let me go. Live your life."

He sighed. If it had been Tiffany left behind, he would have wanted her to let her life move on. He shook his head. He wasn't sure he knew how to let her go.

His thoughts drifted to the young woman he had found, or who had found him. *Who was she?*

The door opened, and the sound pulled Charlotte's gaze to it. She watched as Tyler strode through the room to her.

"So," he said. "Ready for lunch? You should be hungry by now." He acted as if he hadn't been pulled from her and into his memories and gotten stuck there for hours.

"Lunch?" Charlotte glanced down at the book, surprised at how few pages were left to be read. And at how little she remembered of the secrets the poets had shared with her. She was glad that Tyler was back from his place. Back here. Back with her.

"Yes, lunch. You know, the second meal of the day." He smiled. She smiled back and glanced at her watch.

"I didn't realize it was so late." She stretched, and her sweater pulled tight across her body. She held her breath as Tyler's stare caught on her movement. Then his eyes moved back to her face and held her gaze. Charlotte tried to let out a breath, but she felt her throat tighten.

Tyler blinked, and Charlotte saw the sadness return into his eyes. She saw it push away that other look that had flitted across his face before it disappeared.

She tried to relax. The air moved in and out of her body as if it had suddenly remembered that it was supposed to.

"Time goes fast, and all that," Tyler continued in a voice that had rubbed against something that had roughened it. "Want to come help me decide her royal highness's lunch?" He bowed low and chuckled just enough to tickle Charlotte's ears. She liked the feeling. She was glad he was back.

"Sure. The Queen must be well informed if she is to make an intelligent decision." She was glad for this mood that now skipped around the room.

She followed him into the kitchen and tried hard not to notice how smoothly his legs glided as he walked. He could be a dancer. She tried not to notice the way his slacks showed every muscle they covered. Lord knows it wasn't a lack of trying that made her fail.

"Let's see." Tyler looked into the open pantry. "We seem to be all out of caviar. How about one of my famous grilled cheese sandwiches and a salad with my special dressing on it?"

"Those aren't in the cupboard."

"No, but neither is anything more interesting."

"Then grilled cheese and salad it is." She bowed her head and smiled.

While Tyler pulled out what was needed, Charlotte set the table. She felt at home in this house. Cold or not, it felt like she belonged here. She wrapped the feeling around her. She moved the tea kettle to the hot part of the stove. Then she sat to watch Tyler.

His strong fingers moved as efficiently in the kitchen as they had at the piano. Charlotte found herself watching their every movement. They were strong, yet gentle, as if it were a person and not vegetables he was touching.

Tyler placed Charlotte's salad bowl in front of her. All she had to do was move her hand just a few inches forward and she would feel the strength in his hands. . . . She clenched her hands in her lap and watched as Tyler put his own salad on the table.

The tangy aroma of grilled cheese with tomato slices filled the room.

Charlotte's stomach reminded her of how long ago breakfast had been. Her mouth watered in agreement.

"Here we are, grilled cheese specials coming up." Tyler put down the platter as the tea kettle whistled. "Don't trouble yourself," he said as she began to stand. "I'll get it, since I'm up."

Charlotte smiled and Tyler forgot why he was still on his feet instead of in the chair. He shook sense back into his head and got the kettle.

"It's still coming down." Charlotte nodded toward the window. "The hungry snow clouds should have emptied every stream for miles around by now and filled them up again."

"Don't worry. It has to stop sooner or later." Tyler's grin crinkled the skin at the outside edges of his eyes. "And since sooner has passed and later is here, it can't go on much longer." He filled their cups and sat in the chair opposite her.

* * *

Through lunch, they talked about the snowfall that had to have been setting new records, even for the mountains.

"Bet you it stops at two and a half feet," Tyler challenged. "Three feet tops." Charlotte looked out the window.

"No, more than that. You're on. It has to be almost that already if it's been coming down as long as you say." Charlotte frowned. "But I don't have anything to bet." Her words fell heavy between them. "I probably don't have anything worth betting in my car, either. But I don't know. I don't know what's buried out there. I don't know what I have at home. I don't even know where home is." Her eyes found tears to fill them. "Oh, Tyler, what if I never. . . ."

"Not to worry." Tyler' s voice was soft as he patted her hand. "There is something you can bet. Something that will be highly valued by me. Loser does the meals and the dishes for three days." He squeezed her hand. "You're not going to try to back out of our bet, are you?" His voice made her worries small enough for her to manage them.

Charlotte blinked through the brightness in her eyes.

"No." She swallowed. Her smile tried to return. She wiped her eyes and her smile found strength. "Okay," she said softly, "it's a bet."

Tyler looked at her for a while. He nodded, took a deep breath, and released her hand.

"I'd better get back to work. There's a section in my new piece that's been giving me trouble, but I think I can handle it now." Pain, left behind when the hurt had finally gone, flickered across his face. "Will you be all right out here without me?"

"Yes." She was telling the truth. Her smile was a little stronger this time. "I'd better get to work on these dishes." She looked at him. "Since these are the last ones I'll have to do for three days." A twinkle found its way into her eyes and attempted to wipe away every trace of the tears that were still shining there.

"Just consider it practice for the next three days," Tyler answered. He turned away but quickly turned back. "Don't count on too much more time being in your favor. I'll be out in a few minutes and then we'll go measure the snow. I need twenty minutes tops. Okay?"

"Take as long as you want. Take an hour or two. That would be fine with me. Or take the rest of the day."

"Sounds like you're not so sure of your bet." He smiled. "I'll see you in about twenty minutes."

Charlotte watched him go. She liked the way he moved. She liked a lot about him. She shook her head.

Do I have someone waiting for me? She looked at her bare ring finger. She wasn't married, but there was a lot of space between seeing someone regularly and being married. *Wouldn't I remember if I had someone special? Wouldn't that memory be so strong and tied to such feelings that it would never let anything lock it away? If I do have someone, would I still feel this pull toward Tyler?* She shook her head. *How can I expect to remember anything else if I can't remember my name?*

Who am I? The question popped up as if a minute hand on a clock was pushing it along ahead of it. This time, Charlotte let it stay out.

Why was I out in this storm? How long was I out in it? Tyler said it had been coming down long enough for me to have left the road hours before I did. Why didn't I? Was I coming from some place or going to it? And why? Who am I?

A shy smile pushed itself among the questions and shoved them aside. Tyler called her Cleo.

The smile was pushed away by the questions shoving back toward the front. No matter how nice it was, that wasn't her name. It didn't feel right. She frowned. *Would it feel right if it were my name?*

An ache jabbed her, poking its head up like a seedling seeking the sun for the first time.

What was her name? Why wouldn't her mind let her memories show themselves? Her head wasn't hurt that badly. Was it?

Tyler looked as if his memories felt like broken glass, yet his mind showed his to him.

The ache blossomed in Charlotte's head and spread like a fast-growing weed. She closed her eyes and placed her fingers on the sides of her head. She tried to rub her pain away as Tyler had done so magically for her the last time.

Four

"Okay." Tyler stepped into the living room with the grace of a sleek jungle cat. "Ready to go out and meet your fate?"

Charlotte traced a final circle on the back of her neck. Her hands weren't as good as Tyler's, but they had pushed down the ache so she could live with it.

"I'm ready to see you lose," she said. Tyler's voice helped her forget the ache and what had caused it.

"I gave you a little more time than I had intended to." A frown creased his forehead. "I always take more time than I mean to." He pulled on his jacket and zipped it up.

Charlotte smiled. "Don't try to make excuses for your loss before we even go outside." She stood and stretched. "Let's go, so we can end your waiting and put you out of your misery." Her dimples joined her grin. "And so you can prepare yourself for three days of hot, soapy dishwater. Three times a day. For the next three days." Charlotte laughed and put on her coat. "Oh, and don't forget the three days of slaving over a hot stove. For all meals."

"I can see that if you win, you won't be gracious about it."

"Oh, no. Of course not. Part of the joy of winning is rubbing the loser's nose in it. And it's *when* I win, not *if* I win." She led the way to the door.

Tyler grabbed the yardstick from just inside the garage and followed her out.

He pushed his way through the drift that nearly filled the small porch under the overhang. Charlotte followed in his path.

Sunlight allowed shadows to steal small sections of the shallow hollows and to hint at the covered landscape.

"It's beautiful." Charlotte's face looked like the sun had given her a bit of its light to put inside her to add a glow to her cheeks. "It looks like someone sprinkled gold dust over everything. It's like a picture from a kid's storybook."

Tyler stood beside her. He felt as if he almost belonged here in the picture with her. Almost. He watched Juno force herself across the white, away from them. She leaped and barked, as if that would make her way easier.

"I wish . . ." Charlotte stared down to where she thought the driveway was. "I wish we could go to my car and get my purse." She rubbed her head as pain tried to start.

"We don't even know for sure exactly where the driveway is," Tyler said. "It has twists and turns. Even if we were crazy enough to try to make it to the bottom, we'd have to find the car, uncover it, and open it." His voice softened. "As much as you want to and as much as I want to help you, we can't manage that with just shovels." He touched her shoulder. "We can't. I have a man who clears my driveway. He'll be here as soon as he can. Try to hold on until then. Okay?"

Charlotte nodded. She didn't try to force words out. She needed everything she had to push the pain further away.

"Now to continue the business at hand. No more stalling. We measure. Then we admire the beauty."

He trudged through the drifts until he was standing away from the house and the porch.

Charlotte followed in the trenches he had made. "I'll do the honors, if you don't mind." She pushed her disappointment away with the rest of the pain. "I want to be sure it's a fair measure."

"You don't trust me to measure correctly? You think I'd

shortchange you?" He placed a hand over his heart. "You hurt me to the quick." He handed her the yardstick. "Here you are. Your wish is my command, Your Highness."

Charlotte shoved the yardstick into the snow. She gave it one last hard shove and watched it disappear.

"Ha. Look at that. Look at all the space above it." She peeked into the hole to the top of the yardstick. "The snow is more than three and a half feet deep." She raised both hands above her head, imitating a boxer being declared the winner. "I am the winner and champion." She smiled at him. "So sorry."

"I can see how sorry you are by the look on your face." He let out a deep sigh. "It's just what I was afraid of. A gloating winner." Tyler watched as she pulled out the stick.

"Not gloating. Celebrating my victory, that's all."

"I should have come out as soon as we made the bet." His next words pulled a cloud over his face. "Sometimes I think I spend too much time with my music."

"That's your job." Her voice was soft. "You do it so well. It would be awful if your music didn't exist. Artists have to spend time on their art. Everyone knows that." She smiled again. "Besides, you still would have lost." Charlotte looked up at the sky. Lazy flakes drifted down. "I think it's slowing." She frowned at her own words and stood as if frozen in place.

"What is it?" Tyler was beside her.

Charlotte looked at him.

"It's nothing." She shook her head. "For a minute I thought I'd said that before." She shrugged. "Nothing's wrong. Not with me. I intend to enjoy the next three days. It will be nice getting the royal treatment: meals and kitchen cleanup done by someone else. All I have to do is sit around and read my way through your library."

"You do like to rub it in, don't you?"

"I don't know." She frowned. "Do you think I do, Tyler? Do you think I'm like this for real?"

"No," he shook his head. "I don't think so. No matter what happens, your true self would come through."

"But what if I am like that? What if I'm obnoxious? What if I'm ruthless? What if . . . ?"

"I thought we agreed. No more 'what ifs.' " He gave her shoulder a little squeeze and looked into her eyes. "Do you know what I think? I think we need to do something with this snow."

"Do something with it?"

"Yes. When was the last time you built a snowman?"

"A what?"

"A snowman. When was the last time you . . ."

"I heard you. I just don't believe you."

"Why is that? Don't you think we have enough snow for one?"

Charlotte laughed for the first time since she had gotten there. It wasn't strong, but it felt good.

"I would say there is enough snow for whole families of snowmen. Snowpeople," she corrected, then frowned.

What kind of family do I have? She wondered. Do I have brothers and sisters? Are my mother and father waiting and worrying somewhere? If so, where are they? Who are they?

"I stand corrected." Tyler's words pushed apart Charlotte's thoughts. She shook her head as he bowed slightly. It was his turn to frown. "Are you all right?"

"Yes. I was just thinking of my family, wondering if I have one. Wondering who they are where they are." She blinked twice. "If I do, I know they're worried about me."

"We'll find out all that, I promise you." He touched the side of her face. "Now, who shall we make first?"

I think we should each make our own people."

"Competitive, aren't we?"

"Don't you think we have enough snow for two people?"

"We have enough for a whole town of people."

"Let's get to it, then. Our people are waiting to be born.

Or made. Or whatever." She scooped up some snow and rounded it between her hands.

Tyler watched as she bent over and rolled the ball in a circle. Then he did the same. They repeated the task over and over. Charlotte felt some of her tension leave as she went about rolling little balls of snow into big balls.

"That's it." Charlotte clapped her gloves together and snow sifted down. Tree shadows were starting to creep over the yard. "I think that's enough. Especially since there isn't a town." She looked around. Several snowpeople stood around as if waiting for something. Charlotte shivered. "I think even if there aren't enough people, I'm finished for the day. I'm cold."

"That, I agree with." Tyler clapped his own hands together. "A cup of hot cocoa would taste good right now."

"I guess since that's not a meal, I can fix it. Just to keep my cooking skills in order," Charlotte said. "You do have marshmallows, don't you?"

"Of course. What would hot cocoa be without marshmallows?"

"In that case, let me do my last cooking for three days." Charlotte led the way back through the snow, now not as deep as before.

They sat in front of the fire, the last of their chill gone. "I hate to do it," Tyler said as he put down his empty cup, "but I really have to get back to work."

"Don't apologize. I understand."

Tyler blinked.

"What's the matter?" Charlotte frowned. "What did I say?"

"Nothing." Tyler shook his head. "Someone else used to say that to me all the time."

"Then it must have been okay."

"Yeah, I guess." He sighed. "I really have to go work."

"Then go on. The sooner you start, the sooner you'll finish."

"That's true."

Charlotte watched him go. When he closed the door, she went to the library.

She spent the rest of the afternoon on the living room couch, reading and dozing. The sounds of Tyler's piano, sometimes loud, sometimes barely there, reached her, where she was curled up under the quilt. From time to time, she put more wood on the fire. She looked out the window.

Flakes drifted lazily past, but still they came. How much longer would this go on? How much longer do I have to wait to find out who I am?

Late in the afternoon, she went to the kitchen. The chicken that Tyler had taken out was on the counter. Charlotte rummaged through the spice jars as if she knew what she was doing. Tyler could start his three days in the morning.

She set to work. She didn't think she had ever cooked on a woodstove before, but how difficult could it be? That's all that people had for years and they did all right.

She found a large pot with a cover, put the chicken she had diced into water, and placed the pot on the stove. While the chicken simmered, she peeled carrots and found a can of sweet peas in the cupboard.

"Dumplings," she said. "Chicken cooked this way must have dumplings." She almost remembered long-ago dumplings, but they stayed away and let the new ones keep her attention.

"What else?" A box of cornbread mix stared at her from a shelf. She busied herself with that.

"Now the tricky part. Baking on top of that stove." She stared at it as if expecting suggestions. None came; she was on her own. She set the pan close to the side of the heat. If it didn't turn out all right, the birds would welcome it. She kept busy stirring pots and turning the pan. The smells rising from the food seemed familiar, but no memories came to explain them.

"That smells delicious." Tyler came into the kitchen as Charlotte put the last piece of bread into a basket. "I won't mention how I thought I would have to do kitchen duty to pay for my stupid guess."

"I hope it tastes as good as it smells. And your kitchen duty starts tomorrow. I want to make sure I get my full three days out of you." She smiled as Tyler took a serving bowl to the living room. Charlotte followed with the bread and set it on the table. Maybe she wouldn't be here for three more days. Maybe by then, she'd be back home with her family. She wouldn't examine how she would feel about leaving Tyler. Not right now.

She sat and watched Tyler heap his plate and taste a forkful of food.

"I didn't think it was possible, but this is better than the smell had promised," Tyler said. He took a piece of cornbread from the basket. "Homemade bread, too?"

"Chef Cleo aims to please. I'm sure it was easier than that breadmaking machine."

"The breadmaker isn't complicated."

"Neither is building a spaceship, if you know what you're doing." Charlotte tasted the chicken. "This is good, if I must say so myself."

"You didn't have to. I already did." Tyler smiled.

"What are you working on in there that keeps you so busy? Or can't you tell me?"

"It's not a secret. I'm behind in my work. I'm working on an album of new music and the deadline is barreling down on me."

"How's it coming along? I hope I haven't taken up too much of your time."

"It's coming." He gave her a hard look. "Time with you has been well spent." He smiled. His voice held a huskiness that Charlotte hadn't heard before.

The warmth that Charlotte felt flood her face wasn't from the stove or the fireplace. She smiled back.

"Now," Tyler said, "I have a suggestion. Since we don't know what you do for a living," he looked at her, "or even if you work at all. . . ."

"I'm sure I work for a living. Despite your nickname, I don't feel like a woman of leisure should feel."

"Okay. If you had a choice, what you would like be?"

"I don't know." Charlotte frowned and shrugged.

"You like poetry. Of all the books on my shelf, why did you pick a book of poetry to read?"

"I got cold while I was looking and took the next book my fingers touched." Charlotte grinned and her dimples deepened. Tyler caught his breath.

"I like that."

"What?"

"The way your face looks when you smile."

Charlotte felt like the sun had touched her cheeks.

"I like it when you blush, too." Tyler's voice was huskier than before. His eyes sparkled as Charlotte's new color covered her face. "You could have taken the book before or the one right after. Why the book of poetry?"

"I don't have a clue. Nothing else seemed interesting. I am enjoying it." She frowned. "I don't think I could write it, though. Even if I did, I doubt I could be making a living at it." Her voice was barely heard. "I just wish I knew . . ."

"Maybe you do something else that has to do with writing. Maybe you write stories?" Tyler's question came quickly, before Charlotte could finish her wish.

"I don't think so. It doesn't feel like it." She sighed. "But then, nothing feels right." Her mind went to Tyler. Almost nothing. She blinked. Things were complicated enough already.

"If you could be anything you wanted, what would you be?" Tyler was persistent.

"I would be . . ." Charlotte's eyebrows pulled together. "Like I said, I like reading. Both poetry and prose. I really did decide on that book because I got cold while looking, but I was in your library, and I don't think it was just because I didn't have anything to do." Her eyes sparkled. "Yes, something to do with words. I don't think it's what I do, but if I could pick, I think I'd like to try writing." She nodded and reached for her cup. "I think that would be an interesting career."

Tyler's jaw tightened. He sat very still for a while. His hands held his cup as if he thought it might try to get away.

"Did I say something wrong?" Charlotte looked at him.

"No." Tyler shook his head. "I guess it depends on what kind of writing you do." He took a sip of coffee. He looked as if something had suddenly hidden his supply of smiles. The new look on his face was a fence that kept Charlotte from asking him to explain what he meant.

"Tell me what happened after your first music lessons," her soft voice prompted.

Tyler shook his head and a smile slipped out.

"My lessons continued through my school years. I won a scholarship to the local music school for Saturday lessons. Then came a music scholarship for college." He laughed. "I think Mrs. Stanton was as proud as my mother was. And rightfully so. She had a lot to do with it." His look softened. "I won a competition when I was a senior in college, and a recording contract was part of the prize. That was the beginning of my career. The record did well enough for me to do another."

"It's great how everything fell into place for you, how you knew from the time you were little what you wanted to be and how you stuck with it." Charlotte took in a deep breath. "I wish I could remember my childhood. I wish I could remember anything about myself besides odd bits and pieces. Most of all, I wish I could remember my name." Her eyes filled with tears.

"Hey," Tyler took her hand. "Don't worry. When the time comes, you'll remember." He smiled. "You'll probably remember things you wish you could forget."

Charlotte managed a weak smile.

"I doubt that." She sighed. "Any memory will be welcome. I hope it comes back soon. You don't know how this feels. Every time I try to remember, I get this headache."

"Then stop trying. When it's ready, it'll come back. Okay?" He stood.

"I guess it has to be okay." She stood, too.

"Now to change the subject. I've been thinking about our sleeping arrangements." Charlotte stared at him. "I don't guess you'd want to repeat the arrangements of last night?" He tried to look hopeful.

"I haven't been here long, but you know better than that."

"That's what I thought." Tyler nodded. "I have a backup plan. I'll go through all the time and trouble it takes and all the strain it will be on my back, and I'll bring my big, heavy mattress down all of those stairs."

"Nice try." Charlotte smiled. "And good idea. Need any help?"

"You don't have to be in such a hurry." He smiled back. "I can manage by myself."

Charlotte's smile widened.

"I wouldn't want you to strain your back. I'll come, too. At least I can give moral support."

"If you insist on giving support, you can carry one end of the mattress."

Charlotte followed Tyler up the stairs. She stopped at the top and grabbed the bannister, waiting for a wave of dizziness to leave.

"What's the matter? Are you all right?"

"I'm fine."

"You sure? You don't look so great." He went to her and lifted her face to him. His frown met her gaze.

"Yes, I'm sure." No sense worrying him. She had caused enough trouble. "Go ahead. I'm with you."

He stood staring at her for a minute. Then he went into the room. She followed.

Five

A king-size bed dominated the room. It drew Charlotte's gaze and held it. Orange, brown, and dark green stripes marched down the quilted spread and were boxed in by thick black stripes around the edges. An impressive bed for an impressive man.

Charlotte made her eyes look somewhere else. Anywhere else but on the bed. But not on the man who usually slept there.

The window in the bedroom was as massive as the ones throughout the downstairs. Drapes at the floor-to-ceiling window echoed the same pattern as the bedspread. Charlotte looked back at the bed. She couldn't help it. Two pillows spanned the head of the bed. Two. As if that was how many people were meant to share this bed.

"If you're going to help me . . ." Tyler's voice broke into her thoughts.

Charlotte blinked and made herself listen to him.

". . . grab the back end," Tyler said as he wrapped his fingers around the edge of the mattress. He didn't see how the bed, his bed, had her stare pinned in place. "Come on, Cleo. It's too cold to stay up here."

She pulled her gaze from the carved mahogany headboard and tried to lift her end.

"No, no put it down," Tyler said almost immediately. "It's too heavy." He let his end drop back into place. "I wonder.

Maybe we can push it down the stairs." He rubbed the side of his face. "No, the turn after the landing would give us trouble."

"Well, what are we going to do?"

"We are going to forget this and put it back." He shoved his end back onto the bed then did the same to Charlotte's end. "I know when to say 'when.' When."

"But what will you sleep on?"

"It's so nice of you to be concerned about my comfort." He frowned. Then his eyebrows lifted. "I have another idea. I hope it's a better one than this. Follow me."

Charlotte followed him to one of the rooms they had passed.

"Let's try this mattress." He went into a guest room, pulled the bedding off the smaller bed, and put it on a chair. "This one should be easier to handle."

Charlotte grabbed the other side. Tyler looked at her.

"Are you sure this isn't too much for you?" He asked.

"I can do this. Let's go."

"You're sure?"

"I'm sure."

Still Tyler stared.

"I'm not. I'm afraid you might do more damage to your head or your ankle."

"I'll be all right."

"I'll feel better if you just direct me. Walk in front of me and keep me on the right path." He shoved the mattress to the floor and stood it on its side. He didn't give Charlotte a chance to disagree.

"What are you going to do?"

"I'll slide it down the hall. You can act as guide. I'll stop it on each step."

"Are you sure this will work?"

"Nobody said anything about 'sure.' " He smiled. "I just think this way is best."

Alice Wootson

Charlotte did as he said. When they reached the steps, she moved aside.

"Why don't you go in front and let me push. That way you can stop it from getting away."

"That will work. Whoever said two heads are better than one was right in this case." He moved in front. Charlotte pushed and stopped as the mattress reached each step.

"I'll take over now," Tyler said when they reached the bottom. He slid it into the living room.

"I have to put it here." He pushed the mattress to the space in front of the couch. "I can get heat from the fire, but I won't block it from you. Will you move the fire screen closer to the hearth?"

Charlotte did as he asked and then looked at the mattress. There was only enough room between the mattress and the couch for her to walk. The mattress looked like a lower and narrower twin to what would be her bed.

She breathed deeply. They were closer than twin beds would be, but Tyler was right. There was no other place for him to sleep if he was to get heat from the fire. She wasn't sure if she was happy or sad about the arrangement.

Tyler came back down with his arms full of bedding.

"This should do it. Still want to help?"

"Sure."

"You do that side and I'll do this one."

Charlotte took the side of the sheet he tossed her and tucked it in. Then she took the blanket and did the same. She tried not to think of how it seemed right to be making a bed with Tyler as if they would share it. As if they were . . .

"Hey, don't quit on me now. We're almost through." Tyler shook the spread so one side landed near her.

Charlotte blinked and smoothed the spread out.

"Perfect." Tyler leaned back on his knees. "We work well together."

"Yes." Charlotte didn't want to think about working with Tyler. Things were muddled enough already. Too confused.

"This is bound to be more comfortable than the hard ground we used to sleep on when I was in the scouts."

"You were a boy scout?" Charlotte's eyes widened. She sat on the end of the couch.

"First I was a cub scout, then a boy scout," he corrected her. "Why do you find that so hard to believe?"

"I just can't picture you camping in your little uniform."

"I'll have you know I was a good scout. In fact, I earned quite a few badges. I was very serious about scouting." His dimples deepened. "Some of those badges were pretty tough to complete in the inner city, but I was determined to earn them. And I did."

"Inner city? You grew up in a busy city, with something always going on, and you ended up out here in the country all alone?"

"I think the camping I did in the scouts was one of the reasons I moved out here to the country." He frowned. "But I wasn't alone when I bought this house. I had my wife."

Charlotte wanted to ask about his wife, but his face said he was closed to questions about her. Safer questions came out instead. "Camping was one of the reasons you settled here? What were the others?"

"Only one other. I work better if it's quiet." The muscles in Tyler's face tightened for a few seconds. "We moved out here together. Just Tiffany and I." He stared at the flames. "I stayed by myself after . . ." He swallowed. "I stayed because I was already here."

Charlotte opened her mouth, but closed it before any words could come out. She looked at Tyler, who still stared into the fire. Charlotte couldn't see it, but she knew a wall had sprung up around Tyler as surely as if a bricklayer had been hard at work making sure that questions about Tyler's wife wouldn't get to him. Charlotte cleared her throat.

"I guess you got used to being alone. You like being out here all by yourself."

"Yes. I like being away from everything. And everybody."

"Don't you ever get lonely?" Her question was almost too weak to be heard. Should she apologize for being there?

"When I do get lonely, I go into town. And every few months I go visit Mom." A soft laugh found a crack in his brick wall. "I can't get her to fly out here. 'Not unless I can keep one foot on the ground,' she says whenever I try to talk her into coming for a visit." He shook his head. "It's too far for her to travel any other way from Oregon."

"You grew up in Oregon and found this place?" Charlotte frowned. "I didn't know that Oregon had inner cities."

Tyler's laugh had broken through the wall and was in full force this time.

"I guess any place with a city has to have an inner city, doesn't it?" He shrugged. "But no, I didn't grow up in Oregon. Mom's sister, Aunt Kate, moved out there. Kate said she'd always dreamed of living in Oregon. She didn't know why, but she followed her dream. Mom moved out there a few years later. It took weeks for me to drive her out and get her settled in, but every time I compare the drive out with my flight back, she reminds me of her rule of keeping one foot on the ground. She loves Oregon." He looked at Charlotte. "Enough about me. Do you remember anything about your childhood? Maybe you were in the scouts, too."

Charlotte's body tensed. She tried to dig up at least one childhood memory, but couldn't. Had she been a scout? What had she been like as a girl? She sighed.

"Not a thing. I can't remember even one little thing. Not about childhood, not about family. Nothing." She shook her head. "I don't even know if I have brothers or sisters. And what about my parents? Are they still alive? I still don't understand how I cannot know something as important as my . . ."

"I'm sorry. I should have had more sense than to ask. I

didn't mean to upset you. I don't have brothers or sisters,"
Tyler said, "so it's all right even if you don't have any."
He chuckled. "I know people who wish they didn't have
brothers and sisters. Some people wish they didn't have any
family at all." He stared at nothing. "Some people would
like to forget parts of their lives but can't." He blinked and
looked at Charlotte for a long minute. "Don't worry." He
touched her arm. "Here." He handed her a bundle. "Here's
a T-shirt and robe of mine I brought down for you." He
put his hand on her arm. "You shouldn't get cold if you
sleep in them, and you can save your clothes. Actually, you'll
probably get rid of the robe during the night. It might be
hard to believe, but it gets mighty warm in front of the
fire."

Charlotte felt a warmth go through her already. It started
at that place where his hand had touched her arm, and was
spreading itself out. Fast. She felt cold a second later, when
he took his hand away and stood.

"I'll sleep on the mattress."

"No, you won't. Hosts don't let guests sleep on the floor."

"If the host is over six feet tall and the guest will fit a
twin mattress better, he should."

"No . . ."

"Don't be stubborn. It makes sense. It's a nice, thick mattress. It will be very comfortable."

"Are you sure?"

"It's one thing I'm positive about."

"I guess if you're sure . . ."

"I'm really sure."

"Okay then. Now I think it's time we called it a night.
You've had a long day. We both have. How many other people have been responsible for an entire population? And in
only one day?"

"Not many, I'll bet." Charlotte hid a yawn. "You're right.
It has been a long day, and I'm tired." She tucked the

clothes Tyler had given her into her arms. "I'll be back in a little while."

Tyler sat on the couch and tried not to think of what she was uncovering to the empty bathroom. He definitely didn't want to think about his T-shirt caressing her bare skin.

Tiffany's smiling face came to him. It looked to him like she nodded in approval. He imagined her voice saying, "It's about time, Tyler."

He sat on the sofa, his bed, and waited for Charlotte to come back to him.

"Perfect fit." Charlotte pushed one turned-up sleeve of the robe up off her hand. Then she did the same with the other. "Just my size." She giggled and touched the robe that was doubled over in front and tied at her waist. The ends of the belt reached the hem. There was room inside the robe for at least one more person her size.

"It couldn't fit better if it was made for you." Tyler grinned. He was glad she was back.

She slid under the covers and pulled them up close. She watched as Tyler turned out the lamp. The firelight gave a glow to his bronze skin when he pulled off his sweater and knit shirt. Light bathed his chest but allowed shadows to caress a share of his muscles.

He pulled on a T-shirt of his own and Charlotte wondered if the skin he was covering would be silky to her touch. Would he feel as strong as he looked coming toward her? She shifted on the mattress as Tyler stretched out under the covers on the sofa.

"Are you all right down there?"

"Sure." As all right as she could be with him so close. She tried to forget he was there, that he was only touching distance away. A very, short touching distance. She shifted her gaze from him as if that would let her ignore him.

The crackling fire snapped and popped its song into the room, releasing the pungent burning wood smell and letting it drift out to touch her.

Charlotte slipped off the robe and let it slide from under the covers to the floor. She was warm already. Too warm, in fact. A lot of the heat had nothing to do with the wood fires. She hoped she was tired enough to forget the real heat coming from the couch so close to her. She needed to get some sleep.

Charlotte was running hard but couldn't get away. Huge letters, newspapers, and books were chasing her. In the midnight black of her surroundings, only her bright pursuers were visible, and they were flames reaching after her, trying to grab her. The stench of ink filled her lungs each time she took a breath. Her legs couldn't go fast enough. Her heart was pounding, and still she couldn't get away. They were getting closer. If they would just stop. If they would just give her a chance to explain.

She turned a corner and ran into a funeral procession. As she watched, a carved, white coffin was taken from the hearse and placed on a cart. In slow-motion, the heavy cart rolled toward her. Charlotte tried to call to those chasing her. She tried to warn the men to stop the coffin coming at her from the front, but no sound came from her. "I'm sorry," she wanted to call out to all of them. "Let me explain. Please, let me explain. I'm so sorry." But her voice wouldn't work.

Tears rolled down her face. She wiped, but they kept coming, more and more pouring from her eyes and flowing down her cheeks. She turned to the side and ran from it all.

"What is it?" Tyler's strong arms held her from behind as she gasped and struggled to get away.

"I'm sorry. I'm sorry. If you won't let me explain, leave me alone." Her hands pushed against the air in front of her as she tried to push her followers away.

"Hey, Cleo. It's all right." Tyler pulled her up on the sofa with him and gathered her closer. He smoothed her hair from her damp forehead. His strong hands wiped her face dry. Each new tear was wiped away as gently as the last. "It's all right. Nothing will hurt you. I promise." He eased her to him, and rocked her slowly back and forth.

Gradually, her heart slowed to his lullaby rocking rhythm and she stopped trying to pull away from him. Her eyes opened a bit.

"What happened?" She blinked rapidly and looked around through the tears clinging to her long lashes.

Tyler held her close, and she felt his strength. His arms gave her safety. Nothing would reach her here. Nothing could harm her. Tyler wouldn't let it. She took a deep breath and let it out, but she stayed close to him. She liked the way his arms felt around her, the way she felt in them. She closed her eyes again. She didn't have anybody waiting in her old life. She could never forget somebody else if they made her feel this way.

"You had a dream. A bad dream." Tyler's soothing voice pushed the last of the nightmare away. He stroked her arms and back as he held her against his chest. "What frightened you? Do you remember?"

"They were chasing me." Her words floated out. She pressed herself against him. "I-I tried to tell them I was sorry, but they wouldn't listen to me." She wiped her eyes, still closed. "It was so sad. So very sad." She yawned and turned in his arms. Her hands brushed back and forth across his chest as if looking for a spot it had found before.

"Who was chasing you? Do you remember what it was about?"

"I don't know who." Charlotte yawned again. "It's fad-ing." She sighed. "It's gone. All of it. I don't remember it. I only know it was sad and it was my fault. It was all my fault." She took in a breath that trembled its way in. "I was to blame."

"Try to forget it. It was just a bad dream. If something really happened, there's nothing you can do to change it. No matter how you try or how much you want to, you can't change something that has already happened. No one can." He reached over and turned out the light. Then he pulled her back to him and held her close. "Try to get back to sleep. I won't let anything harm you."

Still in his arms, Charlotte relaxed. She believed him.

"Nobody can change anything that already happened," he said again, "no matter how badly they want to."

Charlotte didn't hear these last words from him, but Tyler wasn't talking to her. He was trying to convince himself.

The firelight spread its softness over everything, wrapping the two of them in its glow. Tyler felt as if this was where she belonged. With him. Always. Tiffany would understand this.

He looked down at Charlotte. Tears still clinging to her lashes sparkled in the firelight like tiny diamonds. He wiped them away with a soft finger. Then he brushed his chin across her head tucked so close to him and gently rocked the woman in his arms.

"It's all right," he said over and over, even though she was asleep. Her heart slowed in a rhythm matching his. It felt to Tyler as if their two hearts were playing a soft, slow duet.

She moved against him. Her eyelids blinked several times. Then they stopped fluttering.

* * *

After a while, Tyler eased her from him and gently laid her down beside him on the sofa.

"I wonder what monsters are after you?" He leaned down and stared at her. "And why? What terrible thing do you think you did?"

He looked at her curled against his spot, her head on his pillow. He hesitated. Then he sighed. He tucked the covers around her and moved away. She stirred.

"Don't go," she mumbled. Her hand searched the bed beside her, but her eyes remained closed.

Tyler looked at her. Her eyes were shut in sleep.

I know I'll catch the devil for this in the morning. He remembered her reaction when she'd learned that he had slept beside her. He sighed again, deeper this time. Then he slipped beneath the covers beside her.

She moved close to him again, wrapping her arms around him and stroking his back before they stilled.

"But it will be worth it," he whispered.

The night was already half over, but Tyler knew it was going to be a long one.

Six

"How long have you been staring at me?" Charlotte stretched and covered a yawn.

"Not too long." Tyler smiled and shifted in the corner of the couch. Not long enough. "How do you feel?"

"I feel that you shouldn't dazzle me with your smile so early in the morning." Her eyes widened and she put a hand over her mouth. "I-I didn't mean for that to come out." A blush raced from her neck and covered her face. "Please forget I said that, okay?"

"I don't think so." He moved his head slowly from side to side. "I liked the sound of it too much. I think I'll keep it."

His wider smile reached her and her blush deepened in answer. Her pulse acted like he had kicked it into high gear.

"You're not doing too badly in the dazzle department yourself, this morning." His gaze locked with hers for several breathless seconds. "I'll get things started for breakfast," he said, but he sounded like those words weren't what he meant. Charlotte guessed they weren't even close. Finally, he looked away and freed her from the hold his gaze had on her.

"Tyler, how did I get here on your bed?"

"Do you remember waking up during the night?"

"I don't know." She frowned. "I remember some bits, but I thought I was dreaming. . . ."

"You did have a dream. A bad one." Tyler stared at her. Then he sighed. "It's a long story. I didn't take advantage of you. I just tried to comfort you. Let's talk about it after breakfast. Okay?"

"I don't believe you'd take advantage of anybody, but why can't you tell me about it now?"

"It's going to take a while. It's not going anywhere. Wait until after breakfast, okay? I promise we'll talk all you want then." He stood.

Charlotte looked at him. Why not now? Was it so terrible? She sighed. If he thought it best to wait, she'd trust him on it. "Okay. Right after breakfast." She stood, too. "Oh, look." She pointed to the window. "It stopped snowing." She ran over to look out.

Tyler's gaze was drawn to the slender legs exposed below his T-shirt, which fit her much more interestingly than it did him. Snow? What snow? Who cared what it looked like outside when the view inside was so beautiful.

His body tightened. He saw where the shirt—his shirt— caressed her high breasts before it worked its way down to the tops of those perfect legs on a perfect body.

He tore his gaze from her legs and went to stand close to her at the window.

The snow families greeted them. The thick white carpet still tucked over everything muffled the birds' singing, but they were singing. They, too, were glad that the sky had finished emptying itself.

There was no one else in the world. No one else but Tyler and Charlotte. And that was enough. Enough. He moved close to her. For the first time in too long a time, he felt his world was complete. This woman, his snow treasure, was the reason for that feeling.

His hands found her shoulders and folded over them. It felt perfectly natural for her to lean back against him. His arms pulled her closer and held her against his chest. He could feel her heart beating beneath his arms. His heart adjusted itself so its beat matched hers.

They stood close, looking at Mother Nature's work in front of them, so like a masterpiece in their own private art gallery.

Tyler looked at their reflection in the window. He saw a portrait of two people who belonged together like this.

Juno padded over and settled at their feet. Tyler felt more at peace at this moment than he had in a long time.

Charlotte turned to face him and her gaze bonded with his. His hands trailed up to her shoulders again. They belonged on her. They had a right to be there, touching her. Slowly, painfully slowly, he eased her even closer to him.

She leaned forward. Her head tilted up. Tyler's mouth lowered toward hers.

"Tyler." The sound whispered from her and floated up to him like a snowflake going in the wrong direction. She stood on tiptoe to meet him. He was taking too long, much too long to find her mouth.

Feelings long put to rest awoke and spread through him as her lips finally, finally touched his. The kiss deepened and exploded through him like fireworks on the country' s birthday.

Her arms burned a path of their own as they found their way around his neck. Her fingers stroked the curls waiting for her. Heat flared through her skin. He felt like Charlotte had held a match to him. Tyler liked the way her hands felt on him. He liked the fire that made him feel like he was standing in the full sun in the middle of an August heat wave. He liked feeling alive again.

He deepened the kiss to taste more of her sweetness. She was offering it to him. He was taking it. Her hands clung to his hair, the only way she could keep from falling. She didn't know that he was falling, too, and was taking her with him.

'Too much, too fast' raced through his mind. This was happening too fast.

Slowly, not sure it was the right thing to do—or maybe he knew the right thing but didn't want to do it—he made his hands ease her a breath away from him.

Charlotte blinked rapidly, her blinks matching the rhythm throbbing through him.

"I didn't mean for that to happen," he said. He stroked her shoulders, but he didn't let her go. "I have been wanting to do that since I brought you up here." He shook his head. "But I still didn't mean for it to happen. I don't want to confuse things for you."

"It's . . . it's all right." She managed a smile. "I didn't mean for it to happen, either, but I'm not sorry it did. I don't understand what's going on between us. We just met and I . . ." She shook her head. "I mean I'm not . . ." She took a step away from him and a draft troubled the edge of her nightshirt, pulling her glance down. "Oh." She blushed. "I-I think I'd better go put something on."

"Don't feel you have to on my account." Tyler smiled. "I like the view just as it is. But I don't want you to freeze." Tyler's smile deepened. "Besides, if you don't cover up, we might never eat in time to call it breakfast." He watched her blush thicken. "Go on, Cleo." His voice roughened over the words. "I'd better get breakfast started."

Charlotte watched him go into the kitchen and close the door. He seemed to have taken what warmth she had with him. She hurried over to the fire and stared into it, hoping to see an answer burn to the top. Maybe the answer to the confusion over what was going on inside her was hiding there.

She touched her lips. The tenderness her fingers felt reminded her of what Tyler's lips had just done to hers. What had just happened? She sighed and put on her robe, took the hot kettle, and went into the bathroom.

This is insane. She poured water from the kettle into the basin. I don't even know if somebody is waiting for me. Is there anybody out there who makes me feel like this?

Feelings are feelings, she reminded herself. Memory or not, you can't feel what you don't feel. There was no way she could have ever felt like this before and not remembered. This felt too new, too right, too perfect.

The memory of Tyler's kiss, of his hands on her, had her warm enough to melt ice cubes. She should take time to cool off before she went back. That would be the sensible thing to do. Instead, she hurried. She shoved her arms into the sleeves of the robe and tied the belt quickly. She had to get back to him.

She set the table later, hoping . . . Hoping what? She shook her head. Just the thought of Tyler tied to her hope was making her heart beat like it was playing catch-up. She was in trouble. Big trouble. She sighed. And she didn't care one bit.

"Okay. Breakfast is over." Charlotte put down her empty cup. "Tell me. How did I end up in your bed? I don't remember much of last night, but you didn't rescue me from a blizzard again, and I remember being so warm that I took off the robe, so I wasn't cold. What happened? How did I end up on the couch?"

"You had a nightmare. I know all nightmares are bad, but yours really disturbed you." Tyler shook his head. "You talked about somebody or something chasing you—a lot of them. Do you remember any of it?"

The previous night drifted back to her and tried to get comfortable. She grabbed at it.

"A little. I was being blamed for . . ." Charlotte frowned.

The nightmare drifted away as quickly as it had come and settled away where it belonged without sharing its secret. "I don't know what I was being blamed for." She shook her head. "It's gone."

"Not to worry. It wasn't anything nice to remember, anyway. I tried to leave you after you seemed awake, but you asked me to stay. I don't think you were fully awake and you were still upset." Tyler raised his hand. "I swear I only stayed with you because you asked me."

"I believe you." Charlotte nodded. "I remember that part. I felt safe. I felt you would protect me from them if they came back after me." She frowned. "Whoever 'they' were."

"It must have worked." He smiled. "Afterward, you slept right through the rest of the night."

"Thank you."

"My pleasure. Believe me, it was my pleasure." His voice found a roughness and was showing it. "You do that so well."

"What?"

"Blush."

"Oh."

Tyler felt rewarded when Charlotte's face reddened.

"Come with me." He held out his hand. She put her hand in his, where he felt it belonged.

Together they walked to the window.

"Do you know what I think?" Tyler asked. "We should put some more snow to use. What we need is a snow fort to protect our town. I think we should go out and build . . ."

"Race you getting ready." Charlotte grabbed her clothes and rushed toward the bathroom. A quick glance back showed her that Tyler still standing by the window, but facing her. The strange look on his face held her. Her pulse leaped for several frantic beats before it slowed back to normal.

"Go on, Cleo. I'll let you have this one." His low voice

rumbled softly. Charlotte blinked to remind herself that she was going somewhere. Then she hurried from the room.

Charlotte glanced down the hill where her car was buried. She shook her head and refused to look there again. Her mouth thinned in a narrow line as she turned back to her task.

"This is how you do it." She stretched out in the snow near the porch and moved her arms up and down. "I can't believe you've never made snow angels before. What a deprived childhood you had. This is one of the requirements before you can move on to being an adult. I don't know how they let you slip by without it."

"I guess they made allowances for me. It was hard finding a patch of untouched snow to take the test in." He looked at her. "I'm glad. The guys on the block would have enjoyed seeing me stretched out on the sidewalk in the snow, flapping my arms like I was trying to do the backstroke without water."

"Well, now's your chance to fulfill the requirements. It's never too late to learn, you know."

"Especially a skill like this that will come in so handy." Tyler picked a spot and copied what he saw Charlotte do.

"Good. Now stand up carefully so you don't mess it up."

"Yes, teacher." Tyler stood up beside her.

"They look like they're holding hands." Charlotte looked at the two angels in the snow.

"Smart angels." Tyler took her hand. He liked the feel of it even through the gloves.

"We have to make a few more just in case." She got down and moved her arms up and down.

"In case of what?"

"In case the bad snow guys try to move in. Come on. Just two more."

"Two more and that's it. It's too cold to lie in the snow.

Besides, one angel would be able to give all the protection my folks need, but I'll go along with you." Tyler quickly kept his agreement.

"Okay. Now for the fort." Charlotte pushed together a pile of snow and patted it in place.

"They need angels and a fort? What did these folks do to make someone so mad?"

"Sometimes people get mad at others just because. Maybe they didn't do anything wrong. Maybe it's a misunderstanding."

"My people would never do anything to make anyone mad, but I'll help you with your wall to protect yours." Tyler rolled a ball of snow across from Charlotte and patted it into place. Then he started another.

Two sides of the wall were finished and Tyler was working on a third when Charlotte stood.

"That was my snow you just used." Her glare was offset by the gleam in her eye as she knocked Tyler's new section apart.

"Hey, cut that out." He tried to fix it. "What do you mean, that was your snow?"

"See right here?" She pointed to the ground between them. "You got that snow from over the halfway line."

"The halfway line?"

"Don't tell me you can't see the line that divides the yard at the middle of the picture window?"

"Tell you what, I'll give it back. All of it." He picked up an armful of snow and dumped it on one of her people.

"How can you be so mean!" Charlotte laughed as she scooped up a handful of snow, rounded it, and threw it at him. Little clumps clung to his eyebrows. Bits slid inside his jacket at the top of the zipper.

"Oh, so it's like that, is it?" He started toward her. "If

they act like their creator, no wonder your people need protection."

"No, don't." Charlotte backed up into the small clearing they had made. The back of her legs bumped into the high snow of her wall. "No," she squealed as Tyler picked her up.

"You know that wasn't very nice." He held her with one arm.

"No, don't. Please don't." Charlotte's giggle bubbled out. "I'm sorry. I'm really sorry." She giggled again. "I didn't mean to do it."

"Didn't mean to do what? Tear down my wall or hit me in the face with the snow? Or throw the snow?"

"All three. I mean none. I didn't mean to do any of those things. It was an accident. They were an accident. Accidents."

"I'm sure you didn't mean it. You just accidentally picked up the snow and threw it at me after you accidentally knocked over my wall."

"Yes." Charlotte ducked under his arm when he loosened his hold to reach for a handful of snow. Her foot tangled with his and threw him off balance. He went down.

"Oh." Charlotte laughed as she scampered away. She almost made it to the porch, but Tyler's hand grabbed her foot. He pulled and Charlotte landed on top of him. That suited him fine.

"I'll bet a little snow down your neck would cool your giggles down a bit. Probably more than a bit."

"You wouldn't do such a terrible thing to poor little me, would you?" Charlotte turned in his arms, giggling.

"Wouldn't I?" Tyler's hand reached her collar. His gaze met hers and his hand stopped in midair. The snowy ground beneath them was forgotten as they lay locked together. Neither noticed the snow escape through his fingers like flour through a sifter. Neither noticed the cold surrounding them.

It didn't matter, since their warm bodies were getting warmer by the second.

Tyler almost forgot to breathe.

"I think we should go in." His husky voice finally broke the bond between them.

Charlotte blinked. "Yes, we should." Her voice was barely above a whisper. Slowly, she rolled off him.

Tyler got to his feet and reached down to her. She took his hand. His arms went around her and met at her back before one settled at her waist.

They walked into the hallway. Tyler shut the door and turned her gently into his arms. Slowly, too slowly, Charlotte watched his mouth come toward hers. She closed her eyes and stretched up to meet him.

The touch of his lips on hers was gentle. Charlotte leaned closer. The kiss deepened. Tyler explored the sensitive inner flesh of her mouth. Charlotte's body tightened as lightening sped along her nerve endings until her whole body was warmer than the fireplace in full force. If she were outside, she could melt the snow covering the yard. The driveway, too.

The kiss went on and on, building this new feeling in her, but it didn't last long enough for Charlotte.

Tyler pulled back from her and his hands shifted to her shoulders. His fingers brushed back and forth there, not sure of the exact spot to settle for.

"I did mean for that to happen," he said. His words were as rough as the bark on one of the logs used to feed the fire.

Charlotte smiled at him. Her mouth felt different. She touched her fingers to her lips. She felt different.

"I'm glad it did." Her words slipped out.

Tyler's hands tightened for an instant before they pulled away from her.

"I think we'd better get out of these wet clothes." Slowly, he pulled down his jacket zipper. Charlotte's hands were just as slow as they eased the zipper down on her own jacket. She felt her face flush. She knew it wasn't from the cold that she had spent so much time in. Something sped through her and settled in her bones, her innermost parts.

This wasn't a new jacket she was wearing. She must have worn it many times, yet her hands fumbled before they could tug it loose. She held it for a second, hoping the cold fabric would cool her off. When it didn't, she reached to hang it up anyway. The tremor in her hands made it hard for her to find the hook. Maybe it was the tremor, or maybe it was because she wasn't watching what she was doing. Her gaze held Tyler's. Was there a chain and padlock fastening them together?

They sat down on the bench at the same time and in slow-motion, like a hidden director had given them a signal. Charlotte tore her gaze away and fumbled with her boots.

"Here." Tyler's husky voice slipped into the air. "Let me do that." His hands were full of promises as he slowly tugged first one and then the other boot off. "Seems like I did this before." His voice sounded like Charlotte felt.

Charlotte watched as his hands laid down the second boot, and returned to her foot. Tyler rubbed slow circles on her foot, then up and down and around her ankle. Then he did the other one. If she hadn't been looking at his hands performing their task, she would have sworn that he was moving a heater over her feet. It didn't feel unpleasant, though. Far from it. She could hardly breathe. His hands on her didn't help her find air. The hall was suddenly too small. How did it shrink? And when?

"We'll find something for you to wear." His finger was like a lit candle as he traced around the side of her face. "You can't keep on those wet jeans."

Charlotte could see in his eyes that he was remembering when he had taken her jeans off her. She didn't remember

Alice Wootson

that time, but the memory in his eyes stoked her imagination.

"Cleo . . ." Tyler shook his head. It must have been as foggy as hers. He swallowed. "I better go find you something to put on."

He took his hands from her and Charlotte was suddenly aware of the cold, damp fabric clinging to her legs. She tried to find cooling air. With the heat blazing inside her, her legs should have the pants dry in less time than it would take to pull them off. She tried again to catch her breath as she watched Tyler walk away. That helped her.

"Pull yourself together," she muttered. She moved to the living room and over to the stove.

She stood in front of the fire even though she didn't need what it was sending out. Still, she stood staring as she tried, as best she could, to find a way to do just that.

Seven

"I put a shirt and a pair of sweats in the bathroom for you." Tyler's voice pulled Charlotte's attention from the fire.

She didn't mind at all. If she stood there until summer, trying to get it together, she wouldn't be in any better state of mind. She turned to Tyler and put her efforts on his words.

"I don't think you can use the pants at all," he explained. "I'm not even sure if you can do anything with the shirt, so I hung a heavier robe in there, too." His gaze started fires flaring up inside her that she had just managed to contain. She looked away from his face and tried again for control. His next words waded through the flames to reach her.

"I think you should go change now."

Tyler didn't sound as if those were the words he meant to let loose. He cleared his throat. Was it to keep the real words he meant to say inside of him?

Charlotte guessed that Tyler hoped to give full strength to the words he'd set free. His next words sounded more sure than the first ones.

"I think I'd better go on into the kitchen and start lunch." His words sounded like he was in a hurry, but his look said he didn't want to be anyplace in the world but here with her. Charlotte understood that completely. She was there herself.

"Good idea." She guessed she meant it. She needed to do some mental clearing of her own. "You fix lunch; I'll go change. I'll be back soon."

"Yes. Good." Tyler's look was as intense as a flare-up. Charlotte's look matched his.

Their stares pulled together and held as if an elastic band had been snapped in place around them.

Charlotte forgot that she had to leave the room. She forgot everything but the strong gaze holding hers. Holding her. She blinked herself loose.

"Okay. Okay." She shook her head. "I'm . . . I'm going to . . . to change now." She said it again, more for herself than for him. Finally, she broke away and stumbled her way into the hall.

"Girl, you better get it together," she told her image in the bathroom mirror. She hoped she would take the advice, but she wouldn't bet on it. Things weren't any better in here than they were at the fire Tyler was stoking.

She peeled off her jeans. They clung to her legs all the way down, but the wet pants were the easiest thing she had to struggle with.

She picked up the shirt but dropped it. She flopped down onto the edge of the tub. Janet had give her a blouse last Christmas this same shade of deep green. She frowned. Janet was her sister. A dull ache started in the back of her head, but she ignored it. What was her own name? How could she remember her sister's name and not her own? Who else was waiting for her? She shook her head. No one. She knew that. There was only Janet.

These last memories left and she felt more alone than before. When would the rest of her past come back? How long would it take if it teased its way back a little bit at a time?

She held up the pants. They fit Tyler's frame but there was no way she could get them to stay up on her. She pulled on the robe that was the same shade of green. It must be his favorite color. She fastened it and went back to the living room.

She spread her wet clothes on chairs to dry by the stove, turned them over, smoothed them out, turned them back over and stretched them out again. She untied and retied the belt around her waist twice, checking the overlap each time. No more memories came.

She went to find Tyler.

"I have a sister. Her name is Janet."

"Another memory?"

"Yes." She swallowed. "She's all the family I have." She shook her head and stared at him. "There is no one else waiting for me." His stare held hers. Finally she blinked hard. "No more memories, though."

"No one special waiting." He nodded slightly. "Good." It was a whisper, but loud enough for her to understand. He smiled. "The other memories will come. Be patient. Now let's look at you," he said, trying to take her mind off her missing memories. "The robe's not quite a fit, is it?"

Charlotte tried to smile. The thick, dark green terry fabric lay against her ankles.

"Not quite."

Tyler's smile doomed any chance she had of fighting the attraction to him that was sprouting and spreading through her by the minute. "Sorry I couldn't do better with the slippers, either," he added.

Charlotte held up one slippered foot. There was enough room in the back for her other foot.

"I feel like a little girl trying to wear grown-up clothes." She laughed.

"My clothes are too big for you." Tyler nodded. "But you don't look like a little girl." Light flared up in his eyes like a Christmas candle in a window. "Not at all like a little girl." He moved over to her and stopped.

Charlotte grabbed a breath and forgot to let it go as his

fingers brushed against her cheek, blazing a fire trail along her face.

"Ready for lunch?" His words asked, but his voice had a different question spread over it.

Charlotte nodded 'yes.' Whether the question Tyler was asking was the one that showed itself or the one waiting back inside him, her answer was the same. Yes.

Tyler's hand moved away like there wasn't any better place it wanted to be than touching her. Finally, he picked up the tray and led her into the living room.

Charlotte had no problem following him. Her hands tried to find a steadiness as she set the tableware and plates in place.

"I hate to say this." Lunch was over and Tyler set his empty coffee mug beside his plate. "I'm afraid I have to do some more work. I'll try not to be too long."

"That's all right. Take as long as you need. I understand." Charlotte frowned at the butterfly of pain that flitted across his face. "I really do understand. Don't worry about me. I'm going to get back to my book."

Tyler's brow smoothed. "It does seem to be a nice book to fall asleep to." He looked over at her. Then he moved over to her, but his gaze never left her face. She looked up into deep brown eyes and got lost. Slowly, he lowered his face to hers and brushed a kiss across her forehead. Before disappointment could find a spot in her, he brushed a matching kiss across her lips.

Charlotte didn't need a fireplace when he was around. She didn't need anything else but him.

"See you in a while." His voice held promises that his words didn't show. "A short while." He smiled and touched her face before he slowly turned and walked away from her.

She watched him go into his studio. If he could package

that power, the gas and electric companies would be in trouble, with him as competition. Trouble with a capital T.

Charlotte picked up her book. She would not think of where things were leading between her and Tyler. She had only known him two days, but it seemed longer. She would not think about later on. What would happen tonight? Her lips tingled. It felt like his lips were still against hers. She felt like his hands were still touching her.

Sure, she wouldn't think of it. Like she wasn't thinking of it now. She took a deep breath. How could feelings like this grow this fast? She let out a hard breath.

What are you getting yourself into? If she had an answer, she wouldn't have had the question.

With the quilt tucked around her legs, she began to read. Music from Tyler's studio wrapped around her, giving her more warmth and coziness than the quilt alone ever could.

"Told you so. A good book to fall asleep to." Tyler's voice interrupted Charlotte's dream. This time, the dream hadn't been frightening. It had been about being with somebody to care about and who cares about her. It had been about sharing the rest of her life, her soul, with someone. It had been about love. This time when her dream faded, all it left was the warm feeling it had been wrapped in.

She stretched. She felt her robe loosen enough to let the cold air touch the swell of her breasts through the shirt. Tyler's gaze found what the cold air touched. Charlotte pulled the edges of the robe together and tried to do the same with herself.

"Make fun if you want to," she managed, "but I feel well-rested."

"Then it was worth keeping that book. It's more harmless than sleeping pills and can be used over and over without being used up." They both laughed. She swung her legs down, and Tyler sat beside her.

"Did you finish what you planned to?"

"You mean my music?" His voice rumbled to her. He smiled as a glow crept over her face.

"You know that's what I meant."

"I had to be sure." His smile widened. "I did get a lot done." He explained what he was working on and what he had left to do.

"What happens when you finish?"

Tyler explained the next step. With Charlotte's questions as a guide, he told her about the steps needed to get from writing at the piano to fitting in other instruments and ending up with the CD on the shelves in music stores. Then Charlotte asked about the music business in general, and was fascinated by Tyler's knowledge.

What seemed like a short while later, Charlotte looked at her watch and was surprised to see that it was time for dinner. As they ate, conversation flowed between them like a smooth path.

Afterward, they sat close on the couch, watching the fire perform as it gave them their only light. The flames danced and sparked, putting on a show for their audience. From time to time, the wood added a cracking note to the show.

"All we need now are some marshmallows," Charlotte said after a while. "Too bad we used them up for our hot chocolate."

"If a certain someone hadn't insisted on putting five in each cup, we'd still have a few left."

"It was good the way we had it. You can't have a delicious cup of cocoa without enough marshmallows."

"It was half marshmallows. You don't do anything part of the way, do you?"

"If you're going to do something, don't go halfway."

"That's a very good philosophy." Tyler nodded. "Nothing halfway."

* * *

His arm went around Charlotte's shoulder. He liked the feel of her. This was where his arm belonged. His fingers brushed back and forth, looking for a path leading to what he was searching for. The way his fingers burned, the robe might as well have not been there.

Charlotte snuggled closer. This felt like it was meant to be, too.

"The next time snow is predicted," Tyler said, his hand moving to the side of her neck, "I'll make sure I have a big supply of marshmallows on hand."

"How long . . ." Charlotte felt her pulse jump. She had to grab the words she wanted before they disappeared into the jumble inside her. "How long do you think it will be before things get back to normal?" Charlotte felt like she had just finished running a marathon. Her voice sounded like it, too.

"I doubt if things will ever get back to normal. Back to the way they were before you came to me."

Tyler's velvety voice made Charlotte look up at his face. Flecks of light sparkled in the soft brown of his eyes. Desire and need were peeking from the edges. He planted a light kiss onto her forehead. She closed her eyes and wished for more.

"But if you mean how long before we get plowed out," he continued, "I don't know. This is a bad one. The worst I've seen." His kiss moved to her cheek. "But some good came out of it." She tried to follow his words, but she was getting lost in what he was doing. "The electricity and phones aren't back on yet, so the roads haven't been cleared." Now his lips were teasing her ear. She was hopelessly lost. "We're pretty far out, so the road past here won't be a priority for the snow plows. It might be another week, at least." He brushed his lips across her mouth. She liked being lost.

His mouth barely touched hers, but Charlotte felt him branding her as surely as if a hot iron had touched her.

She struggled as her feelings tried to block his words. It was a hard struggle: feelings against words. Words were losing fast.

"Do these questions mean you're ready to leave? That you're tired of me?" He stroked a finger across her earlobe.

"No." Her answer burst out on its own. Charlotte blushed. "What I mean is . . ." Her tongue refused to work. Leave Tyler? "I mean I . . ."

"I know what you mean, honey," Tyler whispered. "I feel the same way." He pulled her closer and his hand left her face and moved inside the neck of the robe. He traced circles along her collarbone before returning to her neck. Then his fingers made circles again, bigger, deeper circles this time. His fingers skimmed the tops of her breasts and she moaned her reaction.

Warmth from his hands spread through her and reached places he wasn't even close to touching. Places she hadn't been aware of having until now. But places she wouldn't mind him touching. His hand moved to her neck and she moaned again. Places she wanted, needed, for him to touch.

Tyler turned her to him and slowly lowered his mouth to hers. Gently, he pressed his lips over hers, and she opened her mouth to welcome him. His tongue entered her mouth and stroked hers.

Charlotte had been waiting for this all evening. All of her life. Her hands reached the back of his neck and clung to him as his kiss deepened. She was drowning and she didn't care.

"I-I'm not sure we should be doing this," Tyler said against her cheek.

He pulled back and Charlotte's hands slid to his chest. Her fingers moved frantically back and forth, searching for relief. They didn't find it.

"I know we shouldn't. Things are happening so fast." His voice sounded like it had to struggle for power. Charlotte felt his heart racing beneath her hands like an out-of-control express train. She recognized the speed; hers was going at the same tempo. "Too fast," he managed again. "Aren't we going too fast for you?"

"No. Yes. I don't know." Charlotte managed a small shake of her head. She was surprised she could manage enough control for that. Her voice showed the weakness she was feeling. She knew Tyler was considering, was thinking of, her. But she was thinking of him. Of them. Of both of them. Together. Like they belonged.

"Honey, we don't know anything about you," Tyler reminded her. His hand found her neck and was caressing it.

"But this . . ." She swallowed. "This, with you like this, this feels right. So right." Her voice was only a little louder than the fire. She brushed her hand across his chest.

"Too fast." Tyler forced himself to ease away from her. It wasn't far enough. He stood and moved away. "Not yet." He blinked. "I-I'm going to work for a while."

He walked away before he changed his mind, although he didn't expect to get any work done. If the snow didn't have them boxed in, he could go for a run. But if it hadn't been for the snow, she wouldn't be here. He sighed. She was so vulnerable.

Charlotte stared into the fire, wishing she could send her heat to it. A memory drifted up. An old tan brick apartment building in Glenolden in the outskirts of Philadelphia was as clear to her as if she was standing in front of it. She lived in that building on the third floor. Apartment 3A. She lived alone. Not even a cat or dog for company. Miss Mary, an older woman, was her neighbor.

Then the memory left as quickly as the ones about Janet and her kitchen had.

Tyler came out of his studio.

"I've been thinking." He stared at her for a while. Then he grabbed the edge of the mattress and pulled it away from the couch. He didn't look at her again until he had placed it in front of the stove and as far away as he could get it and still feel the heat. "You take the couch." He shrugged. "I'm going back into the studio. Don't wait up for me."

She watched him go. He was right. She stared at the studio door. Then why did it feel so wrong?

By eleven o'clock, Tyler hadn't come back. No music had come out of the room, but she wasn't surprised. He hadn't gone in there to work.

She put another log on the fire, poked it, and got under the covers.

As soon as Charlotte's eyes opened the next morning, she looked for Tyler. He was sprawled on his mattress. His blankets were twisted around him as if he had the same trouble sleeping as she had. But his face was relaxed. It was the first time she saw him so at peace. It made his face look younger.

Charlotte eased the kettle from the stove and went into the kitchen. She was on her second cup of tea when Tyler came in.

"Why are you out here in the cold?"

"I didn't want to disturb you."

"Oh, you didn't?" His eyebrow lifted.

She looked away. Wrong choice of words.

"Any more hot water?"

"You want me to fix you a cup of coffee?"

"No, thanks. I'll get it." He needed something to do with his hands to keep them off her.

"I better put some more water on." As soon as he put the kettle down, she filled it. She needed something to do with her hands. She went back to the living room. What was she going to do with the day?

Tyler fixed breakfast again. They had barely finished when he stood. He fed Juno and let her out. Then he turned to Charlotte.

"I'm going into the studio." He didn't look at her.

"Okay. I-I'll find something to read after I do the dishes."

He worked through lunchtime. For dinner, Charlotte fixed the chicken that Tyler had pulled out of the freezer section. It had still been frozen. They didn't have to worry. If the freezer stopped keeping the food frozen, Mother Nature had given the whole outdoors as an alternative.

She had just moved the vegetables to the side of the stove when he came out of the studio.

"You're just in time."

"My timing is usually right."

Neither one had much to say. Juno, tired of the silence and seeing no crumbs drop to the floor, went to her spot on the hearth.

Charlotte began to clear the table. Tyler took the rest of the dishes into the kitchen. They cleaned up in silence.

"I guess I'd better go back to the studio."

"Tyler." She took a deep breath. "I-I'm not involved with anyone." Her voice was barely a whisper. She blushed, but she met his gaze and held it. "I never have been."

"I know you aren't wearing a wedding ring, but there's a lot that can be between being married and never having been with anyone. You're sure?"

"Yes," she whispered. "I'm sure."

"Another one of those stray memories? Like the way you know you have a sister?" She nodded. "Like you knew about that tea thing?" He didn't sound like he wanted to talk about tea or anything else.

"You're sure about this?" He asked again.

"Yes." She stared into his eyes and almost got lost.

Tyler wrapped his arms around her. Slowly, he pulled her to him, giving her time to change her mind.

When she didn't, when she stroked her hands across his chest, he captured her lips with his. What started as a light touch gradually deepened.

Charlotte tasted in his mouth the canned peaches they had eaten for dessert. Where did that sweetness from the fruit end and his begin?

Then she lost all thought. Her mind filled with Tyler and the magical things he was doing to her. For her. With her. Then there was just her and Tyler. And that was all she needed.

Tyler pulled away.

"It's been a long time for me." He shook his head. "A long time."

They stared at each other as if time had stopped moving.

"I don't have any protection. I haven't needed it." He reached for her, but pulled his hand back. "Are you still sure about this? If you want to change your mind, it's all right."

"It's one of the few things I am sure of."

Tyler opened his arms and she moved into them. His hands pushed aside the robe that was keeping her from him. Heat flared through Charlotte as his hand cupped the lace-covered fullness waiting for him.

She leaned into his hand, filling it with her breast. She had trouble finding enough air to breathe. Her hands found his shirt and worked the large buttons loose from the small holes. It took too long.

Soon, but not soon enough, her fingers brushed through the crisp thicket on his chest. Her hands glided over muscles that bunched under her touch. Her fingers found his tight, flat nipples hiding in the mat and brushed across first one and then the other. Tyler moaned. She brushed again.

His lips left hers to trail a line of fire down the side of her neck. He circled her ear and darted his tongue inside.

Lightning burned a new path and settled at the soft mound between her legs. Tyler's mouth moved to the hollow of her shoulder. All the while, his fingers were moving back and forth over the pebble-hard tip that pushed against his hand. The lightning moved inside her. Charlotte's moan matched Tyler's.

Her hands tightened at his chest. Her fingers wrapped themselves in the thick curls that welcomed her home. His heart beneath her palm felt like it was trying to break through and touch her hand. She tightened her fingers. She had to find a way to hang on. That was the only way she could keep from flying off the roller coaster that was racing her up, up higher and higher still.

Tyler lowered his mouth to sample the sweetness of her breast. The peak tightened even more as his mouth drew it in, released it, and drew it in again. He let go and pulled back only enough to push aside the wisp of lace that was denying her to him. Then he tasted her, her sweet skin, only her. He went back to her mouth and swallowed her moan. His hand, his fingers, kept the other waiting tip from being lonely. They traced smaller and smaller circles around it, almost skimming the sensitive point, but not quite touching it.

Charlotte pushed against his hand, her breast tip searching for his fingertips.

He moved his mouth to the hard nipple standing firm in the honey skin, waiting for him. He brushed his tongue across it before he drew it into his mouth. He tugged gently with his teeth.

Charlotte cried out as threads of flames flared from her breast and through her. She was hanging on the edge, close to falling off into nowhere. Her hands pulled his head closer. She clung tightly to him. She wanted him to end her torture, but she didn't want him to stop. Not now. Not before he finished. Not before he quenched the flames he had started.

He pulled away from her and eased her to the couch,

away from him. Charlotte's eyes flew open. She blinked as fast as her heart was racing.

"No. Please don't go. Don't stop. Not now." The words leaked out from between her kiss-swollen lips.

Tyler stood.

"It's all right." His voice sounded like a pile of gravel had gotten mixed with his words. "I won't leave you." His gaze bored into her. His smile promised to give her what she wanted. What she needed. Quickly, he shed his clothes.

Charlotte watched, mesmerized by the sight of this bronze god standing in front of her. This perfect man. She looked at his manhood as ready for her as she was for him. Somehow, she knew she had never seen such a beautiful, desirable sight before.

Tyler, never taking his gaze from her, threw the pillows from the couch. Then he came back to her. He reached for her and she went willingly. Gently, he slid her robe down her arms, and she shrugged out of the sleeves. She wanted nothing between her and Tyler.

The robe slid off her hands and pooled around her body. It took too long, but he finally pulled the T-tee shirt off her. Then he unhooked the clasp of her bra. The released fullness tightened under his gaze. He slipped the lace from her. For a brief moment, until Tyler pulled her close again, the cold air covered her skin. Then Tyler was there, holding her, and she was warm again. His hands and mouth were working magic on her body once more, as they were meant to.

"Please," she gasped as the flames grew higher within her and threatened to consume her.

"My beautiful Queen." Tyler's voice whispered a caress into her ear. He pulled her earlobe through his teeth and sparks went through Charlotte. His mouth trailed kisses across her face before stopping at her mouth. His hand stroked her sensitive inner thigh, setting a fire there. She would soon be an ash heap.

He eased her backward and stretched out beside her. His

fingers stroked the crisp, moist curls hiding her secret place before they eased inside. She closed around them, locking them inside her.

Charlotte cried out as Tyler stroked his fingers across the hiding nub. She arched her body up to him and rubbed her female core against his hand. Her legs opened. She offered her most precious gift to him. One she had saved for him. His gaze asked her again if she was sure. Hers answered, "Yes."

"You're so small. I'm afraid of hurting you."

"You could never hurt me. Just love me."

He moved above her and settled between her thighs. She made room for him where he belonged. Where she had been waiting for him forever. His manhood pushed against her secret place. She pushed back.

He lowered his body to hers. Carefully, gently, he entered the place waiting for him. Only him. Ready for him.

A sharp pain flitted through Charlotte before it was pushed away and replaced by longing. Her body welcomed him, closed around him, holding him inside her in a perfect fit.

Tyler moved out, just a little, before he moved deeper inside her. Then deeper still. They held each other, locked together in love. Together. Then he was moving in an age-old rhythm but one that felt new to Charlotte.

Slowly, she joined him in the ebb and flow of the ancient mating dance. Soon they moved together perfectly, even though they had never practiced. It was like this was not the first time they had danced together and this was not the first time Charlotte had danced this dance.

As the rhythm increased, Charlotte arched to meet him. All of him. She followed him. She didn't know it, but she had been waiting her whole life for this. She clung tightly as Tyler took her with him on a voyage beyond reality and into a new world. They rode together, hurtling skyward on a rocket more powerful than one shot on the Fourth of July.

Everything exploded and Charlotte disappeared. Ages later, she found herself drifting back to earth. Back with Tyler. He held her close and she lay within his strong arms, where she belonged.

Tyler brushed his lips across hers and drew her closer still into the world where only the two of them existed.

He pulled the quilt from the back of the couch and enclosed them in a cocoon of love.

Eight

Charlotte smiled, still groggy from sleep. The sunshine slanting brightness onto the floor was welcome after days of absence, but its dazzle wasn't the reason for the smile that covered her face. She closed her eyes again. What an incredible, sensual, realistic dream.

She blushed at the memory of her and Tyler together in her dream, melted so closely together that they were one. He was inside her and she wrapped around him tightly, holding him there, closer than she had ever let anyone get before. Just remembering it enflamed her. Heat and moisture filled the place where she'd dreamed Tyler had filled last night.

She tried to turn over, but something held her against the sofa. Something moved slowly across her middle, bringing more of last night's dream back to her. Under the quilt, against her bare middle a path was traced, igniting a fire as it moved. This was the way Tyler had used his hands, and his mouth, to trace a path—so many new delicious paths—over her body last night in her dream.

Her hand reached her stomach and touched Tyler's hand. His hand captured hers and began stroking her fingers, circling and pulling one gently and releasing and pulling again before moving on to the next one. He stroked the sensitive area between her thumb and finger, and her womanhood tightened. It wasn't a dream that she was remembering. It was something more real, more precious than any dream could ever be. She smiled once more and opened her eyes to Tyler as she had opened her body to him last night.

Tyler leaned on one elbow and looked down at her. His smile matched hers. His warm brown eyes caressed her. Golden flecks beamed on her from their depths.

"Good morning, sugar." Tyler brushed his lips across hers. A perfect way to begin the day. "How do you feel on this morning that is almost as wonderful and beautiful as you?" His fingers found their place on her hip and spread themselves out, resting a few seconds. Then they traced big lazy circles that grazed the front of her thighs before traveling up to her waist, where they burned in place. No memory did this feeling justice. They traced another path following the first one.

Charlotte searched for the question his fingers had brushed away. If she could find it and drag it back, she'd look for an answer to it.

Heat washed over her face. "How do I feel? Is that the question?"

Laughter rumbled in Tyler's chest that nudged at her. "That's it, sugar." His hand moved lower.

"I feel . . ." She thought of the night before. She thought of the lessons Tyler had taught her body so thoroughly. She tingled as she remembered the feel of his hands on her, over her, exploring her body, probing her secret place. She breathed in deeply, but her voice was barely above a whisper. "I can't find the right words to describe how I feel. I don't think there are any."

"I hope you can't describe your feelings because they're pleasant and not because it was a terrible experience for you." Tyler's hand moved up to her face, brushing a path over her cheek. His fingers barely touched her ear, but a path blazed itself down her body and widened to cover all of her like a blanket of glowing embers. He stared into her eyes and she was lost.

"Oh, yes." Charlotte's words rushed out as if to escape the heat building inside her. She felt herself blush when Tyler's smile widened at her quick answer. She remembered how he had given her more pleasure than she had ever imagined possible. 'Pleasant' didn't begin to describe her feelings then or now. It definitely wasn't a strong enough word to describe how he made her feel last night as he led her on a new path, as he taught her, as he satisfied her.

"I'm glad it was enjoyable for you," he said softly. "I can't begin to tell you how pleasurable it was for me. Maybe one day I'll be able to put into music what I can't put into words." He brushed his lips across her mouth again and pulled her closer as if to fasten her to his side. "We know you were right about something besides the tea."

"What's that?" She looked up at him and tried to concentrate. Looking at him and concentrating did not belong together. They couldn't possibly coexist. A slight furrow creased her forehead as she tried harder to follow his words instead of his hands.

"From your reaction when I entered you, we learned you aren't deeply involved with anyone." Tyler smoothed a hand over her forehead and kissed the spot still covered by a bandage. "Thank you for letting me be your first."

She couldn't control the color that washed over her again. Pink under tan was becoming her skin tone. She looked away from Tyler's face and stared at the pattern on the quilt.

"Are you having regrets?" His soft voice smoothed over her.

"No." She shook her head, still not looking at his face. "I'm not sorry about last night. I . . ." She shook her head again. "No, no regrets at all."

"I'm glad." His finger eased her chin up until he could see her eyes. She knew they told him that everything was all right with her. "Because," he continued, "last night was beautiful. More beautiful than I could ever imagine." He placed a kiss soft as a downy feather on her mouth, her cheek, her neck. His tongue tasted the sensitive hollow waiting for him there. Charlotte felt her pulse jump to meet him. He moved his lips and kissed his way back to her mouth. "Beautiful," he repeated.

He shifted and turned Charlotte's back against his chest. She snuggled there. She liked the feel of his silky skin against hers. She pressed her body into his, and his hardness greeted her. A tingle rippled through her and settled in her hot, moist love center.

Tyler's hand moved over her stomach again and traced circles that said there was no reason to hurry. "We learned something else," he whispered into her ear.

Charlotte placed her hand on top of his. Together, slowly, as in a dream, their hands rode across her stomach before stopping on her hip. His fingers moved over her skin, rubbing and kneading in a massage not meant to relax.

"What is . . . did . . . ?" What had she planned to say? His fingers, his hands were keeping her words from forming. Keeping her thoughts away. Keeping everything away except what he was doing to her. "What did we . . ." She gulped. "What . . . what else?"

"We learned how to keep your nightmares away." His hand brushed up to cup her breast. "Like this." His fingers stroked the dark circle surrounding the hard, dark bead in the center, almost touching it, barely missing it again and again. The circle puckered in anticipation. The bead throbbed. The rest of Charlotte's body throbbed with it.

She leaned away from his back and into his hand. His strong fingers continued to trace large, then smaller circles, still carefully avoiding the sensitive tip aching for, begging for, needing his touch.

Charlotte tried to find enough air to take in. She tried to remember to breathe. In and out, in and out. Then her breaths tried to make up for the time lost.

Still, he circled the center. Once, only once, did he allow his hand to brush across it. Charlotte felt the throbbing leap inside the place that Tyler had filled so magnificently the night before.

Tyler's other hand remembered her hidden place that was crying for him. His hand rested gently on the outside of the soft, damp mound. Charlotte arched up and rubbed against his hand. He slipped his tongue into her ear as his fingers copied the movement and entered her waiting place. He brushed the nub he found waiting hard and swollen, and Charlotte gasped his name. He brushed again. Tides rippled fire through her again and again. She dug her fingers into his back and called his name again and again as she rode wave after wave.

The tide slowed and Charlotte drifted back to their bed. Back to the giver of her pleasure. Tyler turned her in his arms to face him.

Charlotte put her hands against his chest. Her fingers twined through the crisp, damp mat waiting for her. The racing of his heart matched her own still rapidly beating one. Tyler lowered his head and drew one darkened peak into his welcoming mouth. His tongue flicked over the chocolate tip. Then he tugged gently. Charlotte gasped. How could something feel so fantastic and yet cause such discomfort? Then she didn't think at all. She couldn't. She wanted him to stop. She wanted him to continue. She wanted him.

She let her body follow Tyler's lead as he led her to the tip of paradise again.

"Good morning again," Tyler kissed the top of Charlotte's head hours later.

"Good morning." Charlotte relaxed in his arms. It felt as if the bones had been pulled from her body while she slept. Tyler reached for the sheet that had fallen onto the floor. He pulled it back into place over the two of them. His other hand stroked Charlotte's thigh.

"I have never seen a bed so messed up." He smiled and let his hand slip under the cover and rest at her waist. "But then I have never enjoyed a bed so much before." He brushed a hand across the rumpled top sheet, but he didn't look away from her eyes. His hand stroked her shoulders.

"That's what happens when people lose control." Charlotte ran a hand across his back. Her smile widened when the muscles bunched under her hand.

"Yes," he kissed her, "but it was worth it."

"Yes, it was." Charlotte brushed her lips against his neck. Tyler lowered his lips to meet hers. Morning, time, the snow—everything was forgotten as they began a journey, not for the first time together, not even for the first time that morning, but one that was new all over again.

Later, Tyler stirred against Charlotte. She opened her eyes. Tyler stroked a warm finger across her forehead.

"Keep my place warm while I let Juno out before she scratches a hole in the door." He hurried and let Juno out. "As soon as things clear up, I'm having a doggie door put in." He wrapped his arms around himself while he waited. "As soon as this stuff is gone."

He let Juno in and was rewarded with a lick on his hand.

"That's little payment for me standing in the cold," he muttered to the dog as he rushed back to bed.

Charlotte lifted the covers and he scooted in beside her.

"Good afternoon. It has to be afternoon, although I can't swear it's still the same day." He smiled at Charlotte. "I realize we have warmed each other"—Tyler smiled—"more than adequately." He kissed her forehead. "Immensely, in fact. But as much as we have warmed each other so thoroughly"—he dropped a kiss onto the tip of her nose—"the part of me that is not cocooned"—he kissed an eye closed—"under the cover with you," he said, kissing the other. Then his lips touched her cheek. "And I admit it's not much . . ."

His lips brushed her other cheek. "But what is not under the covers"—his lips returned to hers—"is freezing. Getting up with Juno didn't help." He eased her from him and stood.

Charlotte couldn't take her gaze from his firm body as he walked over to the glowing coals of last night's fire and laid several logs on them. That majestic body had given her more pleasure than she could ever imagine. She stretched beneath the covers. Her muscles were sore from the new task she had given them, but she felt so . . . She smiled and sighed. So satisfied.

Tyler returned to her. He picked up his clothes and sat on the edge of the couch as the fire licked at the fresh wood as if grateful for its meal.

"I know it is unromantic," he continued, "but I am starved." He smiled. "For food." His smile widened. "For the body."

"Me, too." Charlotte smiled back.

"I'll give you first dibs on the bathroom." He brushed the hair from her forehead. "It's the least I can give you after the wonderful gift you gave to me."

Charlotte hesitated in her shyness to let him see her body. He had traveled over it but he hadn't seen her. She took a deep breath and sat up clutching the quilt to her. She swallowed hard and opened her hands. The quilt formed a puddle around her hips as if she were a gemstone set in a display case.

Tyler looked at the treasures the quilt had been hiding. Her breasts were high and full and were drawing up as if in anticipation of his touch. Or the memory of it. His own body tightened at his memory of the same. He had explored her with his hands and his mouth, but never fully with his eyes. He let his eyes feast, then he slowly pulled the robe off the floor and gave it to her.

"You'd better go ahead before we miss a late lunch as well."

Her eyes told him she was remembering why they had missed breakfast.

A peach glow washed over her before she pulled on the robe and covered up what his eyes had been caressing. He smiled as she scurried to the hall, then came back for the kettle. His bold smile danced with her shy one as she came back yet again for her clothes.

Charlotte looked at her kiss-swollen lips in the bathroom mirror. She traced them with her fingers as Tyler had done many times last night with his fingers and his kisses and his tongue. And he did it all again this morning. This glorious morning.

She leaned closer and peered into her wide eyes. Surely something would show there to mark the milestone that Tyler's lovemaking had led her past. Surely their passion had left some sign in her eyes to show that she was his, now. That he had made her completely his.

She turned and leaned against the sink. She didn't have her past, but she knew she had never imagined that making love could be the way it was with Tyler. Tyler. Now he was *her* Tyler.

Her body tingled remembering his touch. The tips of her breasts pulled tight and sent ribbons of heat through her as if his hands were caressing them now, stroking over them, rubbing over them, exciting them. She sighed as she wiped the cold washcloth over her face.

I'm a writer. Her eyes flew open as the thought popped into her mind. *I'm a writer and I was going home from an assignment.* She hung up the cloth. Home from where? Where had she been? What had been the hurry, that she'd left during a blizzard?

She searched her mind. Her name still eluded her, but

something picked at her. Her name should have been the first thing to come back. Why hadn't it? Was there something she didn't want to know about herself? No. She shook her head. It would be all right. Tyler said so. Her memories were coming back. Not as fast as she would have liked, but, in bits and pieces, her past was returning.

Tyler would be there for her when she found out the rest. With his help, she would sort things out. Together they'd make things turn out all right. She knew where she belonged now and forever. She belonged to Tyler. With Tyler.

She washed and dressed quickly, not because of the cold room, but so she could go back to Tyler.

"I was about to send out a search party."

"More memories came back."

"Great. Was your name one of them?"

"No." She shook her head.

"Not to worry. It will come in its own sweet time. What do you remember?"

"I'm a writer. I don't know what I write but I was up here doing a story."

"What kind of story?" The smile was gone from Tyler's face.

"I don't know. I don't know why I left during the storm, but I know I'm a writer. Isn't it great?"

"Yeah, great."

"Is something the matter?"

He stared at her a while. Then he blinked loose of what had pulled his mind away.

"No. See you in a little bit," Tyler said.

He dropped the quilt to the floor, but Charlotte's stare didn't follow it. His body commanded all of her attention. She looked at the crisp thicket on his chest and remembered how it had felt to let her fingers trail a path through it. Her gaze followed the hair down to where it tapered low below his waist to the part of his body that had given her so much pleasure. Her fingers curled and opened as she thought of how his firm hips had felt beneath her hands, of how his muscles rippled beneath her touch. Her gaze wandered reluctantly up to Tyler's eyes.

"If you keep looking at me like that," he rumbled, "I won't be able to go anywhere but on another love journey with you."

Charlotte felt so much heat, she could've given some to the fire and still have had too much. She blinked.

"Go get dressed, Tyler, before you catch cold."

She watched him go, knowing that it wasn't what she really wanted.

Ignoring the bet Tyler had lost, she went into the kitchen and began to fix breakfast. One of Tyler's melodies came to her mind and she hummed it into the kitchen air until breakfast was ready.

As they ate, whenever they could pull their gazes from each other, they talked about the now strong sun bathing everything in gold as if trying to pay for the trouble the snow had caused. Animal tracks skipped through the snow, showing the path that rabbits and deer had taken.

Tyler talked about the wildlife that showed itself in kinder weather. He told of trying to rid his yard of the clover the rabbits used as their private garden. Finally he had given up and decided to leave a small clover patch off to the side in the backyard for them.

Charlotte laughed as he told of the time he had found an opossum trapped at the bottom of a nearly empty trash can.

"He glared at me as if it was my fault that he was dumb enough to fall in. He hissed and showed his needle-sharp teeth as if he could do something besides look up at me." Charlotte giggled.

"What did you do about him, Tyler?" She put her empty cup on the table, laughter dancing in her eyes.

"I took pity on him and tipped the can over on its side and came back into the house. When I went out again, he was gone." Tyler laughed. "He didn't even leave me a thank-you note."

Their laughs joined together as if they were connected. As if they belonged with each other, as she and Tyler did.

Charlotte stacked her dishes in front of her.

"That's my job." Tyler reached for the pile of plates. "Tyler Fleming always pays his debts."

"I'm sure Tyler Fleming does, but I know he's working on something he has to finish for a deadline, so we can postpone payment." She looked up at him. "Or maybe, between us, we can think of a substitute payment."

"I'm sure, between us, if we try, we'll be able to think of something." His gaze met hers and held it in a promise. "Something mutually satisfying, of course."

"Yes, of course. I'm sure we can if we try hard enough." Charlotte let his gaze caress her. Then she shook herself loose. "Go on, Tyler. Get to work."

He took a step closer. He was so close, she could feel the heat radiating from his body, reaching out to hers, which was doing some radiating of its own.

He smiled at her and closed his hands over her shoulders.

"Go work on your music, I mean," she added.

"Of course. I knew that." A cloud flitted across his eyes. "I hate to leave you, honey." His sweet breath reached her. Charlotte fought to keep from pressing her lips to his, from tasting to see if his mouth still tasted as sweet as his breath promised. As sweet as it had the last time. And the time before that. She took a step backward.

"You're just going into the other room, not another state." She glanced out the window and back to him. "Not that you could go to another state. Or even into your hidden village, which is really hidden now." Or to my car, she thought. She blinked that away. "You have work to do. And you know what they say, 'It's a tough job, but somebody has to do it.' You're the 'somebody.' "

"Actually, it's not a tough job at all. I get tremendous

satisfaction when I finish a piece and everything fits together the way I imagined it would." Tyler shook his head slightly. "I can relate to the starving artist mindset. I'm so into my music that I have to write it, no matter what. That starving artist could be me if not for the luck of the draw. Sometimes I feel I should be ashamed to get paid for doing something that I love so much."

"I've heard you play. Luck doesn't have anything to do with your success. With your talent, you were bound to make it. People pay willingly to hear it. It would be criminal if it didn't exist."

"Thank you, ma'am." Tyler brushed his lips across hers. "You wouldn't be biased, would you?"

"Who, me? Of course not. Why would I be?" Charlotte's words rasped from her throat and floated to him.

He pulled back his head, and then leaned toward her again. This time, his lips lingered a bit longer.

"I'd better stop before I start something that will take the rest of the day." It was his turn to step back. "See you in a little bit, beautiful."

Charlotte sighed as he walked away. What did she do in that forgotten life to deserve such happiness now?

She put the dishes on the tray, but her thoughts weren't there. This couldn't be love, could it? The question threaded itself through her. *Love doesn't come this fast, does it? It feels like I've known Tyler forever, but it's only been a few days.*

The magic word—love—skipped through her as she did the dishes. Happiness and wonder and uneasiness tumbled through her, taking turns at the front of her thoughts. What about after we can leave here? How much of this is because we're stuck with each other? What will be left of what we have between us when we can get out? What will we have when I have to leave?

Ridges creased her forehead. Then they smoothed out

slowly. Everything would be all right. Tyler said so. She took the bedding from the sofa and folded it.

This was no longer just a sofa. It was their love bed. She stroked her hands across the folded sheets in her arms. Heat radiated through her as memories of their morning loving came back to visit. She closed her eyes and almost felt Tyler's arms back around her.

She blinked herself away from the morning and put the bed linens on a chair. The quilt went over one arm.

She had a quilt. A blue one. She bought it on sale last year and it was on her bed at home.

Then her quilt was gone and Tyler's was back.

Until tonight this would be a sofa. Then tonight, they'd share this place again, and the lack of heat would have nothing to do with anything. If things went like last night, tonight their problem would be too much heat, not the lack of it.

She smiled. She thought of Tyler's hands warming her with their special magic and how it would happen again tonight. She drew in what she hoped would be a cooling breath.

Keep this up and Tyler can save the rest of the wood for another time. Until after I leave. This last thought popped up in her mind, and she pushed it back down. She didn't want to look at it now. She'd face it when the time came. Later. Not now.

"I'd offer you a penny, but I know by the look on your face that your thoughts are worth much more."

"I thought you were working."

"I was getting ready to, but I think I should put more wood on the fire before I get too much into the music. I don't know how long I'll be and I don't want you to get cold."

Charlotte laughed.

"That's funny?"

"No." She shook her head. "Maybe I'll explain later, when you have enough time. Thanks for thinking of me."

"All the time." He kissed her quickly. "Got to go."

* * *

Charlotte got another book from the library and tried to concentrate, but the questions that had formed in her mind before still swirled through her head. They often mixed with the words on the pages in front of her. When they did, she had to read the sentence over to try to find its sense.

Janet lived in Atlanta and had a little shop named Why Not Whatnots? She was married to . . . Charlotte frowned as the name eluded her. She remembered the name of the shop but not her brother-in-law. And not her own. She shook her head.

Soon Tyler's music crept out, shoved the questions aside, and filled the room.

Today there was a lightness to the music. It reminded Charlotte of a sunny spring morning. As Tyler's fingers flew over the keys, releasing the tune they held, Charlotte pictured a wooded glade with squirrels scampering through the leaves and rabbits chasing each other under the trees.

Then that scene faded and the music painted a mellow summer night all silver and shimmery with moonlight.

She closed her eyes and let the music transport her to their own Eden, hers and Tyler's. Arms around each other, they strolled beneath a canopy of rustling branches holding hands in the air as the two lovers did the same on the ground.

The music released pine, mountain laurel, and honeysuckle perfumes to twine together with love and play tag on the gentle breezes.

In her daydream, she and Tyler stopped under a maple and held each other as birds wrapped their songs around them. Names weren't important.

Nine

Evening was taking over and pushing the daytime away when Charlotte closed her book. Sounds from Tyler's studio escaped now and then, but mostly the air was silent. She fed the fires, let Juno out and back in, and looked toward the studio. *He must be writing.* She hesitated only a moment before she went into the kitchen. She ignored the bet she'd won and started dinner.

As she worked, she thought of how they had played in the snow like a couple of children. She smiled. Snow angels. She had taught him how to make snow angels. Her smile fled quicker than it had come. She had remembered something as simple as snow angels before she remembered the few important things that had come back. When would she get her whole life back?

The frown in her forehead deepened. How would this new life fit in with her old? How would what she and Tyler were building fit with what was already in place and waiting for her to rediscover?

She shook the worries away. Everything would work out fine. It had to. Life wouldn't be so cruel as to snatch away this wondrous love she had found. Her smile came back. Their love was new, but it was too strong to be troubled by whatever lay hidden in her past. She shoved away her doubts as she had done before, and set her mind on the meal she would fix.

* * *

Tyler was still working, but after the hours he was spending in his studio, Charlotte knew he would be hungry when he came out. She wanted to have his dinner ready. She wanted to do something for Tyler. He deserved it. He deserved anything, everything, she could do for him. He had opened up an entirely new world for her. A world she couldn't, not even in her hidden life, have known existed.

He had introduced her to the joy of lovemaking and shared its beauty with her. And it was love they had shared, not just sex. It had been . . . She shook her head. It *was* wonderful, glorious, sensuous love. She smiled at the memory of being sheltered in his arms, and wrapped her own arms around herself until Tyler could come out and replace hers with his. *Enough for now. Get to work.* Her mind told her and she followed orders because she knew the present wouldn't last longer than she could stand. He'd come out and when he did . . . She shook her head. When he did, he'd be hungry. For food. She smiled at the remembered conversation. She flushed and her body tightened at the memory of the lovemaking they had shared before that conversation. The kitchen was warmer now. Much, much warmer.

She pulled out leftover chicken and put it in a casserole. Tears flowing down her face were caused by the onions she was chopping, not by any feelings inside her. Her feelings were so happy that she had trouble keeping them inside. She wanted to dance and leap and shout to the world how happy she was. Instead, she did a couple of quick twirls over to the pantry to get a can of cream of celery soup.

As she moved about the kitchen, she thought of how wonderful it would be if she and Tyler lived here together. If together they watched from this house as the woods changed with each season. Even snowstorms would be welcome. After all, a blizzard had brought them together. How wonderful it would be if she had the right to fix Tyler's dinner for the rest of her life.

She would be here for him. He wouldn't have to be concerned with anything but his music. She looked at the appliances lined up on the counter. She'd even learn to use the bread-making machine. Tyler loved the bread made in it, so she would learn to use it. She would work quietly while he was in his studio so she wouldn't disturb his concentration. She would do all she could for him. In return, he would do for her. He would love her and share his world with her. She would know what 'happily ever after' meant.

She frowned. What was my life like before? Is there something to get in the way of this new life? Something to interfere with a future with Tyler?

She shook her head from side to side. There's nothing that could destroy what she and Tyler had growing between them. How could there be? How could anything tear apart what they were building together?

She pushed away the doubts and questions as she always did when they came up. Together the two of them would work out any problems that might come when her past showed itself. Fear of the unknown was all her apprehension was. Nothing in her old life would matter in this new one. She found the ceramic canister used to store rice, then she almost dropped it.

Flea markets and yard sales. She loved to shop flea markets and yard sales. Lace doilies she'd found were on her end tables and her dresser and chest. She remembered a music box she had been happy to find. That memory left. Another piece in place. Soon it would all be back.

She hummed as she worked to cook a delicious meal for Tyler. She was glad that her knowledge of cooking wasn't lost with her other memories.

She put the last chicken piece onto the bed of saffron rice and poured the sauce over it as Tyler entered the kitchen.

"Something smells delicious." He pinned her in place with

his gaze as he walked over to her. "Almost as delicious as the cook looks." He wrapped his arms around her waist and pulled her back against his chest.

She leaned against his solidness and fit her body to his. He kissed her jaw and her neck, then held her. Both of them forgot, for the moment, the dinner, the room, everything but each other. Then Charlotte turned to face him. The light in her eyes matched that in his.

"Why, thank you, kind sir." Her words sounded as if she had just raced around a long country block. Her heart beat like a race had just ended for it, too. "It's . . ." She lost the rest of her sentence and had to search to find it. She was doing a lot of that since she had found Tyler's love. "This is poor payment for the beautiful melodies I've enjoyed while I worked."

"The muse was with me today." He cupped her chin in his hand. "Actually, I think my inspiration came from a closer, more real source than a mythical muse." He kissed her. "Much closer, much more real." He kissed her again. "One I can touch."

"The food is getting cold." *One touch from either of us,* she thought, *and we could melt an iceberg.* She smiled. "You carry the tray and I'll get the rest."

"Yes, ma'am." He stepped away from her and picked up the tray. "Let's get this onto the table. I'm starved."

"For food," they said together. They smiled then and throughout their meal.

"Did you get much done?" Charlotte asked. Dinner was over and they were cleaning the kitchen.

"Yes. I'm pleased with what I was able to do." He smiled at her. "Actually, I'm surprised at how much I accomplished. I'm surprised I was able to keep my mind on my work when I knew what a delightful armful was waiting for me out here."

Charlotte smiled shyly. "If you weren't able to block things out, I'm sure you wouldn't have succeeded as you have."

"Ah, but I've never had to block out such a delectable distraction before." His eyes burned into hers as he took her hand and let the heat from his reach her. Or maybe it was her own heat he was feeling. What did it matter, anyway?

He tucked her hand under his arm and walked with her into the living room. When he sat on the sofa, he pulled her close beside him. She fit there perfectly, as she did every other place in his life.

Tiffany's smiling face floated up in his mind. He closed his eyes. For once, her memory brought peace instead of guilt.

What I had with you was great, Tif, but that's in the past and nothing can bring it back. This is now and I have such deep feelings for this woman that it scares me.

In his mind, Tiffany nodded approval and faded away, leaving him with his new life.

"If I had a penny, I'd give it to you, though I'm sure your thoughts are worth more." Charlotte said quietly.

"What?" Tyler looked down at her.

"You were so deep in your thoughts, I'm sure they're worth more than the usual penny offered."

"I was thinking how lucky I am that I found you."

"I'm the lucky one, and not just for being rescued from the blizzard." She laced her fingers through his and brought his hand to her lips. After she kissed each knuckle, she lowered their hands to her lap. "And you mean Juno found me."

The dog thumped her tail and looked at them, but she stayed at her place in front of the fire.

"If the storm hadn't brought us together, if we hadn't met this way," Tyler squeezed her hand and went on, "we would have met some other way. We were destined to meet."

"You think so? You believe in fate?"

"I know so. This is too important not to have happened." He shrugged. "I guess that means I do believe in fate." He rubbed a finger over her hand. "Sometimes fate causes good things to happen, just as it does bad."

"That's true." Charlotte nodded. "I would never have thought something good could come out of the snowstorm, but it brought me here to you, so it was worth it." She turned his hand over in hers. "I can't imagine never meeting you, never knowing you."

They sat staring into the fire, this time not looking for answers, but enjoying the light display. This time they waited patiently for the night to come.

"Popcorn," Tyler said as darkness draped itself over the sky, leaving the fire to do the job the sun had quit.

"What?"

"Popcorn. What we need is hot buttered popcorn. Come on." He stood and pulled her with him into the kitchen. "You look over there," he said pointing to the cabinet to the side. "I'll look over here."

He began moving things aside in the pantry while Charlotte did the same in the cabinets on her side of the kitchen.

"Got it." Charlotte pulled out a canning jar. She wiped off the top. "How long have you had this?"

"I don't remember." Tyler took the jar and opened it. He sniffed. "It smells okay. It looks okay. It's okay. Get the butter, please. And the dishcloth. And pot holders. Two of them."

"Tyler, how does popcorn look if it's not okay?"

"I have no idea. It should at least look different, shouldn't it? Anyway, what could go wrong? The kernels are seeds. What harm could they do us? I know how we can find out if it's okay, though. Come on with me." He took her hand and pulled her back to the living room.

"How are you going to do this? Isn't the stove too hot to get close enough to shake a pot? And where is the pot, anyway?"

"We don't need a pot. And we don't have to worry about getting close because we are not going to use the stove.

"Then how?"

"With my handy-dandy fireplace popcorn popper, that's how."

"Your what?" Charlotte watched him take down a long-handled device that was hanging on the side of the fireplace.

Tyler went to the kitchen to wash it. When he came back, he covered the mesh bottom with yellow kernels and snapped the top into place. He put butter into a tiny pan and set it to the side on top of the stove.

"First batch will be ready in no time." He checked the lid one last time. "How about getting a bowl. A big bowl. I'm in a popcorn-eating mood right now. And bring the salt shaker, too, please.

"You have faith that the old corn will pop? You even expect enough to fill a big bowl?"

"You gotta believe, sugar. You gotta believe." He held the basket over the flames and shook it back and forth. Charlotte waited, but the only sound escaping from the basket was kernels sliding across wire mesh and bumping into the sides.

She shrugged and went to the kitchen to humor Tyler.

When she came back, he was still shaking the popper. A few white kernels stood among the yellow. Every so often, several more pops sounded, and more fluffy white kernels stood above the yellow. Charlotte sat on the sofa with the bowl in her lap and wondered if the bowl was big enough. She had caught some of his faith.

When the white outnumbered the yellow, Tyler walked over to Charlotte, gave her a quick kiss, and dumped the popcorn into the bowl she held. The smell of hot popcorn filled the room.

Charlotte took the little pan of melted butter from the

stove, poured some over the kernels, sprinkled salt over it, and sat back down. She watched as Tyler started another batch.

After several more batches, Tyler set the popper on the hearth and walked over to Charlotte.

"I guess that's enough for now."

"I would say so." Charlotte looked at the overflowing bowl on her lap. "I was wondering if you were trying to get enough to match the snow in volume."

"I thought about it. Then I decided to let the snow have the spotlight alone." Tyler ate a few kernels. "It's just as good as I expected it to be." He shook his head. "We need one more thing, though." He started for the kitchen. "Keep it warm until I come back."

"I'll do my best." Charlotte put a few kernels in her mouth.

"Don't eat it all. Save me some. I'll be right back."

Charlotte looked at the huge bowl still filled to the brim and laughed. She was still laughing when Tyler came back with a tray.

"This is what we need." He filled two mugs from the kettle and put the tray on the coffee table. "If a certain someone hadn't insisted on having six marshmallows in each cup of her cocoa, we'd have some left for now."

"You said that the last time. Besides, I only used five. You exaggerate something terrible." She took a sip. "I guess this would have been a little better with marshmallows." She took another sip. "But it is good."

"So it is." Tyler sipped from his mug. "And so is my old popcorn."

"Yes, so is your old popcorn." The fire crackled as they took turns dipping their hands into the bowl. Whenever their hands reached the bowl together, Charlotte and Tyler kissed.

* * *

"I guess I've waited a proper amount of time," Tyler said later as he put the still half-filled bowl aside.

"Proper amount of time for what?"

"To suggest it's time for bed." His husky voice took her back to the morning. And the afternoon. He leaned over and kissed her. "Notice I didn't say it's time to go to sleep." His lips parted hers and she let his tongue dart in. Then he pressed his mouth to the side of her face.

"I noticed that." Charlotte pressed her lips against the side of his face. "You smell like popcorn."

"And you taste like butter, and salt and promises. Sweet, sweet promises."

"I always keep my promises." Charlotte had trouble finding the right words and enough breath to push them out as Tyler's lips worked their magic across her face. He reached her neck and nibbled his way down to her shoulder.

Charlotte brushed her hands across his chest. Then she allowed one to make a path down his body. She hesitated when she reached his waist, then her fingers moved timidly lower, until they rested on the hard bulge that was waiting to be freed so it could join with her. Tyler moaned as her fingers brushed across their new discovery. His hand cupped her breast. Her moan joined with his just as their bodies would join once again.

Soon she was fulfilling her promise and he was showing his pleasure with her once more.

Charlotte turned under the cover Tyler had thrown over them after they'd returned from their lovemaking. She covered her eyes.

"Tyler, what's the matter with you? Turn out that flashlight."

"Covering your eyes doesn't work, love. I already tried it."

Charlotte opened her eyes and looked at him. He smiled at her.

"I guess I forgot to turn that lamp off when the electricity went off. It just let us know the electricity is back on." He sat up, taking Charlotte with him, and tucked the quilt around them both. "We are now back in the machine age." His arm curved possessively around her waist. His hand rested on her hip and rubbed back and forth.

"The house is humming."

"It does that when it's happy to be working again. After all, it did have a long enough rest. The furnace kicked in. The stove will be working. No more pioneer-style meals."

"It's still dark outside." Charlotte looked to the side. Only night showed itself outside the window. "We're going to have trouble getting back to sleep."

"I don't think so." Tyler's hand left her hip and stroked across to her inner thigh. "I think we can think of some way to avoid a bout of insomnia." His hand stilled but his fingers were busy.

"You're insatiable." Any other words Charlotte had planned to say were stopped by Tyler's mouth on hers.

"Are you glad?"

"Yes," her answer whispered out. Then there was no need for more words.

"Good morning, sunshine." Tyler kissed the top of Charlotte's head. "It looks like our oasis of love is operating on limited time." The phone rang. "Civilization is quickly crowding in on us." He walked over and picked up the receiver.

As Charlotte watched him, mixed feelings flooded through her. *Things will never be like they have been these past glorious days. They can't be. There's so much about me we don't know. It has to make some difference. Not much.*

Please, not much. She sighed as she watched Tyler come back to her.

"They were letting me know the phone is back on. I guess . . ." The phone rang again. He shrugged and went to it.

Real life is back. Charlotte sighed. No more make-believe.

Tyler walked over to her and picked up his robe from the floor.

"That was Jake. He clears my driveway. He said he hopes to get to the driveway no later than tomorrow. I told him about your car and asked him to see if he could at least try to get to your purse, even if he can't do the plowing. He said he'll see what he can do."

"That's good." Charlotte didn't feel what her words were saying. She wasn't sure what she felt. She knew she should be relieved that she would finally learn her identity. Relief wasn't the only thing she felt. Fear of what they would learn was mixed in with it.

"What's the matter?" Tyler climbed in beside her and tucked the covers around them.

"I was just wondering."

"About what?"

"About us. How much of what we feel is because of the storm, because we were snowbound? How will things between us change?"

"Why should they?"

"They have to."

"Why?" Tyler asked again. He pulled her close. "Being snowbound had nothing to do with how I feel. I'd feel the same way about you if we were in a skyscraper apartment building in the middle of Manhattan in June." He kissed her.

"But I'm sure I'll have to leave. There has to be some reason why I was in a hurry to get home. I don't think I'm stupid enough to go out in a storm like that unless I had a good reason."

"You are many things." He pulled her closer. "But stupid is not one of them. You'll leave to tend to whatever you have to, but you'll come back to me. You'll take care of whatever there is, tie up every one of those loose ends dangling in your life and then you'll hurry back here to me because I will be waiting." He brushed his lips across hers. "Impatiently." He brushed his lips back the other way. "Promise me you'll come back."

"Yes, I will. You know I will."

He pulled her closer and kissed her again. "Maybe I'll drop everything and come with you. I won't be able to concentrate on music or anything else except you, anyway. Why shouldn't I go with you?"

"No reason. No reason at all."

Together they forgot, for a little while longer, that reality was fast closing in on them. They showed their love to each other again and let it grow a bit more.

Tyler stood, eased Charlotte up with him and held her close.

"Because you are a guest, a most welcome one I might add, I will let you have the honor of taking the first hot shower. I would suggest that we take it together, but I know we'd just need another one afterward."

"I know you're right." She planted a quick kiss on his lips and hurried upstairs. She didn't want to waste any of this last private time they had together.

Later that evening, a knock on the door followed the sound of a truck coming up the driveway.

"Mr. Fleming, I was able to get to the lady's handbag. I knew you were in a hurry, so I came over before the night chased me home." He handed the purse to Tyler. Charlotte grasped Tyler's arm as he held her past in his hands.

"Thanks, Jake. We really appreciate this."

"No problem, Mr. Fleming. I can't pull the car out today. I'll have to do that when I come back to clear the driveway."

"Thanks for taking the time to get this. I know you have a lot of people left to plow out."

"That's true, but not as much as I had. I've been going nonstop since before the snow quit falling. The state hired all the independents to help out." He wiped his forehead. "I'm not complaining, mind you. Fact is, I can sure use the extra money, what with the new baby coming and all. About the car. We might have a caved-in fender, but that will probably be it. I don't reckon it will be much of a problem to get her up and running."

"No rush on the car. Whenever you can do it will be fine." Tyler wrapped his hand around Charlotte's shoulder and squeezed. "We're in no hurry. The electricity is on."

"It didn't take much time getting the handbag. After I found the car, the hardest thing was guessing just where the door was. I got to it, though. I figured it must be important if you asked me to get it out for you."

"Yes, it is." Tyler smiled at the man. "It has very important information." Tyler looked at Charlotte and back at Jake. "We'll see you when you can get back here."

"Yes, sir." He looked from one to the other, and Charlotte felt heat flood her face. "I'll see you folks tomorrow."

"He knows about us," Charlotte said after Tyler closed the door.

"Probably so." He smiled at her. "Especially after you blushed so prettily for him."

"Tyler . . ." Charlotte clutched the handbag tightly. She took a deep breath. "I don't know why I'm afraid."

"It's all right. Go on. Open it. Everything will be okay."

"Okay." Charlotte took another deep breath and let it out slowly. "I will."

"Go ahead and look. Let's see if we can clear up the

mystery of Cleo. I want to see how far I was from your real name."

"Here goes." Charlotte took the purse in hands that weren't sure of what they should do. Her fingers fumbled with the catch before managing to turn it to the proper position. Finally, shaky fingers dipped inside and pulled her wallet from its hiding place.

"It's all right." Tyler smiled down at her. "Do you want me to help?" He gave her shoulder a squeeze.

Charlotte couldn't find words, so she nodded.

Tyler opened her wallet to the driver's license. His breath rushed in harshly.

"No." He looked at it again and shook his head. He dropped the wallet to the floor as if it had suddenly burst into flames. "Charlotte Thompson. No. You can't be her." He let his hand drop from Charlotte's shoulder as if flames had flared there as well, and he couldn't touch her any longer. He took a step away and stared at her.

Charlotte saw him shut her out quickly, as if a glass wall had sprung up between them. The look newly planted over Tyler's face said 'stay away' as surely as if it had been spoken.

"Now I know why you didn't tell me your name." He moved even farther away from her, as if he couldn't stand to be close. As if she had suddenly become something distasteful.

"You . . . you know me?" Charlotte took a step back of her own. The ice in Tyler's eyes pushed her away from its chill.

"Come off it. You know me, Charlotte. After all, you took my picture. You knew I would recognize your name. That's why you so conveniently forgot it. You knew I could never forget the name of the woman responsible for my wife's death."

Ten

Charlotte stared up at the stranger Tyler had become. The coldness coming from him was too strong for the fires that had been more than warm enough to fill the room. She shivered as the freeze touched her. This was worse than any nightmare she could ever have had.

"I don't understand. What are you talking about? I lost my memory, but I know I never killed anybody. I could never murder anyone."

"You're good. You're very good. It might not have been murder, but it wouldn't have happened if not for you." The fire of the hate Charlotte saw in his eyes should have melted the stones of ice showing themselves above it. "You missed your calling, Miss Thompson. That was one award-winning performance you put on for me these past days." He pointed to the couch. "You even sacrificed your body to try to prove your amnesia lie."

"No." Charlotte tried to shake his words away. "I . . . really lost my memory. I didn't know my name. I wasn't pretending with you. You must know that." The words dropped from Charlotte in a whisper. He couldn't think that about her. Not after the way he had held her. How could he? How could he forget so easily the deep experience they had had together? What about the love they gave each other?

Tyler went on as if Charlotte's denial had never come. He acted as if her questions had never been put into words.

He went on as if his words were the only thing that mattered and he had to let them go. He had been waiting too long to face someone about it.

"After what you did with your story, I don't know why I'm surprised at how far you would go to try to add strength to your lie. If I had an affair with you, you figured, everyone would believe I had one with my agent. Right? That would mean the article was not slanderous and the court would rule in favor of you and that trashy publication of yours. Is that what you and your paper thought? Did they help you with your plan, or did you come up with it all by yourself? How smug you must have felt. I'm surprised that didn't sneak out when I could see it."

"Tyler, it's not true. None of what you say is true. It couldn't be." Her words tried to reach him, tried to grab him and make him understand. "After what happened between us, you know me better than that. You have to know I wouldn't do anything that would hurt anybody." Tears started a new path down her cheeks.

"Besides," Tyler's words pushed on past Charlotte's as if hers had never left her. "At the least, the story about your affair with Tyler Fleming would give you another dirty tidbit for your readers to snatch up to feed their need for scandal. This time there would be no question of whether or not the story was true, would there? And I fell for it. All of it." Disgust filled his voice. It left no room for words of love to come out like those he had spoken to her not long ago. But long enough ago for him to have forgotten them. "I've heard of women like you." More loathing entered his voice, if that was possible. "I've just never had the displeasure of meeting one."

Charlotte wrapped her arms around her middle. How could he accuse her of such things? How could Tyler, her Tyler, after what they had between them, say such things about her? To her? How could he accuse her of murder? How could he believe such things? How could he? She shook her head. She had to make this bad dream go away. It was worse than that other one, the one where she was being chased. In this one, the man she loved was killing her with his verbal attack.

"I-I don't know what you're talking about. I didn't kill anyone. I-I . . ." Charlotte tried to make sense out of what he was saying. The rest of her memory was pushing at the edge of her mind, still trying to find a way back to her. She needed it. She needed answers to counteract Tyler's accusations. She needed her memory so she could prove how wrong he was. "When I came to, I really couldn't remember anything. Not even my name. I only know it now because of my driver's license." She shook her head. "I wasn't acting with you. Never with you." Her voice dropped to a whisper. She swallowed hard. "I-I slept with you because of my feelings. Because of my love for you." Somewhere she found the courage to look at his face again. When she did, she was sorry she had.

"As I recall, we did very little sleeping."

Charlotte drew back as Tyler's sharp words hit her as if they were cutting into her skin and piercing through to her heart. How could he make something so beautiful seem so sordid?

"Still don't remember? Let me see if I can help the rest of your 'lost memory' find its way back."

Charlotte watched Tyler walk over to the hutch. If the floor were alive, it would have flinched under his punishing steps.

He jerked a drawer open, but nothing dared tumble out. He tugged at the back until he pulled out a folder that had trouble holding all the clippings that had been put into it.

Papers poked out on all three sides as if trying to escape. They looked as disorganized as Charlotte felt. She felt like she was in a fog, but a fog would let her hide from the hurt slicing through her.

"Here." He stood in front of her, but no warmth reached

out from him. "Refresh your forgotten memory. Start with this clipping. You'll find it interesting reading."

Charlotte took the paper he thrust into her hands. She was careful not to let her fingers touch his. He wouldn't like her touch. Not now. Not anymore. Not ever again. She looked at the picture near the top. A beautiful brown face with a wide smile looked back at her. Charlotte's memory pushed a little harder at the edges of her mind, scrabbling to escape from its hiding place.

"You remember Tiffany. You never met her, but I know you remember her."

The headline above the picture shouted at Charlotte:

WIFE OF WELL-KNOWN COMPOSER/MUSICIAN TYLER FLEMING KILLED IN ONE-CAR ACCIDENT

"I'm sorry about this, but I didn't have anything to with it. I couldn't . . ."

"No?" Tyler shoved another clipping at her. The headline blared: Tyler Fleming Blames Wife's Death on Newspaper Story.

Under the headline was a picture of Tyler at a candlelit table in a restaurant. The woman smiling across from him was not the woman smiling from the first clipping.

"I don't understand. Who is this? What does this have to do with me?" Charlotte frowned. The picture looked familiar. She had something to do with it.

"You took that picture. You didn't bother to find out what I was doing in that restaurant or who I was with. You took the picture, made up a lie to go with it, and turned it in to your paper. It probably earned you a fat bonus. Remember now?"

Charlotte started to shake her head. Her frown deepened. "No. I . . ." Her head went still. Her eyes widened. "No," slipped out weakly. She shook her head. "No." This last word exploded from her as more of her memories found a way to escape from the darkness and burst out at her. Char-

lotte grabbed her head with both hands. The paper drifted
to the floor. Thunder pounded in her head.

Tyler watched her plop to the couch. He started toward
her, but stopped. She was sitting on their bed. He pulled
in a big breath. It wasn't a bed. It was a sofa. Just a sofa.

Her face was as pale as when he had put her there the
first time. He would not let his hand brush back that curl
that had welcomed him back then as it had many times
after that. Too many times after that. Earlier today. Was it
just today?

He pulled himself away and stood. He looked at her before he got a glass of water for her. He looked at her forehead. Anyplace but her eyes. The scar had healed nicely.
Soon it would fade completely away. He wondered if his
memories of her would ever do the same.

He stepped back, trying again not to remember the first
time he had placed her on this couch. Or the times after
that. Or the times when he had lain beside her and gathered
her to him. Times when he became one with her as they
traveled on a journey of love. He tried not to remember
that just this morning, his hands had touched the face that
he now knew as well as his own. He tried not to think of
the scars he would carry inside from this woman who had
reached deep inside him and touched his soul as no one
ever had before. This was just part of her act. That's all it
was. It had to be. He couldn't be responsible for tearing
her apart like this.

He stared at her. Feelings of certainty warred with feelings
not so sure inside him. He wished one would hurry and win.

Charlotte stared straight ahead. She wasn't strong enough
to look at him. Not yet. Maybe not ever again.

Tyler took the glass from her shaking hands, but he didn't

touch her. She was glad. She couldn't stand to feel him draw away from her.

"You're better than I thought."

His voice didn't sound as sure as it had before. She sighed. Maybe she was just used to this new harshness coming from him. Or maybe it was only wishful thinking on her part. What did it matter, anyhow? Nothing did. She didn't say anything. What was left for her to say that would make any difference? His next words reached through her thoughts.

"Your acting, I mean."

Charlotte heard him take in a breath. He let it out slowly as if it was a fishing line and he had his catch in sight. Her.

"Can I assume you . . . shall I be kind and say 'remember' everything now?"

He stood over her blocking out the light, but that wasn't why shivers rippled through her.

She didn't know this Tyler. He was nothing like the one who had held her in his arms and covered her with kisses. This wasn't the man who made sweet and tender love with her. This wasn't the Tyler who had promised to protect her. This was a stranger she was stranded with.

"I-I'm not sure. I . . ." She shook her head. "I don't know if. . . ."

"Here. Let's make sure." He held out the folder. His hand didn't look like he knew her or how to caress her. It didn't show any gentleness at all.

Charlotte's own hand shook. She managed to close her fingers enough to hold the folder that seemed to burn her hand. If she was so terrible, did she want to know? A breath wobbled in. Another wobbled out. Then she took in another and dared a glance at Tyler.

His gaze still held as much ice, now as when he had looked at her license. His gaze would be at home outside buried in the snow. He didn't try to let any words out to help melt the ice inside him. Maybe he didn't have any such words. Charlotte looked away again.

She set the folder on her lap. Her hands and fingers shook, but she managed to open the flap. She tightened her whole body and let the tightness spread to her fingers. Then she lifted the top clipping. CHARLOTTE THOMPSON shouted in bold ink under the headline. She was listed as contributing to the story. The story told of how Tyler Fleming was caught in a romantic setting with a woman other than his wife. The story hinted that they had chosen this restaurant because of the motel nearby.

It's not the setting you'd expect to find Mr. Fleming in, but then you shouldn't expect to find him romancing another woman, either. This man who writes so much about finding true love must still be searching for it.

Charlotte read the next article. It was about Tyler's wife's death. A tear slipped out. More tears followed as more memories came creeping out. As they came, they dragged others with them. Before she finished the second paragraph, a wet trail ran down her face.

Angry music came from the studio. When had Tyler left the room? The music formed a background for her as she read of how the paper with the picture of Tyler with the other woman had been found in the house after the accident.

Charlotte closed her eyes. The rest of her memories decided they had hidden long enough and came crashing back. Her anger awoke and matched the music.

She remembered the picture. She remembered taking it, but it wasn't the part of the picture she wanted.

Charlotte swiped at her face. She looked at other clippings. They told of Tyler's wrongful death and slander lawsuit against the paper, the editor, and the photographer/reporter. Her. She put down the clipping.

The open folder still lay on her lap. She stared at the

cold fireplace. Newer memories mixed with the older ones that had been dragged out by the papers and put in their proper places. The newer memories from the past week hurt more than the old ones did.

She thought of her and Tyler being warmed by the fireplace. Her and Tyler being warmed by each other. Her and Tyler getting lost in each other's arms. Her and Tyler. She let her head drop back against the couch. Then, although she didn't want to, she picked up another clipping.

She read through the rest of the papers. Then she shut them away and put the folder beside her. She wanted to put it away from her, but she didn't dare try to walk. Her legs would never make it.

Shadows lengthened in the room and then darkness took over. No matter. She had already read everything. She wished there had been less. She remembered everything. She was as sorry about finding her memory as Tyler had told her she might be. When he had said it, he was trying to reassure her. He didn't know how right he was or what she didn't want to remember. If she just hadn't taken that assignment. If she had let someone else have it.

She sat in the dark listening to the music escaping from Tyler's studio. The angry piano had been replaced by sounds of an orchestra. This new music made new tears start to flow.

Charlotte recognized the song. Each time a newscaster reported an update after Tyler filed his lawsuit, they played snatches from that song, "Suite for Tiffany."

The music tugged at Charlotte and pulled her mood down even lower. It sounded as if Tyler had poured his sorrow into the song he had written for his wife.

Charlotte let the music talk to the sadness still growing inside her.

She sensed rather than heard Tyler come into the room. She tensed before he dropped his words as cold as a ball of the snow that imprisoned her with this man who now hated her.

"I guess your memory is back. Am I right?"

"Yes." Charlotte couldn't nod. "I remember this."

"Sitting in the dark won't help. I know." Tyler reached past her to snap on the lamp.

Charlotte blinked at the sudden glare. She swallowed hard. She glanced at him but quickly looked away. This was the same lamp that had shone in her eyes when the electricity had come back on. Way back in time. So far back, Tyler hadn't learned to hate her yet. That time, he had turned off the light, held her close in his strong gentle arms, and loved her back to sleep.

She looked at him now. Gentleness wasn't coming back. Not for her. He looked like he was carved from the same stone used for his house. That was her fault, too. She took a deep breath. Her mind raced, searching for a path to get past the barrier he had built between them.

"This picture . . ." She held up the clipping. It wavered in her hand, but still she held it up. "I wasn't taking your picture. This was in the background. I hadn't even noticed you. I was concentrating on my story. My editor is the one who recognized you." Charlotte made her gaze stay on him, hoping to see the barrier drop just a little. It didn't. Not one bit. His cold mask was still in place.

"And I just happened to be there."

"I guess so." His face didn't change, but Charlotte made herself explain the story she had been covering.

"The paper was looking for a photojournalist to cover filler stories. I needed a job and this one seemed ideal. I got to travel a little. Only in the Philadelphia area, but that was okay. I visited small towns that I wouldn't have known existed if I hadn't been working on a story." She looked at him then. Her chin lifted and her gaze never wavered. "I got to meet people who were flattered to have somebody interested in their stories. They were glad to be in the paper. They were happy with the stories I wrote." She looked away.

"The paper got a call about a woman who was celebrating her anniversary ten years after she had been given six months to live. They sent me to Newark to cover her story." She blinked. "I did my own photos. They weren't important enough to have an assigned photographer." She shrugged. "Sometimes they used them; sometimes they didn't."

"This time they did. They must have been pleasantly surprised when you handed them the picture."

"I didn't know what I had. They always developed the film."

"Did they give you a bonus, or was sharing credit for the leading story enough for you? I'll bet you got bigger stories after that. Whose life were you messing up this time? Or did you come up here to find me?"

"I don't work for them anymore. I quit. I work freelance now. I heard about a couple in Lackawaxen who were saved from a fire by the stray cat they took in. I was covering that story."

"Another 'feel-good' story."

"I didn't know you were up here. Thornhill Township. I never even heard of it. I wouldn't have come to you if I had. I must have taken a wrong turn somewhere while I was trying to make it back to the turnpike."

"You sure did." He glared at her. "Did you hope to persuade me to drop the case? How much did they promise you if you did?"

She shook her head. It was no use. She quit trying.

Tyler didn't say anything else. He didn't have to. His stare spoke more clearly than words ever could.

She didn't blame him for not believing her. If she didn't know what she had told him was true, she wouldn't have believed it herself. Coincidences, especially ones with terrible results, were hard to accept.

She swallowed a lump the size of a grapefruit. Then she had to try again.

"I knew that paper's reputation, but I only did human interest stories."

"I doubt your paper would be interested in anything that had human interest. Its purpose is to tear down people's lives. To destroy whomever it can."

"Tyler, I . . ." She stood and reached to him.

His stare held hers for many heartbeats. Finally, he unfolded his arms and shrugged.

"It doesn't matter now, does it? It's too late."

He turned from Charlotte and strode away. His heavy footsteps on the stairs told her where he was going. Charlotte sat back down. She waited . . . for what? She didn't know. There wasn't anything else she could do.

Tyler was right. It was her fault. It was all her fault. She hadn't written the story, but if she hadn't taken that picture, Tiffany wouldn't have died. If Charlotte had not given up with her editor, if she had argued longer, harder, maybe they would have dropped the story and the woman with the wide smile would still be alive. Charlotte knew the kind of stories the paper was known for when she went to work for them, but she figured it wouldn't matter as long as she didn't write them.

She stared into the cold fireplace and felt colder than it could ever be.

Silence hung heavy in the air now empty of music. More memories bubbled up and showed themselves, mostly the ones about Tyler, but an old one, too.

The memory of her argument with her editor over the picture and the story came back like a constant rerun of an old movie. It kept shoving aside the memories of Tyler. Her and Tyler. Tyler smiling at her. Tyler kissing her. Tyler. Then her editor's face would show itself again.

She closed her eyes and let her head rest on her arms

on her knees. Closing her eyes made things worse. The next memories brought more pain with them.

She remembered how long it took her to find another job after she had quit that one. Nobody wanted a journalist involved in a legal scandal. Her savings disappeared dollar by dollar as if some evil magician was at work.

She remembered the move to a smaller apartment outside the city. One not so upscale. Then came her job as a waitress. She remembered her first sale of a freelance article after she had almost given up writing. Those were hard times.

Things were only a little better now, but she wasn't sorry she'd quit that job. Tyler was right. The story was her fault. She never should have gone to work for them.

She opened her eyes and again stared into the dead fire and felt just as dead inside.

She was still staring when Tyler came back and lifted the mattress from the floor and stood it on end. It hadn't been used much. They hadn't needed to.

Charlotte opened her mouth to offer to help, but closed it without speaking. Tyler's look had stopped her words.

She watched him push it to the stairs. As she heard the mattress scrub along and land on each step, she folded the bedding he had ripped off it and placed it in a pile on a chair.

It wasn't long before he was back. Not long enough. He hesitated, darted a look at her, then grabbed the pile of bedding from the chair.

"I'll fix up the guest room for you." The word 'guest' came out as if Tyler wanted to be rid of it, just like he wanted to be rid of her.

Charlotte watched him go and tried not to think of last night. Last night and again this morning, when the two of them had filled this house with love. When she and Tyler had made glorious, heated love. Afterward she had fallen asleep in his arms. Then her world was perfect even without her memories.

She thought of how, surrounded by cold snow, their love had created a place as warm as the tropics for their paradise.

Electric heat hummed and filled the house now, but the atmosphere was as cold as the snow blanket covering the world outside.

Charlotte was dragged back to the present when Tyler's footsteps told her he was back.

"I'll fix something to eat."

"I'm not hungry." Charlotte remembered that Tyler hadn't paid for the silly bet he had lost. Now he never would.

"It's been a long time since we last ate."

"I know." She shook her head. "But I-I couldn't eat anything. Don't bother for me." He wouldn't bother with her, either. Not ever again. She glanced at him, prepared this time for the cold she would still find in his face.

"You should eat. You should . . ." Tyler shrugged. "It doesn't matter. I'm not hungry either." He stared at her. Then he blinked and looked away. "I'll show you where your room is."

Charlotte followed Tyler upstairs and down the hall. They had carried his mattress the other way down this same hall. She tried to keep from remembering how she had started the night on its softness in front of the fire downstairs. That was another lifetime. Another part of her. One that didn't exist anymore. Juno nudged her hand as if it would help.

"In here." Tyler stepped aside at a doorway and let her into the room. He didn't look at her as she passed.

The thick area rug covering most of the floor should have welcomed Charlotte with its warmth as she stepped onto it. Floor-to-ceiling drapes in shades of blue covered the wide window, but Charlotte imagined the view of Mt. Pocono hiding in the darkness beyond. A lamp glowed at her from a nightstand, as if trying to be cheerful for her. Its effort was wasted. Nothing could have made her feel welcome, now that the one person who mattered didn't want her anymore.

The muted color of the drapes and matching bedspread should have soothed her and let peace wash over her. She should have felt welcomed by the soft light reaching from the lamp. Instead, all of it made her aware of how different this room was from the storm churning within her like a disturbed sea. She sighed and let her feet take her farther into the room. Her hand brushed slowly over the smooth top of the dark oak dresser, stopping at a bowl made of swirling blues and reds and purples. She traced one of the swirls and felt more at home with the coldness of the glass than with the warmth of the dark maple.

"I'll see you in the morning." Tyler's words bounced off Charlotte's back. "If you need anything else . . ." His words stopped but his stare went on.

Charlotte knew what wasn't included in his 'anything else.' Him. She would never be allowed to need him again.

He walked away from her and into his own room that they were never able to share. The door clicked, shutting him away from Charlotte, closing her off from him.

Charlotte picked up the robe draped over the small blue and red upholstered chair in the corner. Tyler's robe. She held it to her as she wished Tyler would come back and hold her. Her fingers tightened in the fabric. Never again. He'd never hold her again. He'd never want her again. The only thing he wanted from her was for her to be gone. For her to have never touched his life.

Charlotte picked up her nightshirt. Tyler's shirt. The shirt he had eased off her when they had made love the last time. For the last time.

She closed her eyes, but not tight enough to keep a tear from escaping. The spicy scent of Tyler's aftershave came to her. She pictured his warm brown eyes full of love. Overflowing with love for her.

Her eyes opened. The last time she had dared to look

into his eyes, she'd found no warmth for her. His eyes had looked as if ice chunks from the frozen outside had moved in, but Charlotte knew the cold was only for her.

She clutched the shirt and robe to her and went into the bathroom, wondering how she would get through the night.

The steaming shower cascading over her did nothing to warm her inside. Her tears, finally allowed free, rolled down her face and mixed with the water pelting her. Something Tyler had said when he was trying to reassure her, when he cared about her, when he loved her, came back.

"Some people have memories they wish would stay away," he had said. Then, she hadn't believed that was possible. She did now. Her memories of her with Tyler hurt too much. But did she wish them away?

She dried off, pulled the nightshirt over her head and thrust her arms into the robe. She wrapped it close, as if it could protect her from more hurt, and plodded down the hall. She hesitated outside Tyler's door. Then she forced herself to move on.

She put the robe back on the chair and slipped between the cold sheets. After the couch, the bed was too big. After sharing her sleeping space with Tyler, this bed felt as wide as a night desert. And just as cold and lonely.

She turned over and wished for a quick night. She wished for a quick escape from Tyler in the morning. She wished she had never met him. Didn't she? She sighed. Then she never would have lain in his arms, exhausted from glorious lovemaking. Did she wish that away, too? In spite of the hurt now and Tyler's hate for her, the answer was still 'no.'

Tyler sat up. The quiet of the house usually comforted him, but not tonight. He glanced at the clock and saw that it was early morning. The quiet was just quiet. Nothing more. Sleep was eluding him as the muse rarely did. What he did, what he said to her, didn't have anything to do with how he felt, did it?

He pulled on his robe, trying not to think of his other robe, and left his lonely room.

He stole a glance at the door he had closed earlier. He tried not to think of the woman inside the room and how she had felt against him when he'd held her before . . .

His trying wasn't working. He drew in a deep breath and went down the stairs.

He stood looking at the fireplace that was as dead and cold as he felt. He forced himself into the room that held so many memories and sat on the sofa. More memories, vivid ones, flew up to greet him as if he wanted them.

Visions of Cleo . . . He shook his head. Not Cleo. Charlotte. Her name is Charlotte. Visions of Charlotte in his arms flew at him. He closed his eyes and imagined her smooth skin against him, her body under his hands. Her under him.

He remembered the passion, passion for him, in her eyes when he'd entered her. He remembered how they'd ridden the waves of love together to paradise.

He opened his eyes and shook the image away. There was no love in her for him. She had been acting. All of it was an act.

But how could she? another part of him asked. How could she be involved in the cause of Tiffany's death? The police had said it was an accident, but he knew if Tiffany hadn't seen that picture, she would have been driving more carefully, wouldn't she have? He had never doubted that before. Why now? She wouldn't have been out in the rain, would she? The crash would never have happened without that story, would it?

Tyler sat in the dark, hoping it would ease some of the pain of his memories, both old and new. Especially the new ones, with their still sharp corners, that hurt more than the old. Hurting memories of the warm-bodied woman who had just this morning lain in his arms as if she belonged there swirled up and through him. This morning when things were perfect. It was just this morning, but a lifetime ago.

Had she really lost her memory? Was a photojournalist a good enough actress to make him believe her memory was gone? Wouldn't there have been something in her, a look, something in her eyes, some little thing to give her away? Would someone, would anyone be foolish enough to travel in that storm and deliberately run her car off the road in a blizzard to prove . . . To prove what? Tyler shook his head.

How would she know where he lived? Few people did. Would she take a chance on not being found? If she had been coming to him, why did she wait until a terrible snowstorm to do it? She was unconscious when he found her. That much he knew for sure.

He tightened his hands together. What would be her reason for doing what he had accused her of? Of coming to him now? It was a civil case. She didn't have to fear jail. And she had no money. His attorney told him that. She had nothing to lose.

His jaw tightened to match his hands. She had nothing but her reputation. But would reputation matter to someone who worked for a paper like that, a person who wrote stories like her paper printed? He shook his head and stood.

Slowly, he made his way up the stairs. Confusion stayed with him. He tried to turn off the two sides battling inside him as memories walked along with him.

The lovemaking was real. Her inexperience was real. There was no way she could have faked that.

The memory of the passion in her eyes when she was in his arms tore into his mind. He sighed. It had been just as real for her as it had been for him. Oh yeah, it had been real, sensuously real, for him.

His hands opened and closed as if they were around her smooth shoulders. He could almost feel her satiny skin under his hands, could almost see her body bathed in the sheen after their lovemaking.

Her image came to him as real as if it was there and she was catching the glow from the fireplace now.

He swallowed hard, wishing the memory would pull back, if only a little bit, and take its hurt, its agony with it.

In the hallway, he paused outside her door again. He imagined her in bed trying to sleep. No matter what, after the sharp words he had thrown at her, sleep couldn't come easily to her. No easier than it did to him.

He forced his feet to carry him to the end of the hall and into his room. He didn't expect sleep to visit anytime soon. He wasn't sure he deserved for it to come and give him even just a little peace.

He opened the drapes, and moonlight splashed into his room as if it was glad to have the snow curtain gone. As if Tyler cared one way or the other.

He crawled into his king-size bed and tried to will his mind to stay away from 'what ifs,' but he couldn't do it. 'What ifs' flooded his mind.

What if things were different between Charlotte and him? What if she had been just what she had appeared to be: a reporter caught in a blizzard coming from covering a make-you-feel-happy story? What if she wasn't in bed down the hall? What if he was waiting for her to come share his bed, a real bed for the first time, with him so he could love her?

He turned over and punched his pillow. Every last person on earth had a head full of 'what ifs.' *'What ifs' could drive you crazy if you let them.*

He pulled up the covers and smoothed them out, wishing he could smooth his thoughts as easily. It was going to be the longest night of his life.

Eleven

The new morning finally had pity on Charlotte. The sun poked its fingers of light into the room, copying the pattern of the curtains onto the wall, hinting at the brilliance to come. A bird sang and another answered as if glad the morning had arrived.

Charlotte was glad, too. She was glad, after turning in the lonely bed through the night, that she didn't have to go on pretending she expected sleep to come to her. She was grateful the night had decided to have mercy on her and end its stay. Would she ever get used to sleeping without Tyler's arms wrapped around her? How had she gotten so used to his body cuddled close to hers in such a short time? It had only been a few days. Just a few days. How had his roots anchored themselves in her heart so deeply that removing them ripped her heart to shreds?

She sat up. Wondering wouldn't ease the hurt filling her. Even if she found her answer to the unanswerable questions, it wouldn't change the way things were. Answers couldn't take away the pain. She swallowed a lump. Just a little while longer. She only had to bear it just a little while longer.

With the morning here, she was closer to leaving this place that was torturing her with happy memories of time spent with Tyler. The time when, not too long ago, she could look at him and see only love in his eyes. Love. Only love and concern for her instead of the loathing that glared at her when she last looked. She never thought that happy memories could cause such pain. Part of the pain was because, in spite of Tyler's new hate for her, her heart was still full of nothing but love for him. At least what was left of her heart was; the part that hadn't been shredded to little scraps.

She looked at the light dancing over the walls. So much brightness today. She sighed. She could use some of that brightness inside her to warm the places that Tyler's coldness had touched. She needed a lot of it. Contrary to what someone had once said, things didn't always look better in the light of day.

She envied the early dazzle that promised more to come. The day held no promise for her. It gave her nothing to look forward to. Neither did the future that waited ahead. She could only hope for time to fast-forward to when the tow truck driver came back to free her car so she could get away from here. She shook her head. She'd leave, but she'd never be free.

She wiped at her eyes and hoped the tears wouldn't start. The sun was too bright for tears. Tears wouldn't make her feel any better. They wouldn't change her future. They couldn't. She'd pick up her life and try to forget this past week. She'd try to put Tyler from her mind, try to forget him and what a beautiful thing they had had together. She put on her robe. She swallowed hard. It wasn't hers.

She'd try to forget Tyler, but she didn't expect to succeed. She'd never be able to push him from her mind. She wasn't sure, even now, that she wanted him forgotten like her old memories had been. She loved him. She just wished she could push them far enough back so they wouldn't always hurt as much as they did now.

He would never believe she was telling the truth. That fact put thorns on the memories that pierced her. He believed what had happened between them was based on her deceit. How could he?

She took her underwear from the baseboard heater. At least she hadn't had to depend on the wood-burning stove to dry them last night. She wouldn't have minded using the stove again, though, if it meant other things were like they had been once upon a time. She went into the bathroom.

Any other time, the warm water flowing over her body would have soothed her. Now her muscles, as tense as if they had stood vigil all night, refused to relax.

Charlotte allowed a few tears to mix with the shower water pouring over her, wishing they would empty her misery and let the water take them down the drain with it. It hadn't happened last night and it wouldn't happen now. She wouldn't think of how, if she weren't Charlotte Thompson, but Cleo, Tyler would be in here with her and she would have no tears to shed.

She stepped out onto the bath mat and wrapped a thick towel around her hair. She pulled another from the shelf and rubbed her body dry. She pulled on the robe—Tyler's robe—for the last time. She wished she had brought her other clothes with her into the bathroom. Tyler's robe reminded her too much of him.

Back in the bedroom, she pulled on her clothes, trying not to think of the morning that awaited her and how different it was from the one that could have been. She picked up Tyler's hairbrush, which he had left on the dresser for her. She pulled it through her hair, wishing there was something she could use to untangle her life as easily as the brush did her hair.

"May as well wish for the moon." She repeated the saying her grandmom had used whenever Charlotte had voiced an impossible childhood wish. This adult wish was just as impossible as any of hers as a little girl.

* * *

Tyler lay in bed listening to the shower. He tried not to let his fantasy—from before this nightmare began—find its way to the surface. His fantasy was of sharing a shower with Cleo before she had become Charlotte. The shower with her wasn't real. What he had shared was. He had shared much more than a shower with her. He had shared his soul.

He punched his pillow and shifted in the too-wide bed with the extra pillow waiting. She'd be fixing her hair now. He wondered if that curl, the curl with a mind of its own, behaved any better when it was wet than when it was dry. He could almost feel it wrap itself around his fingers as it did when he'd threaded his hands through her hair. He clenched his hands. His fingers would have to get used to being without that curl, just as his body would have to get used to being without hers close enough to touch whenever he wanted. Would he ever stop wanting her?

He sat up and leaned against the headboard. His hands bunched and smoothed the covers, and then bunched them again. He wondered if she had slept any better than he had. He hoped not. Not after what she had done. How could she do what she did? And why did he still want her?

He heard her pad softly back to her room as if she was trying not to disturb him. He sighed. She was too late for that. About a week too late.

This thing he was feeling started building when he'd uncovered her in the snow. It continued as he carried her into his house. He fought against releasing it, but something stirred inside him that he hadn't been aware he still had. He thought those feelings had been dead and buried for three years. They were dead until almost a week ago. She had come into his life and sparked it awake like a match touched to a pile of shredded newspapers. He had fought the attraction, but he had lost before the battle had begun. He wished he had fought harder. He wished he hadn't let her get close. He remembered how her eyes filled with passion when she was in his arms. He shook his head. He shouldn't have let her reach so deep inside him. It hurt too much to push her away now.

He went into the bathroom and tried to let the shower wash away what was left of his attraction for her. Attraction wasn't the right word. Attraction described something casual, something superficial. It didn't begin to touch what he felt.

He closed his eyes and let the water pour over him, but he didn't expect something so big and rooted so deeply to wash away so easily. It probably never would. And that wouldn't surprise him.

Charlotte went downstairs. The sound of Tyler's shower told her she wouldn't meet him in the hall. She wasn't ready to see him yet. She wouldn't be later, either. She went into the beautiful kitchen, remembering the bit of memory about her own kitchen. It was nothing like this one. At least, when she got home, she wouldn't be reminded of him every time she went into the room. She turned on the burner under the bright red tea kettle. She hesitated. Would Tyler want anything she fixed? Did his hate reach that far? She shrugged, filled the coffeemaker for him and flipped the switch. She tried to make her mind stay blank while she waited for the water for her tea to boil. She leaned against the table. It was a long wait. The old saying was true: A watched pot never boils. She got the mugs, and hesitated before she put hers in front of the chair she had sat in yesterday, when it was her place. Today she didn't have a place here anymore.

Thoughts about Tyler, the past, and the future crept out, but she managed to shove them back. When the water was ready, she poured it over her tea, sat at the table and began sipping. It might as well have been plain hot water for all the notice she gave the flavor. She set the cup down. She heard Tyler's footsteps coming down the stairs, coming toward her. Her fingers tightened around the mug as if afraid it would try to get away from what was coming and leave her here alone.

Please let me get through this, she prayed. Just let me get through this time I have left to spend here. The huge house wasn't big enough anymore.

Tyler stepped into the room and stood in the doorway. He looked at Charlotte. The wariness in her eyes, when she dared to look at him, reminded him of a doe that had wandered out of the woods last spring. Charlotte looked ready to spring away now. With the doe, all Tyler had had to do was stand still to make that look go away. With Charlotte, it would take more than that. It would take more than he had. The words he had hurled at her last night had seen to that.

He blinked. In spite of the way she looked, all covered with hurt, he wasn't sure he'd take the words back even if he could. He wasn't sure they hadn't been right. He wasn't sure of a lot of things this morning.

He walked closer and saw her stiffen. He thought again about his words. Maybe he hadn't needed words quite so sharp as the ones he had used. He sighed. But maybe he had.

"Morning." He filled his mug. In spite of everything he had said, the way he acted toward her, she had thought to make coffee for him. Why?

"Morning." Her voice whispered as if it wasn't sure it was supposed to be there. Her wariness had pulled back a bit, but he could still see it. He wondered if it would ever go away. Would it still be there after she left him? What did he care? He turned from her and started toward the window, but her words stopped him before he got there.

"You have to listen to me. Please, Tyler."

Tyler stopped walking, but he didn't turn back around to face her. She continued to speak anyway.

"What I said last night is true. Everything. You were sitting behind the couple whose picture I was taking. I always did the photos for my stories." She shrugged. "The paper didn't think they were worth the expense of a photographer." She held out her hands. "I didn't even notice you in the restaurant. I was focused on my story. That's the way I work."

Tyler's back tightened as if the muscles were trying for a straight line. His teeth clenched. He would not notice the plea in her voice. He would not let it reach inside him and look for a soft spot to touch. He would not look into her eyes.

"My editor noticed you." Her voice trembled. Tyler tried to ignore it. "The story about you was all her idea. She gave it to a staff writer. She knew I'd never write a story like that. The first I knew about it was when she showed me the galley."

"I'm sure you pleaded with her not to run it."

"I did. I really did." Charlotte hesitated.

Tyler noticed the hesitation. His soft spot hardened a bit.

"At least I asked her not to run the story based on the picture I took. I begged her to investigate first."

Charlotte walked over to him like she was trying not to let the floor feel her footsteps. He wouldn't turn to her. Not now. Not again. She placed her hand on his arm. He looked at it and Charlotte pulled it away. He waited. He didn't know what for.

"I didn't know anything about your private life. I know a lot of people have one face they show to the public and another they wear in private. Still, I asked her . . ." Charlotte shook her head. "No, I begged her not to run that picture." Her voice lost some of its power. The next words drifted out and fell between them as powerful as stray snowflakes. "Whether or not you believe me, that's the truth. That's exactly how it happened. I don't know what else I can do to convince you. How can you believe I'd do something to hurt somebody?"

Tyler moved farther away from her. He walked over to the window and stared out. The green tips of the highest yews were peeking out above the white. The snow had begun to thaw. He didn't know when he would, if ever.

"I quit my job over that story. I spent months . . ." Charlotte's voice broke as if it were a string stretched too tight.

Tyler still refused to face her. He couldn't.

"Oh, what's the use. What's the use?"

Tyler didn't have to see the tears. His ears told him they were there. He listened as she fled from the room and up the stairs. He tightened his feet to the place at the window.

Part of him wanted to believe her. Part of him wanted to go after her and take her in his arms. Part of him wanted to tell her that things would be all right, that he loved her. A big part wanted to admit his love for her, but it wasn't the strongest part of him.

Tyler stared into his now cold coffee. He set the mug down on the counter. Then he put his hands in his pockets and went into the living room.

Memories of the hours he had spent with Charlotte in his arms greeted him when he looked at the sofa. He sat in the chair instead of on the sofa and stared at the cold ashes in the fireplace. He thought of the fires he had built there and the fires they had built together on their sofa bed. He tried to push their fires away. He tried to think about anything else to take his mind away from the sofa and what had happened between them there many times. Too many times. Not enough times.

He was still trying when the telephone jangled later. He had no idea how much later. It didn't matter. Nothing mattered right now. He picked up the receiver more to stop the noise than to talk to anyone. He didn't want to talk to anyone. Maybe he never would again.

The message was only a few words, but it was what he

had been waiting for. Then why didn't he feel happy about it? Why didn't he at least feel some relief? He stopped looking for answers that didn't exist and left the room hoping to leave the memories it held as well.

He took a deep breath and went up the stairs. His footsteps sounded to him like those of a man twice his age. Or twice his weight. Maybe this last was more true. He felt heavier, as if he had the weight of all the snow that had fallen during the storm heaped on his back.

He stopped outside Charlotte's room. The door was open, but he didn't go in. This was his house, but there was no place for him in that room with her.

Charlotte sat on the edge of the bed staring straight ahead. She looked as if, if someone had asked her, she couldn't tell them where she was. Tyler knew she wished she were anywhere but here with him. He knew because he wished that, too.

She looked like she had been crying. Her eyes were dry, but redness gave away their secret. He had been right about at least one thing: Those were tears he had heard mixed in with her voice when she'd tried to get him to listen downstairs. Was that the only thing he had been right about?

He watched Charlotte's hands tremble as they turned a wad of tissue over and over as if looking for a dry spot. Her hands would tighten until the tissue disappeared, then they would smooth and stretch the tissue over her lap before they balled it up again. She looked as if she didn't know Tyler was there, as if she hadn't heard him plodding his way to her as if over thick wooden planks. Maybe she thought if she didn't look at him, he would disappear. She would want him to disappear. She'd be happy to leave him, be glad for his news. He sighed. Maybe happy and glad weren't the right words to use right now.

Tyler looked hard at her before he spoke. He tried not to remember that he had done this to her. He made her like this. But she deserved it, didn't she? He shook his head, but that didn't clear his thoughts. He gave up trying.

"Jake said he'll be here in about an hour."

"Okay." Charlotte darted a look at him, then let her gaze slip back to the tissue in her hands.

"I'll go fix breakfast."

"I'm not hungry." She shook her head and pushed her hair back from her face. Not him. It would never be him again. Someday it would be somebody else. She would look at someone else with the passion she had showed to him. Somebody else would have the right to hold her in his arms and. . . .

He flinched at the stab of pain that shot through him. That wasn't his business. She wasn't his business; she would never be his again. He had made sure of that.

"I'll fix something anyway. You might change your mind."

Tyler felt his hands open and close as if trying to reach her and claim again. Not so long ago, he had had that right. She had been his. His to touch and caress and love. He had to give his hands something to do instead of reach for her and pull her close. He thrust them into his pockets instead. He looked at her a few seconds longer, but she never looked back at him. She never looked up, as if she knew he was still there, staring at her.

He went down to the kitchen feeling no lighter than when he had gone up. He poured out the old coffee and filled his mug again. He set out Juno's food. She'd enjoy her breakfast. He blinked hard. Then he started to cook a breakfast that no one would eat.

Tyler lifted his cup, but put it down after one sip. He looked at the platter of bacon and eggs and the plate of toast. Butter was melting and seeping into the crevices. He set the plate on the table and took out the jar of the mixed fruit jam Charlotte had grown to love. His jaw clinched.

He shouldn't use the word love anymore when he thought about Charlotte.

He looked at the table beckoning to him with its bright, rainbow-colored place mats and dishes full of food. What a waste. He felt as much like eating as Cleo . . . He shook his head. He had to remember. Her name was Charlotte. Maybe the animals would enjoy the food.

He dumped the cold coffee and poured a third. He picked up his mug and left the room that was too bright for his mood.

He hesitated, then went into the living room and over to the window. His coffee was forgotten as he stared out at the snow carpet that had started it all, beginning with finding her. His trip from her car had been the start of what was between them.

It led to the other trips he had taken with Cleo . . . With Charlotte. Trips to glorious peaks where, locked together, they had perched dizzily before soaring to new elevations. Then they had floated lazily back to reality still as one. Afterward, they had lain together in each other's arms. Tyler clenched his jaw.

Reality was the wrong word to use. None of what had been between them was real. It would stay with him in his memory, come out and torture him whenever he wasn't careful, but it hadn't been reality. Reality was that she had lied to him. Reality was that she would do anything for a story, that she had done anything for a story. Look what she had allowed to happen between them.

He set the full mug down. He wouldn't have to worry about too much caffeine keeping him awake tonight. He'd have other things bothering his mind. Things that would disturb him much more than caffeine ever could.

The sound of the brass door knocker roused him from his thoughts. He welcomed the interruption. The knocker dropped a second time and he went to the door.

"Morning, Mr. Fleming." Jake's smile didn't belong here

in this house. "I cleared the driveway and got to the lady's car. I uncovered it the rest of the way so I could take a good look. The right fender is bent in against the tire as I thought it might be, but I'll be able to pull it away enough to drive the car."

"Thanks, Jake. Come on in."

"Not just yet. I'll go work on the fender and make sure everything else is all right. I'll probably have to jump the battery and we'll have to let it run for a while. Wouldn't want the lady to have trouble. If she has to stop somewhere, I want to make sure she can get it started again. I just came up to let you know what's going on."

"Thanks, Jake. How much do I owe you?"

Jake told him. "But I can put it on the tab along with the plowing, if that's all right with you," he added.

"That will be fine, if that's the way you want to do it." Tyler shut the door. He tensed as he heard Charlotte's steps on the stairs, soft, as if she didn't want to bother them. It was too late for her to worry about bothering anything, especially him.

He turned and his stare met hers. He was lost for a moment as he remembered the first time he had seen those brown eyes. They had been so warm and soft. He remembered the body he had warmed that first night before he had even seen her eyes.

He willed that image away, although his body tensed with the memory of her body against his. The warmth was gone from her eyes now. The life was gone from them, too. He had done that, but he didn't try to bring it back. He didn't know if he could if he tried. But he didn't even try.

"Jake got your car uncovered." His voice wasn't as rough as he was afraid it would be. "He went to pull it onto the driveway. He said he has to pull the fender away from the tire and put a charge on the battery. He'll be back up in a little while."

Charlotte nodded. She looked as if it took a great effort.

Her gaze met his and lingered for a few seconds before it dropped away. He stood and looked at her through the wall of ice she had placed between them that was a twin to his. No amount of heat could melt this freeze that had replaced the flames that once burned between them. Sadness grew in Tyler and he didn't try to understand it.

The knocker pushed into the heavy silence and Tyler welcomed the sound.

"Come on in, Jake." Tyler was glad he hadn't taken longer.

Jake stepped onto the mat, stamped his feet and brushed them back and forth. Then he stamped them again.

"She'll be set to go in about a half hour, give or take."

"Take off your jacket and come have a cup of coffee."

"I don't want to track up your floors. I can wait right here."

"The floors are slate. Rock. They're used to all kinds of weather." If Jake didn't come in, what would Tyler and Charlotte do together for the half hour that would feel like a year? "Follow me." He led Jake to the kitchen. "Besides, that's hard work that you do. I'll bet you could use a break."

"You'd win that bet." Jake took off his gloves and stuffed them into his pocket before he took off his jacket. "That stuff is melting, but it's still as cold as a bin of ice cubes." He pulled the cap from his head and stuffed it into the other pocket. "I been working nearly nonstop since before the snow quit. Ain't had a full night's sleep since then."

Tyler tried not to think of the reason he hadn't had a full night's sleep since he and. . . . He took in a deep breath as the nights since he'd found Charlotte flitted through his mind, spiking and swirling as they ran their course, just as their loving had spiked and swirled and soared. He didn't look at Charlotte's face, but he saw water slosh over the sides of the mug as she filled her cup from the kettle. He knew the same thing was romping through her mind, too.

"Sit down, Jake. Do you want cream and sugar?"

"No cream. I like it black, but with lots of sugar. My wife, Mabel, says if I ever give up sugar, I'll put the whole industry into a tailspin."

Tyler managed a smile that he wasn't feeling and set the full mug and the sugar bowl in front of Jake.

"Help yourself to some toast. I don't think it's too cool to eat. And you may as well take the eggs and bacon, too." Tyler pushed the platter closer to him.

"I don't want to take breakfast from you folks."

"Neither one of us is hungry this morning." Tyler knew this was one thing Charlotte wouldn't disagree about.

Jake lifted a piece of toast to his mouth. He chewed a little before he washed it down with a swallow of coffee. Then he started filling his plate from the platter.

"I tell you," he said between bites, "I sure worked up an appetite with all the plowing I already did this morning. I ain't complaining. I can always use the work." He took another bite and another sip of coffee. "If I'm not mowing and trimming in summer and raking and taking down trees in the fall, I'm moving snow in winter and towing folks out." He reached for another slice of toast and smeared jam over it before he took a bite. "But like I said, I'm not complaining."

"Tell us about what you've been doing these past few days," Tyler said. *I'll grab at anything to fill the emptiness waiting for words I don't have,* he thought.

Charlotte sat holding her cup like it was empty. She had fewer words to share than Tyler did.

While cleaning the platter, Jake told them of the world left by the snowstorm.

"All of my customers were snowed in this time, but I clear them on a priority basis. Dr. Bailey's parking lot and his driveway were first. They always are. His patients have to be able to get in to him and he has to be able to get out to them."

"You've been helping with the roads this time?"

"Yeah. The county and state pressed every independent in the area into service. They could have used at least twenty more if they were up here."

Tyler was glad there wasn't going to be a test later on the information. He couldn't have repeated any of Jake's saga, but he was glad for it. He needed for it to fill the wide space between him and Charlotte. Or at least to try to fill it. He appreciated Jake's effort, but nothing could really fill a valley that wide, a chasm as deep as the one he had dug between them.

"I guess I'd best get back to work. The car should be ready to go." Jake gave his mouth a final wipe with the napkin. "Thanks for the breakfast. Don't tell Mabel about this. She fixed me a good, full breakfast before I left the house this morning. She always does." He looked at the platter. A few bits of egg looked lonely by themselves. "Sorry about that, Mr. Fleming. Mabel says nobody should set food in front of me unless they expect me to finish it off."

"No problem. It would have gone to waste."

Jake patted the beginning of a paunch that was out of place on his spare frame.

"I'm afraid it's going to a different kind of 'waist.' " He released a quick laugh. "I got to cut back. My eating is beginning to settle in and make itself at home." He turned to Charlotte. "I guess you're anxious to be on your way."

"Yes, I am." She set her mug on the table, then picked it up and put it in the sink.

Jake led the way to the door. Tyler followed, trying not to notice Charlotte's whispering movements behind him. They were together, but as far apart as if they were in separate rooms.

"Let me just turn my truck around. I turned your car facing the main road, but I left her at the bottom of the driveway so you don't have to drive down the hill. It can

be a bit tricky out there. I'll give you a ride to the bottom
when you're ready."

Silence stayed in control the long few minutes he was
gone.

"We can go when you're ready." Jake didn't bother to
come back inside.

"I'm ready now." If Tyler had been hard of hearing, he
would have missed her words.

Charlotte stood staring out the window beside the door.
Then she lifted her jacket from the hook for the last time.
Memories of snow people and snow angels and closeness
for the first time in the snow flew to her as though set
free by the jacket. She and Tyler wrapped together and rolling in the snow, creating so much heat they must have
melted several inches before they went inside. She tried not
to think of the lovemaking, her first lovemaking, that had
come that evening after their play afternoon. She shook the
images away. They had no place out here. They were out-
dated. Her old memories had shoved these aside. She let
Jake's words reach her.

"I been thinking, Miss. I know you're anxious to get
where you're going, but maybe you should give it a few
more days. It's not going to be smooth traveling out there."

"You got through." She had to get away from here, away
from Tyler. The road couldn't hold as much hurt for her as
this house did with Tyler and her memories of them together.

"That's true, but my vehicle is a bit more substantial than
any car."

"But the road is open. You said so. It's open all the way
to the turnpike, isn't it?"

All she wanted to do was get away. Away from Tyler.
Away from these new and brutal memories that were tearing
into her and ripping her apart. She had to get away now.

"Yes, it's open." He nodded slowly. "But there's open and

then there's open. Like I said, every plow in these parts has been put into service, and we all worked like crazy, but the fact is, it's still not easy driving out there." He pointed toward the outside. "Now you take Mr. Fleming's driveway. I plowed it real good. I mean I cleared it as best I could and mostly I got down to the blacktop. But there are still patches of snow and probably a few of ice. No getting around that. Come nightfall, those that are just snow now will be ice, too. It'll be the same on the other roads. Probably the streets where you're going will be the same."

"I'll be home by the time night comes."

"There's no reason you have to leave now. Today. You can wait until it's clearer, safer," Tyler spoke then, looking as if his words surprised him as much as they had Charlotte.

Her eyes widened. She frowned. She couldn't believe Tyler. He knew better than she did why she had to go now.

"It will be . . ." She took a deep breath. "Now is better."

"Wait a few days more." Tyler's voice sounded as if he had thought hard before he let those words go. It almost sounded as if he meant them. Almost. He turned to Jake. "Will you bring her car up to the house so it will be ready when she is?"

"No." Charlotte shook her head. "I'm leaving now. I'm ready."

Jake looked from one to the other.

"I'll wait outside. You folks let me know what you decide."

Neither Tyler nor Charlotte noticed him leaving.

"I have to go now, Tyler. You know that. You know why." She didn't look at him. She didn't even turn back toward him. She didn't dare. She felt only a thin thread was holding her together, one that was close to snapping. She couldn't spend any more time here with him. Not here, where her enjoyable experiences had been shrouded by his new hate. She picked up her handbag from the table in the hall, promising herself that she'd get rid of it when she got home. Now it, too, held painful memories for her.

"It's not safe. Jake said so. You should wait until . . ."

"I'll get home all right. I'll drive carefully. This is my decision. Only mine. Nothing will happen to me. If it does, it will be my fault." She thought of another woman who drove off while upset and the tragedy that had followed. She was sure Tyler was thinking of the same thing. Why else would he suggest she stay when all he wanted was her gone?

"Cleo . . ."

"No." Charlotte shook her head. She dared a glance at him. His eyes showed something deep down. Something familiar. For a long minute, she stared harder. Maybe if she looked long enough she would see. . . . What? Whatever she wanted to find was dead and thrown away like so much junk.

"I. . . ."

Charlotte shook her head again. "It's Charlotte, Tyler. I know you haven't forgotten my name. My real name." She let her gaze slide from his. "You'll never forget my name."

"At least wait until tomorrow." She knew there was only one reason why he was pushing so hard.

"You know I have to leave. I'll be all right. I know how to drive in the snow. If I had forgotten, that memory is back with all my others. I know how to drive carefully and I will. I . . ." She almost said, 'I promise.' He didn't want any promise from her. He wouldn't believe it if she gave one. "I'll get home safely. I'm not your concern. You're not responsible for me."

"Charlotte. . . ."

"Good-bye, Tyler." She raised her hand as if to shake his, but pulled back and stuffed it into her jacket pocket. He didn't want to touch her. He'd never want to touch her again.

Juno licked her hand and Charlotte brushed it across the dog's silky back.

"Good-bye, girl. Thank you." She didn't look at Tyler's face. She just turned and went out the door, out of his life.

Jake helped her into the truck for the drive down to her car. Charlotte didn't let herself look back to the house. It wouldn't take much for her to fall apart. She tightened her mouth and let out a breath, hoping it would take some of her hurt with it.

"Here we are." Jake stopped and pulled on the hand brake when they reached the bottom of the hill. He hesitated. "Maybe I better check one last time to be sure. This kind of weather is hard on batteries, especially ones that aren't new. I'll turn the motor off and then back on to make sure it starts right up." He got out, but turned back. "Do you know how to get to the highway from here?"

"No." A lifetime ago, she had taken so many turns. Turns that had led her here to Tyler. Now she needed to reverse those turns away from him and the illusion of happiness she had been living this past week. She had to get back to her real life.

"Did you get that?"

"No." She shook her head. "I'm sorry. Will you repeat what you said?" She'd barely heard when he gave her directions.

"Yes." Jake looked at her. "Maybe you might want to write this down. Some of it is kind of complicated. Getting back, I mean."

"All right. Just a minute." Charlotte rummaged in her purse for her little notebook. She couldn't take any more 'complicated.' This time when Jake spoke, she put all of her attention on his words. She was glad he had checked to make sure she got it right. She wasn't doing any clear thinking right now and she didn't need to get lost again. She'd never recover from the last time.

"That's it," he said after she read the directions back to him. "That will put you right on the turnpike."

"Thank you. How much do I owe you?" She pulled out

her wallet, trying not to think of what had happened the last time she had held it. "Will you take a credit card or can I send you a check after I get home?"

"Mr. Fleming took care of everything."

"I'll pay for my own expenses." She didn't want anything from Tyler. Not anymore. "How much do I owe you?"

"Mr. Fleming will have my head if I take your money." Jake smiled. "I won't see you again, but I got to face Mr. Fleming the next time I do some work for him."

Charlotte sighed. She could see there was no use arguing. She didn't have the strength to argue anyway. She tucked her wallet back into her purse.

Jake opened the truck door and helped her down. She slipped a little when she stood, but she didn't go down.

"I just have to ask you again. Are you sure you want to be leaving now? It's bound to be rough going on the roads. Snow is piled as high as your car on the smaller roads. In some places, both directions have to share one lane. The road right off from this driveway is one of them. Maybe you better think about this one last time?"

"I'll be all right, Jake." She glanced up at the house standing guard at the top of the hill. Traveling on the roads couldn't be as rough as staying here.

Jake closed her door after she got in, and watched her fasten her seatbelt.

"Turn it off and crank it up one last time." He watched as she did what he said. "Good." He nodded. "Now you stay to the middle of the road and take it real slow." He laughed. "Not that you could go anywhere else but the middle or any other way but slow even if you wanted to."

"I'll be careful." Not just on the road today, but with everything and everybody from now on.

"I guess I best lead you through the first few turns anyway. I'm kind of going in that direction."

"Thanks, Jake, for everything. I appreciate it."

Jake nodded to her, got into his truck, and pulled around in front of her.

Charlotte put the car in second gear and drove into the snow channel that had been formed by the plows. Jake was right. She couldn't go fast if she wanted to. Her car brushed against the snowbank on the right and she felt like a bowling ball going down an alley with bumpers in place like in a kid's game. This was no game; it was serious, but there was no way she could slide off this road, either.

She inched forward and kept her fingers wrapped around the steering wheel, thinking how much easier it would be if her car had runners instead of wheels. A horn tooted.

Jake waved and pointed to a road to the left that was framed by huge piles of snow, just like on the sides of the road they were on.

Charlotte pried the fingers on one hand loose long enough to wave back before she turned onto the other road. She left Jake and felt more alone that she had in a long time. She shook her head and continued moving away from Tyler.

The next road was only a little better than the first because it was a little wider. The road after that was wider still, but Jake had been right. It was hard going, but not as hard as staying with Tyler would have been, since she knew how he felt about her. She looked at the directions on the seat beside her from time to time and made the proper turns. Turns that took her farther and farther from Tyler.

It took several slow hours, but by early evening, she had reached the turnpike. That road was even better than the others had been and she could go a little faster. She sent up a special thanks to Jake and the others like him who had cleared the way.

She thought ahead to the streets of Philadelphia. They wouldn't be as bad as these roads. She remembered that they never were, but, no matter what condition they were in, she'd deal with them when she got there. She hoped the parking lot of her apartment building had been cleared. She tightened her hands around the steering wheel. If not, she'd manage. No matter what else she faced, she'd manage.

Twelve

Tyler stood in the entry hall until he heard the truck door slam shut. It seemed to take a week before Jake started the motor. It took so long that Tyler had to battle with himself to keep his feet still. He had to fight to keep his hands away from the door knob.

The sound finally cranked into the air as if Jake got tired of waiting for something to change his mind. Maybe he had been waiting for Tyler to come talk to him. Maybe he thought Tyler was going to come running out, shouting for him to stop. Maybe he was waiting to hear: "Never mind, Jake, don't start the truck. It was all a mistake. I was wrong. She's not going away from here."

Tyler clinched his body as if he was expecting a blow instead of trying to keep from moving. He was glad when Jake had gotten tired of waiting. Tyler was still there, standing hard in the same spot, when the sound rumbled off down the hill and faded until nothing was left of it. Just like there was nothing left of him and Charlotte. The air was thin and empty without that noise to fill it. *Just like your life will be without her,* a little voice whispered inside him.

He could still catch her if he wanted to. He could rip open the door and wave them back. Jake would see him in his mirror.

Tyler turned and leaned against the door to keep himself from going after her. From going after Cleo. . . . He shook his head. After Charlotte. Her name is Charlotte. That was her name all the time. And she would never want anything to do with him again.

At the bottom of the driveway, he heard another engine split the air as it started up. He closed his eyes and leaned his head against the solid surface of the door. He listened until that faded away, too, until Charlotte was completely gone from his life.

She was gone. Why did he feel he'd made a mistake? With more mistakes behind him than he could count, why did he feel like this was the biggest one of his life?

He closed his eyes and took a deep breath to try to help sort out his feelings that were tangled like a heap of loose string. Her explanation had sounded sincere, but his anger had kept him from believing her. He had to blame someone.

Tyler opened his eyes and looked into the living room, their bedroom, though it didn't have a bed and they hadn't done much sleeping.

The sofa met his gaze and released snatches of the powerful images it held for him. Charlotte tucked close to him that first night as he warmed her soft body with his. Charlotte, when she'd first opened her eyes for him. Charlotte, whose eyes filled with fires of indignation when she realized he had shared the sofa with her. Later, three days later but at the perfect time, those eyes filled with passion as he showed her how he could make her body sing, as he taught her how to make love. He'd called her Cleo, but she was Charlotte and he'd never see her again.

The quilt neatly folded and smoothed along the back of the sofa was brighter than anything in his dark life should have been right now. But why not? The quilt had only memories of joy to color it. Its only memories were of covering two lovers, of sheltering Charlotte's soft body as it entwined and connected with his in love. It had known only memories of rapture and heat hotter than the fire in the fireplace. It didn't know about the world crashing in on them when her memory returned.

The image of Charlotte flushed with passion in his arms in spite of the cold air surrounding them filled his mind. He could almost feel her body against his. Charlotte, whose hair smelled of his shampoo when he tucked her head under his chin, when he brushed his lips across it. Charlotte, whose lush, full breasts were a perfect fit for his hands. His fingers flexed as if they remembered, too, as if they missed her already.

Tyler turned his back to the sofa, but the memories refused to stay behind him. Memories. Charlotte had lost hers. How was it possible to lose memories, to keep them away? He wished he knew that secret. He needed to use it now.

He closed his eyes, but that didn't stop him from seeing her wrapped with him in their cocoon of love so many times, but not enough times. He couldn't stop the feelings unleashed with the memories.

He could feel Charlotte clutching his back as he filled her; he could hear her make those soft moaning sounds that nearly drove him over the edge before he wanted to go. He could feel her hands, her legs clinging to him as they soared higher than anyone ever had before. He could feel her peacefully snuggled against him after they had returned to this worldly place. Charlotte, drifting off to sleep still nestled against him so trustingly floated through his mind and took a front seat. So innocent. Innocent. But it was too late.

Tyler turned back and walked into the living room. He snatched the quilt from the sofa. The scent of buttery popcorn and love and promises drifted up. He stuffed the quilt into the closet until he could get rid of it for good.

Putting it away wasn't enough. It didn't help him at all. Only the quilt stayed shut away behind a door. His memories were too strong to be held off by any door. He wasn't sure if there was anything, if even time could hold them off forever. He wasn't sure of anything anymore.

He climbed the stairs feeling, and with his footsteps sounding, much older than when he had climbed the last time.

His feet took him to the room Charlotte had used last night. They refused to take him beyond the doorway. Instead they stopped so he could see what his words had done.

The spread was laid smoothly in place and draped perfectly to the floor. The sheets were folded neatly at the bottom of the spread as if to deny that Charlotte had spent the night there alone instead of with him. She should have spent last night in his arms, in his room, in his bed. Was that only yesterday morning? Tyler pushed out a hard breath. She shouldn't have been in bed alone.

The clothes laid beside the sheets pulled him into the room like a kid drawn to a toy store.

His robe and his T-shirt—her nightshirt—were draped over the side of the bed as if waiting for Charlotte to come for them. They looked as if they expected Tyler to remove them from her only a little while after she put them on, as he had before.

She would be sharing his bed with him tonight if he hadn't built a wall between them with his words as hard as stones. She would still be here with him, for him, if he hadn't let his words change her feelings for him. If he hadn't chased her away.

Tyler picked up the nightshirt. He sat on the edge of the bed and held the shirt close to his chest as if Charlotte were in it and hadn't been driven away from him, by him.

He closed his eyes and hoped, prayed, that the pain would dull. Soon. He wasn't sure it ever would. He wasn't sure he deserved for it to ease in his lifetime. Why wasn't he as sure of his accusations now as he had been a short while ago?

Hours later, he was still waiting for release. Juno came to him and pushed her head under his hand and whined. He had to feed her. Somebody should eat.

When had she come upstairs? He patted her head and stroked his hand across her back, trying not to remember that Charlotte's hand had touched this same spot not long ago. He was glad Juno was with him. If she weren't, he might be spending the rest of his life sitting on the bed, waiting for a miracle.

He patted the dog once more and followed her downstairs. He let her out and waited for her to come back. He could handle this kind of waiting. He knew it wouldn't be long, but it wouldn't have mattered if it was. Juno scratched on the door and he let her back in. She ambled into the living room and took her old comfortable spot on the hearth. Tyler went into the studio to look for his.

Notes from the piano tumbled and crashed and pulled at each other as Tyler sought release in his music. No sooner did a note fly up that another didn't chase it in a discordant sound. He let them battle it out.

After a while, the notes and chords got tired of fighting. Tyler's fingers settled into a slow, soft rhythm like rain at the end of a summer thunderstorm.

He lost himself in music as he searched for peace. He tried to make his music enough for him again, as he had been trying to do for three years. He hadn't managed to find it before. He didn't find it this time, either. He'd keep trying, though. What else could he do?

The sun had been gone for many hours when Charlotte's car crept into the parking lot of her apartment building. She barely remembered getting home.

The car slipped on a patch on ice and she had to swerve to keep from hitting a parked car. She stopped counting the spots missed by plows between home and. . . . She wasn't going to think about him.

This was the last slippery spot she would have to worry about driving over for a while. She steered to an almost clear place at the end of the small lot. It looked as if the plow had gotten tired when it got this far. She felt the passenger side brush against the snow piled like the start of a ski slope. She sighed. It spite of the mound and the ice, it was good to be home.

The roads had been worse than she had thought possible. At times, hers was the only car on the road, but she didn't slide off as she had before, when . . . No. She wouldn't think of it. Of him.

In spite of the road conditions, she had been able to keep her car under control. This time, she knew her way and she knew where she would end up.

It had taken her six hours longer to make the trip than it would have on clear roads, but she wasn't sorry she had decided to come home today. She hadn't had a choice. Staying with Tyler would have been more than she could handle.

She got her luggage from the trunk and picked her way to the door by stretching over icy spots and stepping from one bare spot to another. She looked at the elevator. An "Out of Order" sign was on the door, as it often was. "Welcome back," she muttered as she climbed the stairs to the third floor.

The paint was chipped and as old as the building, but the door to her apartment was a friendly sight. She went inside.

When she closed the door of her apartment, she let the last of her tension go in a deep breath. She leaned against the wall in the tiny hallway, her hallway, and let her body finally relax. This was where she belonged. Here she was welcome.

She stayed against the wall in the darkness for a few minutes, trying not to think of that other hallway that had been so wide and so inviting before this morning. This morning, the invitation had been missing.

The phone rang in the apartment next door. Charlotte was glad it wasn't hers. She was glad she didn't have to talk with anyone, glad she didn't have to make sense to anyone. Not that she could have. Everything in her mind was jumbled together like a desk full of papers disturbed by a strong wind.

She picked up her bags and walked toward her bedroom. The answering machine blinked at her. Not now. She couldn't call anyone now. Maybe later. Maybe not ever.

Usually, she found comfort in the blue and white flowered quilt on her bed. Tonight she wished she had bought a plain blanket instead. She didn't need to see or think about a quilt, any quilt, right now.

Her mind ignored her and dragged out for her memories of that other quilt that had done more than given her warmth. She sighed and sat on the edge of the bed. She couldn't block those last memories. What would have happened if her other memories had come as easily as these kept returning? What if the old ones had come back as soon as she had opened her eyes that first morning?

The other quilt, and Tyler's body, had warmed her before she knew either one was there. Charlotte closed her eyes. This time she didn't try to fight the memories unwinding like a ball of yarn rolling across a floor. It wasn't any use. She couldn't win such a fight.

The scent of Tyler's soap mixed with his aftershave mixed with him came to her as if he were there with her now. She curled her fingers as she remembered his solid, wide shoulders under her hands. She remembered how his muscles rippled under her fingers as she urged him closer and he obeyed. She could almost feel his arms around her and her hands against his chest; she could almost feel his crinkly chest hairs against her fingers as she found the flat, hard nubs hiding there and teased them to life as his hands tightened on her.

He had made her trust again. He had taught her how to love. He had shown her how sensuous and passionate she could be. He had created feelings in her she hadn't known she was capable of, hadn't known even existed. She had let down all her barriers and let him in. She had opened herself, her heart, her body, completely to him. She had believed they had forever together. She hadn't known it would just be for a week. Just until her life came back to her. If she had known what was going to happen, she would have . . . What? Not let him into her heart? Not fallen in love with him? Was it possible to not let yourself fall in love? She sighed. She knew it was possible to stop loving somebody. She didn't think she could do it, but Tyler had. He had made the change in an instant.

She could still see the difference in his eyes when he saw her name on her driver's license. He had looked as if something had died inside him when he stared at her after that.

No. Charlotte shook her head. That wasn't right. It was more than something dying. He had looked as if any love he had had for her had changed to hate as fast as the snap of a magician's fingers. That hate was for her, just as the love had been.

Maybe he never loved her. He couldn't have, or he would have believed her when she'd told him the truth. If he loved her, he would have known she could never do anything to cause anybody harm. He would have known she could never do what he accused her of doing.

She blinked hard and dragged the blue lace-trimmed pillow off the bed and onto her lap. She wiped her eyes and clutched the pillow to her. Then she wiped her eyes again. After that, she didn't bother to wipe anymore.

Tears slipped out. Others followed as if the first ones had cleared the way for them. They made two streams that ran down her chin and dripped off. The pillow caught them. Charlotte hugged it closer, glad to have something, anything, to hold on to.

The phone jangled into the quiet darkness, filling the room around her soft crying. She let the phone clang until it got tired and stopped.

Later, a few minutes later, or maybe it was a few hours— it didn't matter—but later, she stood and peeled off her clothes. Tyler had taken them off her when he was concerned about her being cold. Another time, after she and Tyler had played in the snow and her clothes were damp, he had suggested she change out of them because he didn't want her to get sick. Now he didn't care what happened to her. These clothes would remind her of that each time she looked at them. She rolled them into as tight a ball as she could and shoved them to the bottom of the wastebasket. She didn't want to see them again. She couldn't bear to look at them. Tomorrow she'd get rid of them. Throw them into the dumpster. They held too many memories. If she was luckier than she had ever been before in her life, they'd take the memories they held with them.

She wished she could laugh. Not long ago, she was scared that her memories were gone forever. Now she wished these new ones would go, take her hurt with them, and never show themselves again.

She went into the bathroom. It was smaller than the one she'd been using for the past few days, but this one was hers. She turned on the shower. After she stepped in, she learned it wasn't so much different from that other bathroom, after all. Her tears mixed as well with the water here as they did with the water in the other shower.

She wished her tears could cleanse her of Tyler, like the water was cleansing her body.

She wiped her face that was wet from more than just the

shower. How many tears could a body make before it ran out of water?

The tears finally got tired of falling and the shower turned cold. Charlotte stepped out. She wrapped a towel around her body and another around her head. Just like the last time she'd taken a shower. She shook her head. No, not like the last time. She dried her hair and her body and pulled on a nightgown. Her own nightgown. Not a T-shirt pretending to belong to her. Not Tyler's T-shirt.

Go away, she told him as his face appeared in her mind. The thick curls above his forehead seemed to wait for her touch. Leave me alone, she begged. Just go away and leave me alone.

She got into bed and pulled up the covers. It was a quilt, but it was hers, not that other one. This one had no memories to hurt her. She was glad for that. She stared at the ceiling and wished for sleep to come so this day would finally release her from its grip and go away.

The ringing phone shook her awake. She opened her eyes. Sunlight streamed in the windows that she had forgotten to cover the night before. Sparkles skipped gold off the snow piled on her windowsill like thick icing. The sparkles were like the others that had bounced off different windowsills and a porch's snow covering in that other lifetime. She sighed, rolled over, and reached for the phone.

"Where have you been, Charlotte Thompson? I've been trying to reach you for days. I left a dozen messages. Why didn't you call me back?"

"Hello, Janet."

"Don't you 'hello, Janet' me. When you didn't call me back, I checked with all the hospitals in your area. When you weren't in any of them, I called the police to see if they had an accident report about you or if something worse had happened. Answer me, sis—where have you been this past week?"

"I'm okay."

"Do you know how worried I've been about you?" Janet continued. "I called your neighbor, Miss Mary. She said she hadn't seen you since you went on assignment. When she told me that, I was afraid you were stranded out on the highway somewhere buried under ten feet of snow. Where were you, Charlotte? Why didn't you call me back?"

"You sound just like Mom did when we were young, and I seem to remember you swearing you never would," Charlotte said, rolling her eyes.

"The older I get, the more I know she was right. And you're changing the subject the way you used to do with her, but it won't work with me."

"You used to do the same thing and you know it, so don't get in such a huff with me."

"Charlotte Thompson . . ."

"Okay. To answer your questions, the last one first, I think you have made it clear how concerned you were about me." Charlotte managed a smile. It wasn't much, but it was more than she expected to have this soon.

"Well, at least that's a start. I imagined all sorts of terrible things happening to you, you know."

"I know. You always do. Janet, you panic if somebody is five minutes late coming to a party. Remember that?"

"That was justified. You'd had trouble with your car the month before and I thought it had broken down on the road."

"I told you when I got my car fixed. And I didn't have to go on a road, only streets. And I was only fifteen minutes away from your house. What about the time before that when I was five minutes—five minutes—late coming over? Or the time when . . ."

"Never mind any of that. It's all in the past and should be forgotten. Especially by you. Are you okay?"

"I'm okay." Charlotte felt something squeeze inside her. As okay as she could be considering that her heart was in pieces so small it felt worse off than Humpty Dumpty.

"Well, how about it? Did you? Is that where you were?"

"How about what? Did I what? Was I where?"

"Honestly, little sister, it's been a long time since you've had this much trouble paying attention. I asked if you were covering that story up in the Poconos? Is that the assignment Miss Mary mentioned?"

"Yes, that was it." Charlotte took in a deep breath and let it out slowly. "I had to stay longer than I'd expected because of the storm."

"You got caught in that awful storm? It was all over the news down here, but I didn't really think you got caught in it. If I had, I would have panicked."

"Yes, I got caught." Charlotte swallowed. *I got caught by something more dangerous than a snowstorm.*

"Are you sure you're okay? Where did you spend the time? You weren't stuck on the road, were you? Did a rescue team have to search for you?" Janet didn't wait for answers. "You sound funny. Not like your old self. Did you have trouble getting home? How is it there now? When did you get back?"

Charlotte laughed. She was surprised to learn that she still could.

"Typical Janet," she said. "Give enough questions for an exam and don't give space for answers to fit in between them."

"I'm just concerned about you, that's all."

"I know you are." Charlotte's voice softened. "Thank you for caring." She was glad somebody did, now that Tyler didn't.

"That's what big sisters are for. Now when did you get back home?"

"Last night."

"You just got back last night? You had to stay that long?"

"Yes, I had to stay that long." Too long. Much too long.

"There must have been a lot of snow. How much was there?"

"More than three and a half feet." Charlotte remembered how she knew how deep the snow had been. She also remembered later that night when . . . She shook the memory away. "There still is a lot of snow. I had to drive through it to get home. We have a lot here in the city, too." She looked out at cars still buried in the parking lot as if waiting for a massive thaw. "You and I would have thought we were in heaven if we had had this much snow when we were young, although we did have some fun storms, didn't we?" Charlotte tried a smile again. This time felt better than the last time. "I know you deserted us for sunny Atlanta, but you must remember snow."

"Don't get cute. Atlanta might be sunny, and I haven't seen any snow since we moved here, but last night I was very grateful for central heat. It feels good this morning, too. And I still need winter clothes."

"Yes, for about a week, right?"

Janet's laughter tickled Charlotte's ear.

"A bit longer than that." She laughed again. "Listen, I didn't just call to check up on you, although that seems like a good idea now that you told me what happened. After all, somebody has to look after you."

Charlotte winced at Janet's last words, but she made herself listen to the rest.

"What I called for was to remind you that Jim has to come to Philly for his annual conference in two months. I want to make sure you don't take an assignment out of town then. He can stay at the stuffy hotel they usually book the conference into. He's going to be shut up in meetings all day, so I'm coming to hang out with you."

"I wouldn't call the Four Seasons Hotel stuffy. No one in their right mind would, but I'll be glad to have you stay here. You know that. It will be good to see you."

"Same here. Now that I have reservations at Charlotte's Place, I gotta go. I have to go open the shop."

"How's it doing?"

"It's doing great. I have a lot to tell you. And more than about the shop. But it will wait. I'll fill you in when I see you, but you know I'll call you every week before then."

"You always do."

"Keeping in touch with you is a thankless job, but somebody has to do it. Since it's just you and me, the chore falls to me."

"Thanks a lot."

"You're welcome."

"I was being sarcastic."

"I know. But I forgive you. Take care, little sister. Bye."

Charlotte's hand tightened at Janet's last words. She held the humming phone long after her sister had hung up. She swallowed a lump and the tears trying to escape along with it.

Janet's warning was about a week too late. It was too late for Charlotte to be careful.

Thirteen

Charlotte drove into a spot outside her apartment building and felt her car slip to a stop. She leaned her head back against the headrest. Food shopping had made her so tired. Lately, everything made her tired. She felt like she had covered miles instead of only a few grocery store aisles. She only went shopping today instead of waiting for the streets to be completely clear because she had to.

Janet was coming in a few days and Charlotte didn't want to wait until the last minute to get her favorite foods. March in Philadelphia was so unpredictable; one day you would swear summer was here and the next it was like January again. She certainly didn't want to have go near a food store the day the weather forecast said snow was on its way. People were in a frenzy as they piled their carts with enough supplies to last through three winters of nonstop snow.

Charlotte got out of the car. After the way January and February had been this year, she wouldn't be surprised if they got another record snowfall.

A gust of wind blew her raincoat open at the bottom and dampened her slacks, but she didn't notice. For a moment, she was back looking out on the snowstorm that mattered, and not just because it set new records. She thought of strong hands pulling her against a hard body and holding her close as if he would always want to have her with him like that.

Charlotte shook her head. That's what she had thought then,

but she had been wrong. So wrong. The drizzle pelted her face and she brushed a tired hand across the dampness. She felt as if she had just completed the Broad Street Marathon. She took a deep breath, went to the back of the car, and tried not to think of what she suspected was the reason for how she felt.

She lifted two bags from the trunk and hurried through the March drizzle that had spent the last two days trying to melt what was left of the last snowfall. The snow had barely piled three inches deep on top of everything. Usually she enjoyed a snowfall that did no harm, but made everything look like vanilla ice cream. She hadn't enjoyed this one. She was glad when it turned to gray slush and didn't look like snow anymore.

When the flakes had started to fall, they reminded her of that other snow that had covered everything except her heart. It had left her heart open to be broken by . . . *Not now.* She shook her head. *I don't want to think of him now.*

She tightened her fingers around the handles of the plastic bags. When would she learn how to shield herself from these thoughts that came whenever they wanted to? She went inside still trying to figure out how to keep them away.

She breathed a sigh when she saw the "Out of Order" sign gone from the elevator. She didn't feel like climbing steps today. She didn't feel like doing anything today. And she hadn't felt like it yesterday, either.

The phone rang as she reached her door and a grocery bag tipped over from the spot where she set it when she fumbled with her keys. A frantic grab brought it upright, but the keys clanged to the floor.

"Oh, no you don't." She pushed the carton of eggs back down inside the bag as it tilted again. "I didn't slide to the store through that slush to have you fall and break here." She shifted the other bag to her hip and picked up the keys. An orange fell from the bag and rolled across the hall. "Wait a minute," she called to the phone as if it could hear her and obey. "Don't stop ringing yet. I'm coming." The door clicked open. She grabbed the phone from the hall table and set the bags on the floor.

She nodded and scribbled on the message pad as she listened to the first good news she had heard in a long time. She had gotten the freelance job she had applied for with the chain of local neighborhood newspapers. She needed the steady income, but just as important, she'd have something to take her mind off other things. She hung up and went to get the orange that had stopped outside Miss Mary's door.

Then she went back to her car for the other two bags. As she put the milk, cheese and pickles into the refrigerator, she tried not to remember her last assignment a month and a half ago.

Every day, she tried not to think of it. And every day, it came back to her like a boomerang. It wasn't the last story that troubled her mind—it was what had come after it that still had her in a turmoil. Her time with Tyler.

She took a narrow box from a bag and set it on the counter. She pushed it back as if it were as fragile as the dozen eggs she had been afraid would break. She stood looking at the box. Then she turned her back on it as if that would make it go away, even though she knew it wouldn't. The box would wait. She swallowed hard and unpacked the other things.

The old man smiled at her from the package of Janet's favorite microwave popcorn. Popcorn. Sharing buttered popcorn in front of a cozy fire.

Charlotte didn't know what would trigger memories since she got home, but she should have known that popcorn would. A big bowl of popcorn, hands touching in the bowl, and kisses. Butter-flavored kisses. Since all of her old memories had come back, none of her memories, especially the newer ones, wanted to stay hidden. She sighed. Memories were funny, but she didn't feel like laughing. She hadn't felt like laughing since she got back home. Would that feeling ever return? Would laughing ever feel right again? What was he doing right now?

She folded the bags and stored them in the bottom drawer of the cabinet next to the sink. She wiped the already clean counter as carefully as if it were in an operating room. She straightened the toaster, already lined up perfectly with the blender, and the flowered canisters she'd found last summer at a yard sale. She straightened the top on the biggest one, even though it wasn't crooked. She shook her head. No sense wasting time. The truth wouldn't change. She couldn't put it off any longer.

She leaned against the counter and stared at the box she had pushed back, the one she hadn't really needed to buy. When it wouldn't go away, but waited patiently for her, she picked it up and went into the bathroom. Maybe she was wrong.

A few minutes later, Charlotte sat on the side of the tub and stared at the unmistakable mark that told her what she already knew.

Morning sickness—not confined to morning, as she had found out—was as sure a sign as any kit. The first time it happened, she tried to believe it was something she ate. The next time, she told herself she had the flu.

When she considered her need to sleep more hours than a toddler and her constantly queasy stomach this past month, she could have saved the money the kit had cost her.

Sex without protection. Even teenagers knew better, and she was well past her teens. The fact that neither she nor Tyler planned to have sex was no excuse. The fact that they didn't have protection was no excuse. She was an adult.

She hadn't had sex when she was a teen. She had promised herself she would wait until she fell in love and was married. She had lost more than one boyfriend because of her stand, but she never regretted it. She sighed. Sometimes people get dumber as they get older.

She should have had more self-control. She knew the risks

but she ignored them like some brainless creature. Tyler had left the final decision to her and she had made it. *She* had made the decision. Now she'd pay for her irresponsibility. She was pregnant and, as if that wasn't bad enough, her baby's father hated her.

She rubbed her trembling hand over her middle. "Never mind, baby," she whispered to the little one growing inside her. "It doesn't matter," she lied.

Her middle still looked flat, but she could feel a tiny, hard bulge right in the center, just below her waist. Her feelings were no longer mixed, as they had been when she'd first suspected she was pregnant.

She patted the spot again as if it were worth all the gold hidden away by the government. She wouldn't have planned this pregnancy. It would be hard doing it all herself, but now that it was . . . She shook her head. Not an 'it.' Now that *he* or *she* was on the way, Charlotte would manage to take care of her baby.

The new job was more important than ever. Somehow, the two of them would manage. She and her baby would make out just fine alone. It wouldn't be easy, but she would handle it. She would give her baby as much love and care as she could.

She stood and tried to decide whether she wanted a nap or a snack more. In the past week, constant hunger had replaced the earlier nausea, but sleepiness hadn't disappeared. She decided she could have both. First a snack. She went back to the kitchen. A bowl of cookie dough ice cream with chocolate chip cookies would hit the spot just right. She could take a nap afterward.

When she awoke from her nap, the room was covered in darkness. She had done it again. Her nap had run into bedtime. She warmed up the rest of last night's dinner and made plans to call her doctor the next day.

She knew she was pregnant. What she didn't know was what to do to make sure the baby was healthy. Dr. Blake would tell her.

Charlotte thought of the women she saw in the office when she went for her annual checkups. Their rounded middles left no question about why they were there. Charlotte had wondered how it would feel to have a life growing inside her. She didn't think she would ever find out. Now she would be one of those women. She frowned. There were difficult times ahead.

She began her new job at the neighborhood newspaper. The pay wasn't a fortune, but it was regular and she didn't have to go out of town on assignment. And she had no qualms about working for these newspapers.

Dr. Blake gave her guidelines to follow. Charlotte swallowed hard at part of their conversation. They had been back in the private office after the exam that told the doctor what Charlotte already knew.

"I like to have as full a history as I can get on the baby. Do you have any medical history on the baby's father?"

"No." She was embarrassed. She never thought she would need Tyler's medical history. She hadn't done much thinking at all when she was with him. "He won't be part of our lives. He . . ." Her eyes widened. "Is something the matter with my baby? Are you looking for something specific?"

"Your baby is fine, Charlotte." Doctor Blake patted her hand. "We just like to have as much information as we can get. Don't worry if we don't have it. Things will be all right." They set up the next appointment and Charlotte left.

Should she contact Tyler? As she drove home, the question popped up, and the answer came right behind it. No. He wouldn't care. He didn't want anything more to do with her. He'd feel the same way about her baby, too. If Dr. Blake said they could do without any information about Tyler, he could stay in the past, where he belonged.

* * *

She had gotten her first paycheck the day Janet swooped down on her.

"How have you been, little sister?" Janet hugged her close before she sat down. She stared at Charlotte. A crease folded across her forehead. "How have you been?"

"I'm okay." Charlotte moved away from Janet. "Let me hang up your coat."

"Not just yet. I have to let the chill move out of me." Janet shivered. "How could I forget how bad March in Philadelphia can be?" She looked out the window at the rain that had turned everything gray. "How long has it been coming down?"

"This is day five of our countdown. Miss Mary decided we're going to start building an ark when it reaches day twelve."

"Good idea." She turned to face Charlotte again. "Maybe you should consider moving to higher ground, even though you are on the third floor."

"It's not that bad, Janet. You always did exaggerate."

"Maybe so." Janet stared at her sister again. "You don't look so hot. Are you sure you're all right?"

"I'm sure." Charlotte turned toward the kitchen. "Why don't you go get settled while I start on the soup. I think this is perfect weather for a pot of my award-winning soup."

"Award-winning, huh?"

"Sure. You always said my soup could win prizes in a national soup contest."

"Your soup is good, but I was probably just hungry when I said that."

Charlotte swatted her sister's arm before she disappeared into the tiny kitchen.

* * *

Janet's frown stayed after Charlotte left the room. Things weren't right with Charlotte. Something was wrong. Janet hoped she could make herself wait until after dinner to question her, but she didn't know if she could. Patience wasn't one of her strong points. She took her bags into the bedroom.

"Okay, Charlotte, give. What's the matter? I've been here long enough to have dinner and for us to drain the teapot. Still I haven't heard anything important coming from you except about your new job." She put her cup on the end table and tucked her legs up under her. "I think I've given you long enough to talk without me questioning you, but you know I was never patient."

"After having grown up with you, I can swear to that." Charlotte set her cup of herbal tea down. "I'm sure you set a new record for yourself today."

"Don't get smart. And you didn't have to agree with me so quickly." She shifted into the corner of the couch and put the small pillow behind her back. "Don't try to change the subject, either. You know that never works with me. I saw you try it too many times with Mom." Janet leaned forward and touched Charlotte's arm. "Little sister, you look like something the cat wouldn't bother to drag in. What is it? What's the matter with you?"

"You always did know how to phrase things. Maybe you should have been the one to become a reporter." Charlotte frowned. She stared at the braided rag rug at her feet. *Then I wouldn't have had that assignment to cover back in January,* she thought. *I wouldn't have been the one to meet Tyler. He wouldn't have taught me how to trust. He wouldn't have taught me how to love. He wouldn't have made me love him so. And I wouldn't be* . . . Charlotte blinked as Janet's words reached her.

"Well?" Janet put her feet on the floor. "Don't try to get

me off track again. It won't work." Her voice softened and her concern showed itself. "Charlotte, have you been sick? Are you keeping some horrible condition from me? I'm the one who needed to lose weight, not you. Have you seen a doctor?" She shook her head. "I shouldn't have asked that. I know you have enough sense to go to a doctor when you're sick. What did he say? What's wrong with you? How can I help?"

Charlotte smiled and shook her head. She smiled as if she didn't have a problem she was going to have to share with Janet.

"Janet, I changed my mind. You should have been a lawyer. You're so good at interrogation. And if you're going to throw so many questions at me at one time, you're going to have to write them down so I can keep track of them."

"Charlotte . . ."

"Okay." Charlotte took a deep breath. "I have lost a little weight, but I'm working on putting it back on." Janet didn't need to know how much weight she had really lost when she came back from losing her heart. Under Dr. Blake's guidance, she had already put most of the weight back on. As for her heart, at least with it broken, nobody else would be able to get to it. She'd take care of what was left of her. She had to. She had to be healthy for the baby. She brushed her hand across her middle and left it there.

"What made you lose the weight in the first place? Did the doctor tell you the reason for it? Is that what you're hiding from me? You have some awful . . ."

"Janet, I wasn't feeling well, that was the reason. I had a lot on my mind." Charlotte blinked hard. *On my heart, too.*

"It's not just the weight. You look . . ." Janet scrambled for the right word. "You look droopy. Real sad. You look a lot sadder than the last time I saw you."

"I'm okay. Really. At least I will be."

"You will be? What's wrong that you know you'll be bet-

ter? When? How can you be so sure?" Janet sat up straight.
"Is it because of that stupid lawsuit? Is that what's troubling
you? Hasn't that ridiculous thing been dropped yet?" She
shook her head. "I hope that's not what you're worrying
about. You know you're innocent. You could never be part
of such a terrible story designed to hurt the way that one
was. Anyone who knows you knows you couldn't write
something like that. The others will know it too, when you
have a chance to explain. Sis, we talked about this lots of
times. First when you were served the papers and many
times after that. I thought we agreed you weren't going to
let it bother you."

"Yes, we did talk." Charlotte nodded. "And yes, we
agreed. It's not the lawsuit that's on my mind. Not exactly."

She wished she could be as certain as Janet was about
being believed. Charlotte wasn't sure anymore that she could
convince a jury that she was innocent. Janet was sure, but
she didn't know what had happened at Tyler's. She didn't
know that Charlotte had already tried over and over to explain what happened to the person she had let get closer
to her than anyone had before. She had explained to Tyler,
and he hadn't believed her. Not any part of it.

Charlotte remembered how cold his look had been after
she'd finished explaining. She thought it was easy to understand, but it hadn't been easy for Tyler.

She shivered now as she remembered his accusations. He
didn't believe her story then. He never would and he was
the one who mattered most. The one whom she thought
cared about her. Why should anybody else believe her? And
why should she care whether they did or not?

"Well? Has the suit been dropped yet or not?"

"It hasn't been dropped, but that's not all that I'm worried
about."

"So you agree you are worried."

"Yes." She should have used a different word instead of
'worried.'

"What's so heavy on your mind that it's affecting your health like this?"

Only one question from Janet, for the first time, but Charlotte didn't feel like celebrating.

"I don't want to talk about it right now, okay? I can't." She shook her head from side to side. "Maybe later." Charlotte blinked several times and swallowed hard. "Now tell me about your shop. How's business at Why Not Whatnots? What's your latest find that's sure to set a new trend?"

Janet stared at her like she was trying to decide whether to answer Charlotte or wait for an answer to one of her own questions. Charlotte hoped her sister didn't pick one of her own. She needed more time to decide how much to tell Janet and how to say it.

"Business is great."

Charlotte was glad her question won. Now all she had to do was listen to the answer.

"I found a fantastic artist," Janet went on. "Flora uses a pecan shell mixture to make figurines so lifelike you expect the little people to walk around and talk with you. We're starting to do them in a series based on occupations. Let me show you one." She went to the bedroom and came back with a small package wrapped in tissue paper. She handed it to Charlotte. "I brought this one because it reminds me of you."

Charlotte peeled away the paper. A small figure of a woman holding a pad and pencil looked back at her.

"This is unbelievable." She held it up and brought it closer. "Look at the detail. You can see the lines on the paper. And look at the line around the pen point. You can even see her eyelashes." Charlotte hugged Janet close. "It's beautiful. I know just the spot for it." She removed a ceramic cat from the end table and carefully placed the figure in the center of the lace scarf. "Perfect." She gave it a pat and moved back to the couch. "Has she done any more?"

"She just finished an African dancer that's sure to be

popular with people who have two left feet. It's so wonderful, they might expect to touch it and have the dancer's talent rub off on them. She said the next one will be of a mother braiding her daughter's hair as the little girl sits on a rag rug. I saw the sketches. I can't wait to see the finished figure."

"That's great. I'd like to see that."

"It reminded me of how Mama used to have us sit on the floor while she did our hair."

"Yes, I remember that. She'd tell us stories to keep us from squirming around."

"That's how we got a lot of our family history, from Mama braiding hair and weaving stories."

"By the time I was old enough to do my own hair, I felt I knew all about Grandmom and Grandpa."

"And all of Mama's aunts and uncles, too," Janet added. She laughed. "Remember the story about when Uncle Willie climbed down the well and couldn't get out? He said he wanted to see where the water came from."

Charlotte's laughter joined with Janet's as they interrupted each other retelling the story. It felt good to laugh. Janet was good for her.

"So, are you selling anything else new that's as great as Flora's people?"

"There's always something new. I found a young man who does hand-blown glass. He mixes his colors like I've never seen before. Then there's a young woman who makes decorative objects out of handmade paper that looks like Kente cloth. Both of them are great artists. I know they'll move on to bigger places, but for now I have the pleasure of handling their work."

"Tell me about them."

Janet did. Then she talked about the wood carvings and cloth dolls she'd brought from her latest trip to the islands.

Charlotte tried to concentrate on what Janet was saying. She asked questions and tried to pay attention so she could ask more. She tried everything she could think of to put off the conversation she knew would come later.

"How did you decide on which islands?"

"Enough about business." Janet leaned forward. "What I'm working on now is something better that any new or old artwork or merchandise." Her face softened. "No more carefree life for me and Jim." She touched Charlotte's arm. "I have a more important project going on. Are you ready for this?" A wide smile spread across her face. "Oh, Charlotte, Jim and I are going to have a baby. A baby. Isn't that great? We've been trying for three years and I'm finally pregnant. You're going to be an aunt. Aunt Charlotte. At least that's what it will be until the little one is talking and can scramble your name into something else."

"Yes, that's great news." Charlotte felt her head move up and down, but she didn't remember meaning to move it. She tried as hard as she could to find a smile for Janet, but she couldn't. "I'm so happy for you."

"What's wrong?" Janet grasped Charlotte's hand. "You don't sound happy. You don't look happy at all. You look pale. Sis, you've got me worried all over again."

"Don't be." Charlotte took a deep breath. "That is great news. I know how much you and Jim want this. I really am happy for you." She hugged her sister. Janet patted Charlotte's back before she pulled away.

"Tell me what's bothering you. Right now. Whatever is eating at you, I want to know. Maybe I can help."

Charlotte shook her head. "This isn't a broken toy or a lost game piece for you to find. You can't fix this for me like you fixed things when we were kids. You can't help at all." She shook her head again. Even Janet can't mend a broken heart.

"Try me. Tell me. Please."

Charlotte took several deep breaths and let them out slowly. A woman on an exercise show swore that this was the way to relax.

Charlotte swallowed hard. The woman on television lied. She took one more deep breath and closed her eyes.

"Don't judge me, okay? When I tell you, just don't judge me. I don't need you to tell me how stupid I was or what a dumb thing I did. I've been telling myself that since I left . . ." Another deep breath, which helped a bit. "Since I got back."

"That's an easy promise. You know I'd never say anything like that to you any more than you would to me."

Janet's voice was just the way Charlotte needed it to be. Soothing and caring and understanding.

She touched Charlotte's arm and her hand was comforting.

"Go ahead," she said. "I'm listening."

Charlotte started with trying to get home in the storm. She told of her car slipping off the driveway. When she got to the part about her amnesia, Janet stopped her.

"Wait a minute. Amnesia? You said you had amnesia?" Janet's word sliced into Charlotte's story. "Are you sure you're all right now? Do you remember everything you had forgotten?" Janet shook her head. "How would you know if something's still forgotten?"

"My memory's back. All of it. Some of the new memories, I wish would go away." She swallowed hard. "My memories of Tyler."

"Tyler? Who's Tyler?"

Charlotte's voice stumbled when she mentioned Tyler, but she made herself go on. "Tyler. He had this massive house at the top of a long, steep, winding driveway. Of course, I didn't see it when I went up. I was unconscious and he had to carry me."

"Why do you want memories of him to go away? What kind of memories are you talking about? What happened?"

"Janet, he's so handsome in a strong sort of way, and he was just as caring as he is good-looking. He's got these eyes that see right into your soul. I think I was falling in love with him from the time I opened my eyes and looked into his."

Charlotte told of how reassuring he was about her memory coming back. She told of how he seemed to fall as much in love with her as she with him.

"Then he saw my driver's license and everything changed." Her words got caught in the tremble of her voice when she told the part about how his love changed to hate and how different the two feelings looked on his face. Then she sighed. "I know those memories of him won't stay away. I learned that doesn't happen. But I wish they would at least move back far enough so they won't hurt me so much."

"I don't understand."

"Tyler's last name is Fleming."

"Tyler Fleming? Isn't he the one who . . . ?" Janet took in a deep breath. "He can't be the same one?" She shook her head. "But how many Tyler Flemings can there be? Oh, Charlotte. Poor baby."

Janet wrapped her arms around Charlotte as she would a child, but no child could ever feel the way Charlotte did. No child could have emotions that ran so deep in the understanding of what had been lost and what she would never find again.

Charlotte tried to draw some of the strength Janet was offering to her. She needed it. She needed a lot of it.

"Oh, little sister, I'm so sorry." Janet rocked back and forth, still holding Charlotte close. "I'm so sorry that the first time you fell hard, it had to be for somebody like him. I hated him before. Now I hate him even more for hurting you like this."

"You haven't heard all of it." Charlotte pulled herself away. She watched her own hands twist and untwist in her lap as they helped her search for the words she needed to explain things so that her sister would understand. "That's not all. There's something else very important I have to tell you." She didn't look at Janet. She just stared into space as the silence stretched long between them before Janet broke it.

"Charlotte, what . . . ?"

"I'm pregnant." Now Charlotte found the nerve to look at her sister. "I'm pregnant with Tyler's baby and he hates me." Charlotte brushed at her cheek. She looked at her fingers and was surprised to see tears glistening on them.

She hadn't realized they had started. Just like she hadn't realized when her love for Tyler had started. She wiped again. Once started, the tears wouldn't stop. It was like a cork had been pulled from a tipped bottle and everything inside was spilling out.

Janet patted Charlotte on the back, but instead of soothing, it seemed to encourage more tears to show themselves.

"It will be all right." She wiped at Charlotte's face. "I promise, sis, everything will be all right." She eased Charlotte's head to her chest. Neither noticed how quickly Janet's blue blouse darkened with Charlotte's sorrow. Neither cared.

"Okay. Let's do some planning." Janet looked across the small kitchen table at Charlotte's finally dry face. Crumbs were all that were left of the oatmeal raisin cookies that had filled the plate. The aroma of the strawberry tea they both loved drifted from the steaming cups in front of them and from the white porcelain pot on the mat in the center of the table. They had faced their teenage crises over strawberry tea and cookies. Back then, it had helped Janet face the end of her sometimes weekly crushes. Things always got better after strawberry tea.

Charlotte knew that no answers would come from cookies and tea, no matter how delicious the flavor. Still, she bent over her mug and allowed the sweet aroma to enter her and try to sooth her. She let her sister talk because she knew it would help Janet.

"First, you should pack up and come home with me."

"I can't do that." Charlotte sat back. "I just started a new job."

"You can get another one in Atlanta."

"Even if I did come with you, it wouldn't help. Nothing would change."

"I know it wouldn't change things, but I don't agree that it wouldn't help. It would keep me from feeling so useless about helping you. I want you where I can see you and pamper you a bit. I want you where I won't worry about you all the time."

"No. I can't come. I . . ."

"Hear me out," Janet added when Charlotte continued to shake her head from side to side.

Charlotte's words were stronger than Janet's this time.

"I'm not moving in with you and Jim. Even if you are my sister, a third person in your house would still make a crowd."

"Don't be silly. You won't be in the way. We'll lock you in your room, the basement would be the proper place, I think, and only let you out for your meals. Or maybe we'll just throw a crust of bread down to you three times a day. Does that make it sound okay now?"

"Janet, I appreciate your offer, I really do, but I . . ."

"Okay. Truth. I need you."

Charlotte slanted a look at her.

"Sure you do."

"Honest. I need you. That's one of the reasons I came. The shop is much more than I expected. I'm a victim of my own geniusness." She held up a hand. "I know that's not a word, but it should be. It fits. Anyway, success breeds success, period. I've tried several people, but I can't find anybody I'd trust to work full-time in the shop. With my pregnancy, I can't do as much as I used to. After the baby comes, I know I'll be doing less."

"You're making this up."

"I am not. Whenever I need to go on a buying trip, I'm

afraid of what condition the shop might be in when I come back."

"You've never been afraid in your life."

"Only a fool is never afraid. I'm just good at covering it up so you won't notice." Janet placed her hand on top of Charlotte's. "Try it for a few months. If it doesn't work out, I'll let you go. That is, provided you look more like your old self by then."

"I'll never look like my old self."

"Poor choice of words on my part. Provided you look and feel better than you do now. How's that?"

Charlotte stared into her cup. Then she looked at Janet.

"Are you sure Jim is all right about this?"

"I discussed it with him when that stupid lawsuit came up. I didn't mention it to you then because I knew you'd turn me down. Things have changed now. I'm pregnant and I need you. If you'd stop being so stubborn, you'd admit that you need me, too. Anyway, when I mentioned it to Jim, not only did he agree, but he thinks it's a terrific idea. He says maybe if you're there to help out, I'll stop whining to him about how hard it is to find good help nowadays. He also says maybe I'll stop worrying about you all the time, imagining you caught up in one disaster after another."

"You're telling me the truth?"

"Would I lie to you? I mean about something important?"

"I guess not."

"You know not." Janet gave Charlotte's arm a tug. "Come on, little sister, try it for a little while. I promise not to work you too hard. You can probably work for one of the papers in the area. You've been talking about making a career change. Well, here's your chance to try a change of scenery, too."

Charlotte didn't answer. She stared at the table as if looking to see if 'yes' or 'no' would appear.

"You owe me." Janet's voice broke into Charlotte's search.

"I owe you? I owe you for what?" She let her gaze climb to her sister's face.

"I don't remember specifically"—Janet waved her hand—"but I'm sure, after all these years, you must owe me for something."

Charlotte let a smile go free. It felt good. A laugh followed. It was small, but it was a laugh. With Janet here, she was able to find more of those than she expected to.

"A few months, Right?"

"A few months. That's all." Janet nodded quickly.

"Then if I decide to come back here, you won't nag me?"

"Me? Nag? I never nag. You know me."

"Right. I know you. That's why I want your promise. If you never nag, it won't be hard for you to promise not to."

"Okay, I promise." Janet frowned. "I'm not sure a few months will be enough, though. You know that southern living is much slower. Much more easygoing and genteel and . . ."

"I haven't gone with you and already you're trying to make me stay longer."

"All right. All right." Janet held up her hand. "A few months and no nagging, cross my heart and hope to die." Her eyes opened wide.

"Don't try that innocent look on me. I know you have your fingers crossed behind your back like you always do."

Janet's giggle made Charlotte remember when they were younger and her sister had always been able to nudge her out of a blue mood.

She sighed. That was back when a crisis was not having a date for a party. Charlotte smiled, but it quickly flew away. This wasn't something that would go away with time. This would be with her for the rest of her life.

Charlotte cradled her middle protectively with both hands. She could handle this. She would handle things. Without Tyler.

"You're sure Jim is okay with this?"

"Jim will be just as happy for you to come as I will. Of course, he'll have to forego our impromptu sex episodes on the kitchen table and floor. Probably the front porch, too. Oh, and I can't forget the hallway."

"Janet?" Charlotte wasn't sure whether or not to take her sister seriously. She wouldn't put anything past her.

"I'm kidding," Janet said after she caught Charlotte's stare. "Honest." She held out both hands. "See. No crossed fingers. Really, Jim will be glad to have you with us for as long as you like. It's not like we'll be tripping over each other all the time. The new house we're moving into is so big we'll have trouble finding each other."

"If you're sure . . ."

"Great." Janet's face lit up. "The first thing we have to do when you get there is get you to my doctor. She's great." She stopped talking and stared at Charlotte for several minutes. "You are going to have the baby, aren't you? I didn't ask you. You're going to have it and keep it afterward?"

"Yes, I'm going to have it." She placed her hands over the life growing inside her. "And I'm keeping him afterward." She patted gently. "I couldn't do anything else. I never even considered it."

"I'm glad." Janet hugged her. "I'll help you. We'll get you through this together, little sister, and our babies will grow up together. Now I think we should celebrate."

"Celebrate?"

"Sure. We'll celebrate your coming move. A client gave Jim tickets to see one of the top shows on Broadway, so you and I get to go to New York."

"I can't take Jim's ticket."

"He won't go. He doesn't like musicals, no matter how popular they are. I don't know how I missed so big a flaw in him. I guess I was blinded by love."

Charlotte flinched. She blinked hard several times.

"Oh, sis, I'm so sorry." Janet grasped Charlotte's hand. "Sometimes I have a stupid way with words."

"It's okay. Really." Charlotte squeezed back. "I remember the movie musicals we saw when we were growing up. We'd see each movie twice and walk home singing every song."

"You mean we'd dance and sing our way home. No one could tell us we weren't ready for starring roles of our own."

Charlotte blinked away the rest of the pain to make room for a giggle at a memory.

"We'd prance around, singing and acting out each song until the next musical came to the Ritz."

"We almost drove Mom and Dad—especially Dad—over the edge of sanity."

They reminded each other of movie stories and favorite songs as they remembered the reactions of their parents, who had passed away five years before, within a few months of each other.

Charlotte's mood lifted like a lighthearted song from one of those movies.

Fourteen

The cold wind swirled across the sidewalk and down the street before it came back acting as if it couldn't decide which way to go. March was living up to its reputation as the windy month, though at the moment, it felt more like February. Charlotte pulled her collar up around her neck. She wasn't sure she wanted to keep up with Janet anymore.

"We have to buy something from Saks," Janet said. "Just one little thing. I promise. I won't take long. We're on Fifth Avenue. The store isn't far from here." She turned to face Charlotte, ignoring the wind that pressed her coat against her body, showing the soft mound of her middle.

Charlotte stood in place as if she was home and wasn't going anywhere else, no matter what.

"Come on, little sister. It would be breaking part of the sacred shopping oath if we don't go to Saks and buy something." Janet tugged at Charlotte's arm.

"You mean *you* have to buy something. I'm through shopping. I was through four stores ago. And I'm through with these crowds, too." She waved around them. "Look at all these people. How could they all have someplace to go at the same time?"

"It's New York." Janet shrugged before she pulled a little harder. "Come on. We still have time before our train is due."

"That's what you said before you dragged me into the last store. And the one before that."

"It's still true. See?" Janet flashed her watch at Charlotte but pulled it away before Charlotte could see the numbers.

"I'm glad we put our suitcases in a locker at the station." Charlotte sighed. "Just the thought of lugging my bag around while you search for 'something, I don't know what it is but I'll know it when I find it' sends chills through me. And my chills have nothing to do with the temperature," she added as Janet started to speak, "so don't try to blame them on that. It is freezing, though." She looked at the time and temperature marching across the top of a building on the corner down the street. "Actually, it's below freezing." She pulled her collar up closer to cover her ears. "This is absolutely, positively the last store I'm going to go . . ."

Charlotte never finished her sentence. She couldn't have, no matter what was at stake. The music coming through the store window beside her was soft, but it was hitting her like a sledgehammer. Only one person played like that. How could something so soft hurt so much?

She turned toward the store window that was filled with televisions of different sizes for sale. All of them were tuned to the same channel. All were letting go of the same strong sounds to go with the same strong face. All of them were showing Tyler. His face was turned to the side, but Charlotte didn't need for him to face her to see that it was him. She didn't have to see his mouth to remember how it had felt pressed against hers. She didn't have to stare into his eyes to picture them warm after their lovemaking. She frowned. She remembered how his eyes were frozen hard against her when he learned who she was. Words poked at her from around the edges of the music.

"The opening concert was played before a packed house," the newscaster reported, as if her words would have no more effect on Charlotte than a forecast for a beautiful sunny day in the middle of June.

Charlotte stood as if glue dripped from the words and pooled around her feet, fastening them in place.

"Tyler Fleming used his piano to silence every critic who questioned whether or not he had run out of talent," the reporter went on. "His performance was nothing less than spectacular. Stellar is a more appropriate word," she gushed. "I won't dare to hazard a guess as to how many hits he'll get from his new album when he finishes it. We were told that he's working on more songs to go with the ones he favored us with last night. And he did favor us. Yes, folks, Tyler Fleming is back with a vengeance, much to the joy of all of us."

Her words kept coming as Tyler's fingers danced across the keys. His head was bowed in the familiar way Charlotte had seen when he had let her into his studio and played for her. That was before he had learned to hate her. He looked now as he had then, as if he was trying to see the music escaping from the piano and into the open before anyone else did. He had smiled at her when he told her his teachers had given up trying to break him of the habit.

Charlotte closed her eyes so no other pictures could get in. It was not 'joy for all of us' as the reporter had said. *For some, for one at least,* she thought—*for me—it brings pain.*

She couldn't watch anymore. One Tyler would have been too much for her right now. Too much at any time. This many was impossible for her to look at. She shook her head to make his pictures go away. It didn't work, but she hadn't expected it to.

She turned her back and leaned against the huge window that showcased Tyler. Why did the window have to be so big?

It was a struggle, but she found enough air for one breath. Then she grabbed another. If she put all of her attention on that, on just breathing, she could get through this.

"Charlotte? Charlotte?" Janet threw a lifeline of words to her. She grabbed Charlotte's arm and pulled her away from the dark whirlpool threatening to claim her.

Charlotte tried to blink herself away from the edge. She was so close to falling in, she didn't know if she could avoid it. She didn't know if she wanted to.

"Charlotte?" Janet tightened her hand and tried to shake her sister back to her. "Charlotte? Come with me. Come on. Let's get away from this."

Charlotte felt Janet's pull on her arm and stumbled away with her. She'd follow anybody anywhere right now, if they would help her escape from this torture.

She didn't know how, but her feet took her with Janet into a store, a different store. A store that wasn't flinging Tyler's images at her. A store that was playing music that didn't mean anything. That was fine with her. If there had to be music, this was the best kind.

"Excuse me." Janet stopped at a counter. "My sister has to sit down, please." Her words sounded like they were coming from across the room, but she was close enough to push Charlotte into the chair the saleswoman quickly vacated.

Charlotte tried to make her heartbeat slow down. It was racing as if it was trying to catch a train pulling out of Grand Central Station. She tried to make her shaking hands stop moving and the bones come back into her legs. She tried to make all her parts behave the way they should. The way they could before she saw . . . The darkness crept closer as if it was just waiting for the chance to take over.

"Put your head down." Janet's words were an order, but her hand was gentle as she nudged Charlotte's head low. "It will help if you put your head down."

Charlotte let her head droop. It was too heavy for her to hold up, anyway. A paperclip would have been too heavy for her to hold up right then.

"That's it. Good." Janet rubbed Charlotte's back. "Now breathe. In slowly. Now let it out slowly. That's it. Now take in another. You're doing fine."

Charlotte raised her head enough to glance at Janet. She saw her sister take a breath of her own that looked as weak as Charlotte felt. Charlotte wanted to assure Janet that she knew how to breathe, but she wasn't sure that was true.

"You frightened your color away," Janet said. She touched Charlotte's cheek. Then she brushed a curl back from her forehead with hands that shook almost as much as Charlotte's did. She let out a hard breath. "I have to tell you, you scared more than a few years off my life just now, little sister."

Charlotte was sorry she had worried Janet, but she didn't have the strength to tell her that. She needed all of her power to make all of her parts at least try to act normal. Maybe later she would tell her. Later. Much later. She let her head drop back down.

"Here. This might help." The saleswoman handed Charlotte a glass of water. It sloshed over the sides until Janet wrapped her own hands around Charlotte's. She eased the glass to Charlotte's mouth and made sure she sipped slowly.

"Thank you," Janet said to the woman. Charlotte wished she had the energy to say it. Those should be her words. It felt like Tyler should be hers, too, but he wasn't. She took a deep breath without Janet having to tell her to this time. Maybe later, when she was back on hard ground, maybe then she could thank the woman.

Janet's gaze never left Charlotte. Each time Charlotte blinked away the darkness, Janet was right there with her.

Janet bent down again and looked Charlotte in the face. She spoke slowly, and Charlotte was glad. It was hard to hear what Janet was saying at normal speed. As if anything was normal about this.

"I'll go hail a cab. It's time for us to go." She started away, but came back. "You just stay put in that chair. Don't move. I'll come get you. You wait for me here, okay?"

Charlotte still struggled to breathe. If she thought her voice could come out without a wobble, she would have agreed with Janet. If she thought her voice could come out

at all, she'd let it. The best she could manage was a nod.
It was past time to go.

Janet got Charlotte into a cab and into a seat in a rear
car on the train, but Charlotte didn't remember how. A pa-
rade of all of the trombones in the world blaring could have
passed them, and Charlotte wouldn't have been aware of it.

She closed her eyes, rested her head back on the seat
and let the train's rhythm carry her with it. The steady clack-
ing of the wheels over the tracks gave her something to try
to match her breathing to. The side to side sway was almost
like being rocked by her mother when she was a child and
had no worries. Almost. She hoped the sway would at least
last long enough for her to gain control of herself.

"Charlotte? Are you feeling better now?"

In all their years together, Charlotte had never heard Janet
sound so unsure of anything.

"Yes." Her face softened in the beginning of a smile. It
didn't finish, but it was a start. "To tell you the truth, I
don't think I could feel any worse."

"I shouldn't have made you stay. I should have let you
drag me away earlier. You probably had a premonition that
something like that was going to happen. That's why you
kept wanting to go."

"You heard the reporter. Everybody loves his music. They
say he's a genius."

"Don't defend him." Janet's voice held the anger that
Charlotte felt should come from herself but didn't. "Not after the way he treated you."

"I'm not defending him. I'm just telling the truth."

"He is stupid. He should have known you aren't the un-
caring person he made you out to be. I don't care if you
were together for only a week. It doesn't take long to discover that about you." Janet's jaw tightened. "He's a good

example of intelligence and common sense being two very different things."

"Maybe you're right."

"No 'maybe' about it. Look what he did to you."

"Soon everybody will be able to look." Charlotte patted her stomach and let her hands stay over it.

"I'm not talking about that and you know it. I'm talking about how he hurt you. I'm talking about how you trusted him more than you ever trusted anybody before, but he didn't trust you. I'm talking about how you gave him a gift you can only give once and look what he did after that. He was too stupid to know its value."

"It's over with. Everything between us is over. All of it. I can't change things that already happened." She sighed. "Right now I don't have the energy to worry about what it would be like if things were different." Her eyes closed again. She remembered thinking of other 'what ifs' when she was with Tyler.

"Charlotte." Janet took a deep breath. Her voice was gentle when it started again. "You know, with him back in the news, you're going to have to be prepared to hear about him, to see his face. He'll be all over the news, in the paper, on the radio, everywhere. You're going to have to be ready for that. Philadelphia will probably be on his tour." She sighed. "I hope you won't still be there when he comes."

"I hope so, too." She looked at Janet. "I know I have to face those things. He was working on the new numbers when I . . . when I was . . ." She swallowed hard and tried again. "When I was with him. As popular as his music is, I'm not surprised he's all over the news. And I know he will be until his tour is over." She closed her eyes. "I just didn't expect it this time; that's why it hit me like that." She swallowed. Hit was the right word to use. It was exactly how she felt when she saw Tyler's face flash on the screen.

"I think we have to . . ." The rest of Janet's words were lost when she looked at Charlotte. "Later. We'll talk when we get you home. Right now I think you need to get some rest. Try to grab a nap. I'll wake you when we get there." She patted Charlotte's hand as if she expected her to relax enough to sleep. Charlotte let Janet think that that was possible.

"I said I read the reviews." Tyler tossed the newspaper onto the polished mahogany table in his hotel room. Of all the woods they could have picked, why did they have to have mahogany furniture? He thought of soft curls the same rich color that went with warm, wide eyes and skin as soft as satin.

"Well, I'd never know it from the way you're acting." Barbara clutched her own copy of the trade paper with the glowing report about Tyler. "This is fantastic, Tyler. Sam McIntire is a hard man to impress. More than one would-be star can swear to that." She pulled out a chair that was a twin to his and sat across from him. "I don't understand you. This is what you wanted. You said so when you started writing again. What's the matter with you?"

"Let it be. Drop it." Suddenly the chair was too tight for him. He stood.

"Do you realize what this means?" Barbara continued as if she hadn't heard Tyler. "Do you realize how important this is? Do you know how many sold-out houses this will mean? I've been getting calls all morning from people begging for their cities to be added to the tour, and you act as if the critics panned you." She held up the paper again. "These are important people talking. You know what they say about making it here. Well, you've made it here. Again. And even bigger than the first time. You took those years off, but it's like you never left the public's eye."

Tyler shrugged. He crammed his hands into his pockets and walked over to the window. Sunlight glittering off the walls of glass facing him looked the same as when it had bounced off the deep snow in his yard. Somebody else had stood at his window with him back then, back when he still had good sense.

"Tyler?"

"What did you say?" He stared at Barbara's image in the glass wall, wishing it was somebody else's.

"Remember you have that radio interview to tape at three today. I'll come by for you and we'll go together. All right?"

"Yeah." He blinked. "Okay."

"Is it okay if I go ahead and add those new cities to your tour? I want to let them know one way or another today."

"Whatever you want, Barbara, whatever you want." He rubbed a hand over his jaw. Somebody should have their desires satisfied.

"And don't forget the interview tomorrow morning. I know eight o'clock is early for you, but it's worth getting up for." She laughed. "They've called twice already to make sure you'll be there." She laughed again. "The other networks weren't very happy when I told them we had already booked you with somebody else. Still, they all want to set something up before you leave the city."

"I'll be ready in time this afternoon. And I won't forget about the television show in the morning."

Barbara frowned at him. "Tyler, I think if I told you the president just declared your birthday a national holiday, you still wouldn't be excited. Are you all right?"

"Sure. I'm just tired." He turned to face her. "Give me a little time alone, okay?"

"Okay." Barbara stared at him. She opened her mouth, then closed it without saying anything. Then she let loose the words she had been holding back. "Look, Tyler, I know something has been bothering you. I could tell when you brought me the new numbers after that big storm that something heavy was on your mind. It seems to me that it still is." She left room for his answer. When it didn't come, she went on. "If you want to talk, you know I'm willing to listen."

"I know." Tyler turned his back on her reflection and faced her. He nodded. "I know," he said softly. "If I thought it would help, I'd take you up on your offer. But nothing can help me with this."

"Is it the lawsuit that's bothering you? It's coming up soon, isn't it?"

"Yes, it's coming up soon, but, no, that's not what's bothering me. It's not important anymore." He shook his head. "I'll see you later."

She stared at him for long seconds. Then she walked to the door. "I can take the hint." She turned back to him. "I'll give you a call when it's time to leave for the radio interview. If you need me before then, give me a call. I'll be in my suite."

Tyler heard the door click softly behind her, but he didn't bother to look.

The one he needed wasn't there and he couldn't call her. She'd never be with him again. He had seen to that. His words had cut a wedge between them like a sharp axe doing its job. It was all his fault. And all the sorry in the world wouldn't fix things.

He picked up the trade paper again knowing he wouldn't read it, but needing to do something with his hands.

He moved to the couch as if through the deep snow he had once waded through to rescue Charlotte. He had rescued her and then did more damage to her than the storm would have done.

He only sat there in the strange room because he didn't know what else to do. The thermostat was turned to a comfortable level, but the suite felt colder than his house had after Charlotte had come to him. He remembered the heat they had shared during their lovemaking. His body tensed as it remembered, too.

Tyler tried to push away the heat and the memory of her

body, tight against his. He took in a ragged breath. His hands tightened on the arm of the couch.

His whole life, he'd always been so sure of himself, so sure he was doing the right thing. He had even been sure when he ripped Charlotte away from him, from where she belonged.

I wonder if she's all right? I wonder if she's healed from the hurt I did to her? Does she hate me like she should?

He glanced at the paper grasped in his hands. His name shouted from the headlines. He had seen himself on the news programs. It seemed like whenever he turned on the television, there he was. Barbara said she had been flooded with requests for him to go on talk shows and to add concerts to his tour.

Before all this happened, he had thought it would mean more to him when the recognition came again. He had expected his new success to have a sweeter feeling. He had thought showing critics that his talent hadn't died with Tiffany was important. He had locked himself away and created new music to prove he could still make the piano share its magic with him, even though Tiffany was gone. He sighed. He had worked as if proving that had mattered.

His face tried to manage a smile, but failed. He could think of Tiffany now without the sharp pain stabbing through him as it used to. The road leading to her memory had smoothed out and didn't hurt as much as he traveled over it. He could separate the happy times with her from the pain at the end of their time together. The pain of losing her hadn't disappeared, but it had dulled. He had learned he could survive without her. He would never forget Tiffany, but he could manage without her. Tiffany was part of his other life.

He sighed. The hurt from the newer loss was impossible to escape. *Charlotte. Where are you right now?* The pain was still fresh, but he didn't expect it to get any better with the passing of time. It would hurt as much a hundred years from now as it did today; that was one thing he was sure of.

Mahogany curls, trusting warm eyes, a softness he'd never forget—all were gone. They hadn't been taken away by fate. That would have been bad enough. Those valuables were gone, she was gone, because of his doing. He had thrown away what they had had together as if it had been something easy to find. As if it was something easily replaced.

He stared at the carpet, but if someone had asked him later, he couldn't have described it. He couldn't have even told what color it was. He wasn't seeing it. He was looking at his past and wishing he could be the first to figure out a way to go back to the past and undo his mistake.

I wonder what she's doing right now? Philadelphia isn't that far from here. At least I had enough sense to get that much from her license.

He let his mind follow that path. *I could drive there in a few hours. A train would take less time. A plane. It would be even quicker if I chartered a plane. I know I can find her. I didn't notice her address, but I know I could find her if I looked hard enough.*

He shook his head. *And then what? Expect my 'I'm sorry' to erase what I said to her, what I did to her, and make everything perfect again? She wouldn't want to see me. How could she? Even somebody as sweet as she is couldn't forgive me for the awful words I said to her, the way I treated her that last day. Right after the most complete lovemaking of my life, I destroyed everything with my words. I wouldn't even let her explain.*

He sighed. *I can't blame her for hating me. She's better off without me. She'll forget all about me and what was between us. I hope she forgets the hurt I caused her, too. She'll find a nice guy. One who would never hurt her. They'll fall in love and she'll live the kind of life she deserves. The 'happily-ever-after' life that everybody's looking for, but that she deserves.*

Tyler swallowed the bitter taste that filled his mouth. He didn't want to, he couldn't let himself, think of her with anybody else. She belonged with him. They belonged together. Or at least they had before he messed things up so badly.

He got up, grabbed his folder of music and held it as if it might try to get away. He grasped it like it was the only thing keeping him from scattering into small pieces. He could lose himself in his music if he tried hard enough. He knew he could. He had done it many times before.

He rushed to the theater as if afraid it might disappear before he got there. He'd look for peace where he knew he could find it, if only for a little while. He didn't deserve it, but maybe he could find it anyway.

He got into the taxi by himself, but he wasn't alone. The cab could take him away from the hotel, but it couldn't help him leave his thoughts behind.

Fifteen

Charlotte picked up the toaster she had found at a yard sale two years before. She had cleaned and polished it until it was as shiny as it had been when new. It still worked fine, but she wouldn't need it anymore, just as she wouldn't need so many other things she had already gotten rid of. She hugged the toaster close for a minute, then went across the hall and tapped on the door.

"Miss Mary? It's me. Charlotte."

"Just a minute, sugar. I'm coming."

Charlotte heard the soft bumps of the walker coming closer to the door. She smiled when the door opened. Her smile was met by an older, wider one.

"How are you making out with your packing?"

"I'm getting there. I'm just about finished." Charlotte held out the toaster. "I was wondering if you could use this? It works fine, but I won't be needing it."

"Why, I sure could. That old thing I've been using has forgotten how to pop up. I either have to stand watch over it, or try to run over and catch my toast before it's turned into charcoal." Black eyes twinkled in a friendly face. "Running don't come as easy as it used to before I started dragging this old thing around." She tapped her hand on the top of the walker and sighed. "I reckon I should say before it started dragging me around."

"Now, Miss Mary, I've seen how you move with that

walker lately. You know it won't be long before you'll be running on that track at the high school again. Then you can give that walker away to somebody who needs it. Look how fast you got out of that wheelchair."

"My old doctor scared me out of that thing when he started talking about how, at my age, maybe I should get used to it. I won't be sixty-two until my next birthday. That's barely old enough to collect Social Security."

"That's right." Charlotte nodded. "When I reach that age, it won't be old enough to collect."

"I'll tell you what I did get used to," Miss Mary continued. "I found me a new doctor and got used to him. One who believed that the wheelchair didn't have to be a permanent part of me."

Laugher from both of them filled the air. Then the laughter was pushed away by Miss Mary's serious look.

"When I get back to my true self, I'm going to jog down to Dr. Adams's office and show him how wrong he was about me. He didn't know a thing about what I was doing before I took that fall. He, with his fresh-out-of-medical school mindset, took one look at me and figured all I could do was shuffle along from my bed to a rocking chair. I don't even have a rocking chair. I'll jog into his office and let him see for himself. Maybe that will make him think hard before he tells somebody else what they can and can't do. The next poor soul might believe him."

"That's true. So many believe that if the doctor says it, it's true."

Miss Mary moved the walker to the side. "What are we doing standing here in the doorway talking? That draft is whistling around like it's looking for a home, but I don't intend to let it share mine. Come on in. I know you're busy, but you have time to take a few minutes' rest. Bring the toaster on into the kitchen and have a cup of tea with me. I just made a fresh pot of that strawberry kind you brought over here."

Charlotte followed the older woman through the cozy living room. She always felt as if the handmade pillows scattered on the furniture and crocheted scarves on the backs of the sofa and chairs were welcoming her.

"I guess I can take a few minutes off."

"Of course you can. Since the elves have gone out of business like Jackson's Store that used to sit on the corner, your work will be right there waiting for you when you get back to it." She chuckled.

"That's for sure. No more elves around to do the work." Charlotte watched her friend make her way across the small kitchen to the cupboard. "Do you want me to get another cup?"

"No, thank you, I'll get it myself. You just sit down. You look like you need a rest more than I do. You're the one who's been doing so much work. Besides, the more I do, the more I *can* do. I got to get this hip back to normal."

Charlotte watched as the woman took a cup with bright yellow flowers from the dark green cabinet over the small counter beside the sink.

"Did I tell you about the birthday present I plan to give to myself next month?" Miss Mary asked. She faced Charlotte. "Sit on down, child." She waved toward the table. "You know you don't have to wait for any invitation to take your usual seat."

Charlotte sat in a chair with a yellow flowered pad tied at the seat. The small table was covered with a yellow checked cloth that matched the ruffled curtains at the window over the old-fashioned porcelain sink.

"No, you didn't tell me about any gift. What is it?"

"I'm going to get rid of this thing," Miss Mary said, touching the walker. "I'm going to give myself a cane. Actually, I'm thinking about giving it a try in a few days. I don't intend to keep that too long a time, either, though. I can't go around like I'm used to going if I got to be bothered with carrying something like a cane. I need both my hands." Her smile disappeared. "I'm sorry you won't be here to see it and to celebrate with me."

"I'm sorry I won't be here, too, Miss Mary, but your kids and grandkids will be with you."

"That's right. All eight of my kids. This house will be near to busting at the seams, what with them and my fifteen grands. We're going to have a time of it." She nodded. "But there's always room for you. I'm still going to miss you being here with us."

"I'll miss you, too, Miss Mary. You know that. But I have to move away from here."

"I reckon I do know that." She nodded. "But that won't keep me from wishing you were here." She filled Charlotte's cup. "Now tell me what all you have left to do and exactly when you're planning to desert me for Atlanta."

"I have a load of donations to take down to the thrift shop over on Chelten Avenue. You know the one."

"I sure do. It's one of my favorite shopping places. Never know what I'll find there."

"Yes, it's like a treasure hunt each time I go." Some of the things in her donation box were finds from the store. She was doing her own kind of recycling.

Charlotte went over the other things she had left to do. Listing them out loud helped her make sure she wasn't forgetting anything.

Miss Mary listened, nodded, and gave suggestions from time to time. Charlotte added more things to her mental list. Then they talked about the times they had shared, and their memories floated around them. Finally, Charlotte stretched.

"I think I better get back to work. No sense putting it off any longer." She drank the last of her tea. "Like you said, I can't count on the elves to help me finish." She took her cup over to the sink and ran water into it.

"Just a minute before you go. I got something to give you before you finish packing up your things." The older woman left the kitchen. Charlotte followed and waited in the living room.

"Miss Mary, you don't have to give me anything."

"I know I don't. You just wait right there. Don't you go away, now. I'll be right back."

Moving almost as fast as she used to before she got the walker, Miss Mary disappeared into the bedroom.

Charlotte looked around. She would miss this friendly place. She sighed. She knew she'd have to find room for the gift in one of her already full boxes, rather than hurt the woman's feelings.

"Here you are, but this isn't for you." Miss Mary lifted the top from the white box she carried.

"Oh." Charlotte's eyes widened. She looked at the tiny hand-crocheted yellow sweater and hat. The matching booties nestled with them in the folds of tissue paper looked small enough for a baby doll instead of the real baby's feet they were made for. Charlotte stared at them.

"I reckon you might find a use for these things." Miss Mary held up the hat. Pale yellow ribbon ties trailed down from bows made of the same ribbon. "By the time your little one gets here, this should still be warm enough for him."

"How did you know?" Charlotte thought of the times she'd started to tell her friend, but didn't. She didn't think that Miss Mary would understand. Friends or not, they were generations apart. But she was wrong. Miss Mary would understand anything.

"When you've carried as many babies as I have, and you've seen as much as I have, you get so you can recognize the signs. There's a softness that only comes to a woman when she's carrying a child."

"Miss Mary, I'm sorry I didn't tell you, but. . . ." Charlotte swallowed hard.

"You don't have to tell me nothing, sugar." She patted the younger woman's shoulder. "Now don't you start crying on me or you'll get me to crying, too, and I don't need that. Neither one of us does. Tears waste so much effort."

Charlotte smiled as she wiped her eyes. "Thank you, Miss Mary. This is so delicate and beautiful." She touched the crocheted edge of the sweater with one finger. "Just beautiful." Carefully she took the box from the woman's hands.

"Everything will be okay, sugar. You just wait and see. Once that little one is nestled in your arms, you'll wonder what you worried so much about. Things will work out all right, you mark my words. And when they do, you just remember Miss Mary told you so. Now you best get back to work over there if you expect to be ready to leave here in two days' time. I got errands to run all day tomorrow, that is, as best as I can run, dragging this thing with me, but you come over and say good-bye before you go away from here. Don't you dare go away from here without coming over and give me one last hug."

"I won't leave. I'll come over." Charlotte gently held the woman close to her. Then she went back across the hall. She would miss her friend.

Miss Mary had come over and introduced herself the first day Charlotte had moved in, three years before. She had brought a large pitcher of iced lemonade with her.

"I thought you might feel like a nice cold drink this hot July day," she had said. "And I know that old refrigerator of yours hasn't made ice for you yet."

She had made Charlotte's move less painful. They had shared many cups of tea and stories since then.

Miss Mary had told Charlotte all about how her parents had moved up from South Carolina before starting a family. Many of her stories were about her own children and how things had changed in the neighborhood over the years since he had moved in. Charlotte had told her about the stories e had covered and her problems with the paper and why she left. Miss Mary had assured her she had done the right thing.

"Nothing's worth nothing if you can't live with yourself in peace," she had said.

When Charlotte had gone to the older woman in tears about the lawsuit, Miss Mary had found the right words to reassure her that things would turn out all right.

"The truth always shows up when you need it most," she had said at the time.

Charlotte was the one who found Miss Mary on her floor after she had fallen from a ladder while changing the light-bulb in the bathroom ceiling fixture and broken her hip. Charlotte had watched over her recovery in the hospital and after she got home. She had no doubt that the walker and the cane would be gone before long, just as Miss Mary promised. Charlotte sighed. She wouldn't be here to see her friend back to normal. Yes, she would miss her.

She looked around her apartment. She had work left to do, but it would wait a bit longer. She sat on the couch. Her hand brushed over the sweater. She picked up a soft bootie. It felt like it weighed nothing. She brushed her fingers over the side. She imagined how it would be if she were in that large stone house sitting at the top of the hill above the twisting driveway. What if she were there and not here in a small lonely apartment in the city?

If she were there in that house, she would be fixing Tyler's lunch in that kitchen that could hold four of hers. She would look out from time to time to the woods. The new pale green leaves should be showing themselves on the trees and bushes. Maybe a doe with her babies would come out to the edge of the lawn. Maybe the opossum Tyler had freed would come back to finally thank him. Tyler's music would be dancing in the air through the whole house, keeping Charlotte company as she worked. Maybe she'd be fixing her own version of his grilled cheese specials.

She smiled at the idea. She'd pour his coffee into his cup

with musical notes marching all over it. Then she'd put their lunch on a tray and tiptoe into his studio.

He'd kiss her and pat her middle. She'd kiss him back.

"Hello, baby," he'd say to their child growing inside her. He'd kiss her stomach. As they ate, he'd tell her how his work was going. Maybe he'd play one of the new sections for her.

She'd encourage him like a wife who loves her husband would do. After lunch, she'd let him get back to work while she worked on a story, or an article, or maybe knitted a new sweater for their baby.

Charlotte sighed. That was how it could have been, if only things had been different. But things were as they were, and she was here, not there in that wonderful make-believe world.

She laid the box down beside her and put the cover back on it. She still had things to do if she intended to stick to the deadline she had set.

"Yes, Janet." The next evening, Charlotte made one last phone call. "First thing in the morning I'm leaving." Charlotte nodded even though there wasn't anybody there to see it. "Janet, I have done this before, you know. I have moved and I managed not to leave my head behind when I did it. I will see you in three days . . . Yes, I know I can take an extra day if I want to. I can take an extra week, if I need to. Janet, no more. That's it. I'm hanging up. Yes, I'll call you from the road if it's going to take me longer than three days. You can bet I won't forget to do that. If I do, you'll have every state trooper and local police department from here to Atlanta looking for me. Yes, you would. Don't even try to deny it. Janet, take care. I'll see you when I get there."

Charlotte picked up her checklist one last time. She was pleased to see the row of checkmarks marching down beside all of the items. The car trunk was packed. The only thing left to do in the morning was to put the things that didn't fit in the trunk into the backseat.

She went across the hall to Miss Mary's for the last time. Even if the woman did insist that she'd be up early, Charlotte wasn't going to go over there at the time she expected to be leaving. When the door opened, Charlotte's smile didn't reach her eyes.

"I just wanted to say good-bye and get my last hug."

"I guess it is better to say good-bye tonight, sugar. If you come over here in the morning, we might get to talking and half the day would be gone before you get away from here." Miss Mary pulled Charlotte close to her, then let her go. "You drive carefully, you hear? You aren't in any race."

"Yes, Miss Mary."

"And you stop when you get tired, don't matter what time it is. No sense pushing yourself. You aren't on any timetable."

"Yes, ma'am." Charlotte smiled. "Are you sure you didn't talk to Janet? You sound just like she did last night."

"That's because the both of us are talking sense. It's because we both care about you. And right about now, you got to be extra careful. You got somebody else to take care of besides yourself, you know."

"Yes, I know. I'll be very careful. I'll drive as if you and Janet were in the car with me."

"Good." She nodded. "Don't forget to write to me when you get yourself settled in. I mean I expect to hear from you way before you let me know whether it's a grandson or a granddaughter I have." She smiled softly and blinked against the tears filling in her eyes. "Sugar, you know I couldn't love you no more if you were my own flesh and blood."

"I know, Miss Mary. And you know how much I care about you. You're like a mother to me." Charlotte blinked.

Her eyes matched the other woman's. "If you keep this up, you'll have me crying."

"We can't have that. You got to rest your eyes so they'll be ready for that long drive come tomorrow morning." She patted Charlotte for the last time. "You take care, you hear?"

"Yes, Ma'am, I will."

Charlotte awoke just as the sun was winking at her through the new leaves on the huge oak tree outside her bedroom. With no curtains to stop it, morning came earlier than usual. "May as well get started," she told herself. "The day is here."

An hour later, glad the elevator was working, she packed the rest of her things into the car, filled the backseat, and was back in the bedroom. She straightened the now bare pillow on the bed as if it would be used the way she left it. She let her gaze wander around the room for the last time. It had only taken three weeks to strip it of her things, of her life.

The room looked different. It seemed larger and emptier without her belongings scattered around. The furniture looked shabbier with family pictures and knickknacks gone from the tops. Scars and scuffs she had covered with lace scarves now showed themselves. The dresser looked lonely without the perfumes and the mirrored tray Janet had given her one birthday to hold her barrettes.

The little blue and red music box Charlotte had found at a church rummage sale two Decembers before wasn't in its place on the dresser in the corner next to the closet, sparkling light off its gold-trimmed edges. Instead it was packed away, waiting for its new spot in her new home.

Charlotte wasn't sure she'd ever put it out again. Even after she got settled in at Janet's house, she might leave the box with its happy, dancing couple packed away. She didn't know when, if ever, she would be ready to see the man and woman in their evening clothes twirling on top to "Somewhere My Love," as if they had found such a place and it was waiting for Charlotte to find, too.

She turned her back and shut the door because she couldn't bear to look at the room. It wasn't hers anymore.

She went into the living room, picked up her jacket, and walked to the door with it clutched in her hand. She looked around once more at the room with its coffee table and end tables clearer than they had been since she had moved in. The magazines she was going to get to but never did would be enjoyed by the folks in the senior citizen building a few blocks away.

Charlotte pushed her bag up on her shoulder, turned her back, and let the door close on her old life.

In the car, she put the tiny sweater set on top of the pile in the backseat. She looked at it one more time. It meant too much for her to hide it away in a bag. It was the first gift for her baby.

She gave the sweater a final pat and smiled at the thought of the little body that would be wearing it. She hoped it would be a boy who looked like a little Tyler. She let the cover drop to protect the set.

Charlotte pulled out of the small parking lot and headed toward the Blue Route that would take her to Interstate 95. She was glad she didn't have to use the turnpike. She wouldn't have to even see the words "Northeast Extension" on the route she was taking. She didn't want to go anywhere near the exit that would stir up old memories like dust on a dry country road.

Sixteen

"Damn." The lone word bounced off the acoustically perfect ceiling of the concert hall. Tyler clenched his hands to keep from banging on the piano keys, as he did when he was a little boy trying to learn a new piece. He was long past being a little boy, and this wasn't a new piece he was trying to play.

This morning, it was the same as it had been every day for the last few weeks. Every time Tyler tried to warm up, this is what happened. Nothing but garbage came from the piano. The notes mixed together until it was like trash from a compactor. Nothing was recognizable or worth anything to anyone.

He gave in and brought both hands down hard on as many keys as he could cover. The sound of the jumbled notes couldn't be called music by even his greatest fan, but that was okay. It wasn't meant to be music. The last notes finished bouncing off the high ceiling and hung in the air as if they were worth something. Tyler wasn't doing the concert hall justice. Nor the music. He clenched and unclenched his fists.

He had played this number so many times, he should have been able to play it flawlessly in his sleep. He had used it for a warm-up for years, yet today he was making mistakes that somebody playing the song for the first time wouldn't make. What kind of composer can't play his own numbers without mistakes?

One with so much on his mind there was no room to concentrate on anything else. He answered his own question. He was lucky his hands shifted into automatic when the hall was full. At least he was able to give the people their money's worth. Nobody would pay to hear the way he was playing during his practice sessions, and he couldn't blame them. It wasn't worth anything. That was how he felt about himself. Worthless.

He leaned his arms on the keys. Discordant, but now gentle notes this time, drifted up from the piano.

He rested his head on his arms and listened to the silence, the only thing that had been worth listening to this morning.

The reason for his lack of concentration wasn't that he had so many things on his mind. He knew that. He was honest enough with himself to admit that. It wasn't "things" on his mind at all. Charlotte was embedded into his mind and his heart like the taproot of the old oak beside his driveway. Like that taproot of his favorite tree, he didn't want her out. He wanted her in his life. He wanted her, the real her and not just her memory.

He closed the piano, grabbed his folder and jacket, and left the theater. How hard could it be to find her? And even if it was, he could do it. He had to. He didn't just want her, he needed her. As he rode back to the hotel in the cab, his mind sifted through plans, trying to find the best one. He was surprised when the driver told him they'd arrived.

"Tyler, I was afraid you weren't going to show."

Barbara rushed to him in the lobby. "I was just this side of panic," she added.

"Have you ever known me to miss an appointment?" He didn't tell her he had forgotten all about the interview and the only reason he had returned was because he couldn't stand to hear himself destroy music any longer.

"No, I haven't." She shook her head. "But I've never known you to be so preoccupied as you have been lately, either."

"Let's go, Barbara." He didn't need for her to tell him about his recent state of mind. That wouldn't change it. Only one thing—one person—could. And he'd find her. He didn't know how, but he would find Charlotte.

"Do you need to go up to your suite first?"

"What?" He blinked at her. "Oh, no, I'm ready. Let's get this over with."

He saw Barbara shake her head, but she didn't say anything. He was grateful she knew him well enough to leave him alone with his thoughts.

They rode to the studio in silence. He didn't know what Barbara was thinking about, but his thoughts could only stay on one thing. Finding his love. But first he had to get through this interview and everything else in his way.

"One final question, Mr. Fleming. You have had so much success going off away from the city and working in isolation. Do you find that makes your work easier? Do you recommend that others lock themselves away from everyone and everything so they can concentrate on their work? Do you think removing yourself from possible distractions is the reason that you've topped your former success this time?"

The man finally decided to wait for an answer. Tyler took a deep breath and shrugged.

"Different things work for different people." That was the best he could do. He couldn't tell him it hadn't been all isolation. He couldn't say that his best work came from being with and then trying to forget the person he had driven from his life. He couldn't say that, even if his most recent work was successful, it hadn't done what had he needed it to do. It hadn't cleansed him from her. It hadn't made him forget her. It hadn't let him stop wanting her. It hadn't been worth the time and effort it took to write it.

"Mr. Fleming?"

Tyler looked at the man and was surprised to see his hand reaching toward him. Tyler took it, glad for what it meant.

"Thank you for taking time from your busy schedule to meet with us. I know my listeners will be waiting as anxiously as I am for the release of the new album."

"Thank you for having me here." Tyler was glad he could use words he had used so often that they came automatically. He was in no state of mind to try to find new ones.

"I think that went very well," Barbara said after they left the studio, "even though we seemed to have lost you a couple of times and I wasn't sure if you were coming back."

Tyler didn't deny his lack of concentration. He had had a devil of a time finding answers to some of the questions. At least answers that made any sense. It wasn't that the questions had been hard; he just couldn't keep his mind on them any better than he had on his music at practice that morning.

"Why don't we walk back to the hotel instead of trying to get a cab?" He hoped the walk would clear his head and let him sort things out. He couldn't go on this way much longer. He walked faster as if trying to outrun the turmoil inside him.

"Enough, Tyler." Barbara stopped, after they'd walked for a few minutes. "I'm not sure this walking was the smartest decision I ever let you make. I have been trying for three blocks to match my steps to your long strides. If you don't want me to walk with you, just say so. You don't have to run from me." She pointed to her black pumps. "These shoes are as comfortable as the ads say, but they aren't made for jogging."

"What?" Tyler stopped. "Oh, I'm sorry, Barbara." He

looked down at her. He had forgotten she was there. "I didn't realize how fast I was walking."

"It was closer to running." Barbara breathed in deeply, and not just to catch her breath. "Tyler, you didn't remember I was here. I'm not sure you even realize what city we're in."

Tyler didn't disagree. He looked around and noticed the late afternoon crowd for the first time.

"You didn't add a show for tomorrow, did you?"

"No, your schedule is free like it usually is on Mondays. Why? What do you have in mind?"

"I have to go somewhere. There's something I have to do."

"I don't suppose you intend to tell me where?"

"You wouldn't be interested. It's not important." His jaw tightened. *Not to anybody but me. To me, it's the most important thing in my life.*

"Do you want to grab something to eat with me before tonight's concert?"

"No, I'll order something up from room service."

"I guess you intend to get some rest before the show?"

"Something like that."

He set off at a slower pace so Barbara could keep up with him. What he had to do would wait until he got back to his suite. He couldn't go anywhere before the performance, anyway. He let out a sharp breath, glad he didn't need to talk. He was grateful that Barbara left him alone when they got back. He had to make some calls so he could make plans.

"What do you mean, her number is unlisted?" Tyler knew he was bellowing into the phone. He didn't care. He had to make the woman on the other end understand. "This is important." It was hard, but he lowered his voice. "Very important."

"I understand, sir, but as I said, I can't connect you to an unlisted number."

"Let me speak to your supervisor." It wasn't as if he was trying to speak to the President of the United States. He only wanted to hear the voice of someone who had taken a part of him when she left.

"Yes, sir. Please hold."

He waited because he didn't have a choice. His fingers tightened around the receiver as if it was a lifeline.

"Miss Harris speaking. May I help you?"

"I hope so." Tyler gave her Charlotte's name. "I just need her number." He needed more than that, but that was the first step, and this woman couldn't help him with anything else. He doubted if she would help him with that any more than the other woman did. Damn company policy.

"I'm sorry, Sir, but that number is unlisted. I can't . . ."

"Look." He made his words stay slow and low, the opposite of what he wanted to let them do. He needed this woman's help.

"Let's do it this way. You call her and ask her if she'll talk to me. I'll even give you my number in case she prefers to call back." If he was lucky, luckier than he deserved to be, Charlotte would say "yes."

"I can do that for you, sir. Please hold."

As if he would do anything else but hold, if it meant he had a chance of reaching Charlotte. He prayed she'd at least give him a chance. *Another chance. Please.*

"I'm sorry, sir. That number has recently been disconnected at the customer's request," the operator told him.

"What? When?"

"A week ago, sir."

"Did she leave her new address?"

"She wouldn't leave that with us, sir. She paid her final bill when she requested the shut-off. We wouldn't have any need for her new address."

Tyler sighed. Of course not.

"Is there anything else we can help you with?"

"Yes. You can give me her old address."

"I'm sorry. Sir, I can't do that. It's against company policy to give out that information."

"What difference does it make if she's gone?"

"I don't know, sir. I don't make company policy, but there must be a reason for it. Besides, we don't know that she's gone, only that she had her phone disconnected. People have different reasons for taking that action. I'm sorry I can't help you."

"Not as sorry as I am." Tyler sat with the phone long after the tone had changed to a voice telling him to hang up if he would like to make call. He'd more than like to make another call. He took in a deep breath. If only he had the number he needed.

Had she moved? If she did, why would she move? Did she need money? Was that why she had her phone service disconnected? He had more money than he could use in three lifetimes. If she left her home, was it because she needed money? She wasn't sick, was she? Maybe her injuries had been more serious than they had seemed. If they were serious enough to make her lose her memory, maybe something was still the matter with her. She had really lost her memory. He had admitted that to himself. But by the time he had had enough sense to do that, it was too late for it to do any good. He had to find Charlotte.

He finally hung up, as the voice kept telling him to do. Then he picked up the phone again. He wasn't finished. He wasn't giving up yet.

"Yes, that's right." Tyler tried to keep the hope out of his voice. "I need the numbers for the newspapers. Yes, both papers in the city. Repeat that. Please."

Tyler slowed his scribble. The paper looked like he had written on it while riding over railroad ties. The information he was getting wouldn't be any good to him if he couldn't read it later.

"Yes, give me the names and numbers of neighborhood papers, too." Bless the woman for suggesting that to him. "Yes, all of them." He didn't know the name of the paper Charlotte had been doing the story for when she slipped off his driveway, but he doubted a large city paper would have taken her so far from home. He had no idea where she was working now. He didn't know if she was working, or even if she was able to work at all.

"Wait. You may as well give me the information about any papers in the surrounding areas, too. Yes, go ahead and include Jersey in your search."

He didn't know how close Charlotte lived to New Jersey. He didn't have any idea in which section of the city she lived. He wished he had looked at her address when he'd uncovered her license instead of getting stuck on her name. He wished a lot of things that weren't so.

"I guess that's all. Thank you very much for your help."

Carefully, he folded the sheet of paper with his hope written on it and put it into his wallet. Then he sat for a few minutes, sorting things out. He'd use this information later, when he had more time. He picked up the phone for a third time. He knew he'd get some information here.

His fingers missed the right buttons several times and he had to start over, but he kept trying until he reached the person he wanted to call.

"Jerry, I want you to drop Charlotte Thompson's name from the suit. Yes, you heard me correctly. She didn't have anything to do with that story. Never mind how I know, I just know. The next thing: I need her address."

Tyler's head moved from side to side as if he were a pitcher waving off a suggested play from the catcher. "I didn't ask you for legal advice this time. Don't tell me how my contacting her might compromise my case. I asked you for her address. And I want it. I need it. Now. It shouldn't matter anyway, since she's not included in the suit anymore." His head moved faster for a few shakes. "I don't care. I'll take that chance. This is more important to me than any lawsuit."

Now his head moved up and down. "Yeah, Jerry. That's a good idea. You can call her as our witness if you think it will help our case. Whatever you decide. I'll leave that up to you. Now, no more stalling. What's her address?"

Tyler made his hands move the pencil slowly across the pad. He had to be careful. He had to get it right. This was the most important thing he had ever written in his life.

He read it over as if he expected it to disappear like an audiotape on that old television series. He released the first smile in more days than he could remember. The first smile since he. . . . No. He shook his head. He wasn't going to think about that time. He couldn't change it, but he could make up for it, if she'd only let him. Please, let her let him.

He sat and waited for the crawling time to speed up and get him to the other side of tonight's concert so he could get to work on what was really important. Tomorrow he'd get an early start on searching for his lost dream. With a whole lot of luck that he didn't deserve, he'd find it.

The sun had just announced the bright morning to come when Tyler hopped out of bed. Today was the day. He went into the shower and tried not to think of hearing Charlotte taking her shower that last terrible morning that he would give anything to have back. He could have been in the shower with her. His body tightened at the thought. He would have been with her if he hadn't been so stupid. Never mind. He was going to fix it. By the end of the day, everything would be as it should. He couldn't remember when he had last been so anxious for the day to begin.

He hurried and dressed, wishing the car rental agency opened earlier than eight o'clock. He should have gotten

the car last night. Then he could be on his way instead of
stuck there, waiting.

A short time later, but an hour earlier than necessary to
meet the rental agent, Tyler was in the lobby pacing like a
lion in a too-small cage. He looked at his watch often, but
looking didn't make the hour pass any faster. When he saw
the doorman coming toward him, he was out the door before
the uniformed man could open it. Finally, he could do something besides wait.

Tyler stepped on the brake of the rental car again to bring
his speed closer to normal. A lot closer than he was. He
used to wonder why some drivers rode the brake pedal as
much as the gas. Now he understood exactly why. He was
in a hurry, but a speeding ticket would only delay him. The
last thing he needed now that he was so close, was for
something to make it longer before he could reach Charlotte.
He followed the signs hanging over the road from time to
time and drove closer to finding his love. Charlotte.

Two hours later, and after many stops to ask directions
and then more stops to verify directions, he pulled into the
parking lot of her apartment building.

The wood trim around the windows and roof of the building looked as if it had needed painting for years. Bare wood
peeked through in more spots than not and in some places,
gaps between the boards were noticeable.

The lot wasn't in any better condition than the building.
Grass had forced its way through the cracks in the blacktop,
making it look like a green and black quilt. Another quilt
tried to show itself to him, but this time Tyler was stronger
than the memory was. He didn't need to think of a quilt
at this time. That real quilt belonged in the past. He was
here to find his future.

He drew in a deep breath. After he found her, he could think again about the quilt and the sofa where the quilt belonged. After she was back with him, he could think of how Charlotte lay within his arms under that cover. His jaw tightened. He would find her and take her away from here. She deserved a better place than this. She deserved a lot more than that, but at least she deserved a better place than this to call home.

He rode the elevator to the third floor, wishing it would move faster. He walked down the dim, narrow hallway, looking at each door. He stopped when he found the number he had dragged out of Jerry. He stared at the door waiting for his courage to gather itself inside him. Then he took a deep breath and closed his eyes. He knocked. His knocks echoed from the inside as if off a hollow log.

He thought he hadn't been expecting an answer, but he was wrong. Hurt knifed through him when the door stayed shut and no sound reached him from within. He took another deep breath and stared at the door as if, by some miracle, that would make it open. When it didn't, he dragged himself to the door across the hall and hoped to find his miracle there.

"Who is it?" A strong voice reached him through the door.

"I'm looking for Charlotte Thompson. Do you know where she is or what time she'll be home?"

Tyler heard the thump of a walker. A pleasant face looked at him from under the chain lock.

"Who are you, young man?"

"I'm Tyler Fleming, ma'am. I'm looking for Charlotte Thompson. It's important that I find her." Tyler took a deep breath. *It's more than important. It's vital.*

"She doesn't live there anymore, son." Tyler met the eyes looking at him, as if measuring him. He blinked. He couldn't leave with just that. It didn't help him at all. He had to have more. He needed something to keep his hopes up.

"I tried the manager's apartment, but no one answered."

"Mr. Grayson is only there in the evenings and his wife is at work. Besides, he don't know where she went. He don't know much of anything. Never does." She stood looking at him. Finally, she saw that he wasn't going to leave it at that. "I guess if Charlotte wanted to keep in touch with you, she'd have given you her new address. She'd at least have let you know she was going."

"Yes, ma'am." Tyler looked down. Then he looked back at his only chance. "You see, ma'am, we had an argument." Tyler knew that argument was the wrong word for what had ended things between them. 'Argument' was too weak and held a promise for a later chance. Arguments could blow themselves out over time without much help. The damage his words had done needed a lot of help to fix. He prayed there was that much help in the world.

"I see." Her head moved slowly up and down. "An argument, you say?"

She stood as if waiting for more. At least she hadn't shut the door in his face. That was a hopeful sign. He'd take all of those he could get.

"Yes, ma'am. If I could just explain to her, I know I could make her understand." He didn't know anything except that he had to try everything he could think of to get the information he needed.

"I don't have her new address, son. She didn't give it to me before she went on away from here."

Tyler swallowed hard and shook his head as if shaking away the words that were like stones flung at him.

"I . . . I'm sorry to have bothered you. You have a nice day." He turned away, wondering where he was going to go now. The other paper he had thought was so valuable was worthless now. He was almost to the elevator when her words stopped him.

"Just a minute, young man."

He rushed back as if a bag of gold was waiting for him.

"Yes, ma'am?"

"You give me your number where you can be reached. If I hear from her, I'll give it to her. Then it will be up to her. That's the best I can do."

"Yes, ma'am. Thank you." Tyler fumbled for a business card, hoping this woman wouldn't change her mind before he could get it out. Finally, he managed to pull out a crisp beige card. "Just a minute, please." He pulled out the paper with the directions that had gotten him there and to this woman, who was keeping his hope alive.

"Take your time, son, I'm not going nowhere." This time, her voice was as soft and warm as honey.

"Yes, ma'am." He was glad he wasn't at the piano. His hand shook as he copied the hotel phone number from the top of the paper. He took a deep breath and handed it to her. "This is where I'll be. At least for the next three weeks. After that, I'll send you the new information, if that's all right."

She looked at the paper. "That's all right, but, son, you best hand me your pen so I can write this so I can read it. It won't be no good if I can't read it, now will it?"

"No, ma'am, it won't." Tyler did as the woman told him. "I can't tell you how much this means to me."

"Now, I'm not promising that Charlotte will get in touch with you. I'm just saying I'll give it to her when I hear from her, is all. The rest will be up to her."

"I realize that. And I appreciate what you're doing." Tyler held out his hand. "Thank you."

"You're her young man, aren't you?"

"I was." Tyler's words floated out and drifted away. "With any luck I will be again."

"If the good Lord means for it to be, it will happen. You take care, now, Tyler Fleming. You take care of yourself. And keep your hopes up."

"Yes, ma'am. You take care, too." He ran down the steps.

He had too much energy and hope to wait for the small elevator.

Tyler drove into the hotel lot, wondering how he got there. He had no memory of the drive back to New York. His guardian angel must have worked extra hard to get him back safely. He had spent the trip with his mind on Charlotte and what could have been. On what, with a little luck, could still be.

The drive back hadn't been nearly as long as the drive to Philadelphia. It wouldn't have mattered if it had been twice as long, though. He had something to look forward to now. Charlotte would call him. She had to. Everything between them couldn't be gone. If just a sliver of what they had was left inside her, he could make her care again. If she'd only talk to him. If she'd only see him. She had to let him try. He'd keep begging until she did. He would do all in his power to make up for the way he had hurt her. He could make her happy. He would make her happy, if she'd only give him another chance.

He returned to the present long enough to make arrangements to return the car, then he let his mind take him away again.

He was back at his house and she was with him. He worked on his music, but now he knew that she was more important to him than anything—even his music—could be.

He let the hotel elevator take him up to his suite and let his imagination continue to run after he got there.

In his daydream, Charlotte wore his ring on the finger that told the world she was his. At night they shared the bed with the mattress that had become too large for him after he had known her and lost her.

In his fantasy, he wrapped her in his arms and promised
to keep her safe always. A promise he would keep this time.
He kissed her perfect lips and trailed his lips down her body,
cherishing her with the appreciation of a treasure lost and
then found again. Holding each other, they became one as
only a man and a woman can. As only he and Charlotte
could. Afterward he held her close and they drifted off to
sleep.

His fairy tale continued. Soon she would be carrying his
baby. He'd always wanted children. Now he knew he wanted
them with her. A little girl with that same curl that did as
it wanted. A little girl, with warm, trusting brown eyes that
looked just like her mother's, would look up at him. Charlotte's eyes. His house would be filled with happiness again.

His dream had to come true. He couldn't bear to think
of what his life would be like if it didn't. He wouldn't even
consider that possibility. He just had to wait. That was the
hardest part, but he could do it. He could do anything if
it meant he'd end up with Charlotte.

He grabbed his dreams and his music and went to the
studio. His hope came out in the lightness of his practice
pieces that came from the piano perfectly.

He'd find her. Not as soon as he wanted. Not today. But
he would have her back with him again and this time he
would know how to love her as he should have before. He'd
get his second chance. He knew he would. He had to.

"Flawless. Your playing was absolutely flawless tonight.
The old Tyler Fleming is definitely back." Barbara was
standing in his dressing room after the show. She looked
more relaxed than Tyler had seen her in a long time. She
looked like he felt.

These past months, he had felt as if he was carrying a

piano on his back. Now, a little more lightness and Barbara would have to tie him down to keep him from floating off.

His fingers had played with the emotions he had felt when he had written the music. At times they glided over the keys like a skater over smooth ice. Other times they danced as joyously as he would when he held Charlotte in his arms again. He hoped that would be soon, but if not, he'd wait. He'd wait as long as it took to have her back.

From the way her old neighbor had acted, he knew Charlotte would get in touch with the woman. And he knew Charlotte would get in touch with him. She had to. Life couldn't be so cruel as to let him find her and then snatch her away. He just had to find the patience to wait until that day came.

He closed his eyes. *Please let it be soon.*

Seventeen

Charlotte, following Janet's directions to the shop, reached Atlanta without problems, although she had decided to take an extra day to get there.

"It's about time." Janet met her at the door of the shop.

"Janet, I told you I'd be here about this time. You haven't been watching for me all day."

"Of course not. Come on back here." Janet led the way to a small table at the back.

"You answered just a little too fast for me to believe you." Charlotte followed her and plopped down in one of the chairs.

"Maybe I peeked out a time or two." Janet filled a teapot from the electric pot and sat in the other chair. "How was your trip?"

"Long. I feel like I walked the whole way instead of driving." Charlotte took a sip of tea after Janet filled their mugs.

"Well, you're here now and you can rest as long as you want. I can't wait for you to see the new house. We just moved in two days ago. You don't want to hear about the problems we had with the floor finisher. Or the people who remodeled the kitchen. Or the ones who redid the master bathroom." She took a sip from her own mug. "But of course, I'll tell you all about them later." She smiled. Charlotte smiled back. It was good to be with Janet. Things seemed better all ready.

After she was settled in, Charlotte called Miss Mary to let her know she had arrived safely.

"I'm glad to hear that. You know I been worrying."

"I know. How have you been?"

"I've been just fine. I gave myself my present early. I went out this morning and bought myself a cane to lean on. Like I told you before you left, I plan to lay this down real soon. It cramps my style."

"I know it does." Her laugh mixed with Miss Mary's.

"Charlotte, I . . ." The older woman's voice stopped before the rest of her words came out.

"What is it, Miss Mary? Are you all right?"

"I'm just fine, sugar, just fine."

Charlotte heard her take a deep breath and let it out in a heavy sigh.

"I had a visitor. Or I should say you had a visitor."

"A visitor?"

"Yes. He said his name was Tyler Fleming and he had to get in touch with you."

Charlotte was glad she was sitting. Her hands were having trouble holding the phone in place and her legs were rubbery. Miss Mary's voice finally made it through the fog that had formed around Charlotte.

". . . like a nice man. He said you two had an argument." When Charlotte didn't answer, Miss Mary went on. "I promised to give you his number. You take it down, now, and think about talking to him. Are you ready for it?"

She'd never be ready, but she answered 'yes' anyway. She didn't want to try to explain to Miss Mary why she wasn't going to write down the number. She couldn't leave herself open for more hurt from Tyler. She'd never survive it.

After she found the fastest way to do it, she said good-bye to her friend, promised to call her again real soon, and hung up. She sat staring at the blank pad beside the phone. Then

she made herself walk away without wondering if she would
be sorry when she had time to think about it.

Two days later, Charlotte applied for and got a job at a
newspaper over Janet's protests.

"You don't have to do that. Just help me out in the shop."

"Janet, the shop is doing well, but you know you don't
have enough work for the three of us. Besides, I need a
real job. It's only part-time, so I'll still be able to help out
when you need me." She gave Janet a hard look. "Make
that *if* you need me. I'm starting to doubt your desperate
plea when you came to visit me." She held up a hand to
wave off Janet's words. "I'm not sorry I came, even though
I do doubt your claim to need me." She shook her head.
"I got this job because I have to have something to keep
me busy." Maybe work would keep her from thinking about
the phone number she hadn't written down. She wondered
if Miss Mary still had it. She shook her head. Probably not.
She sighed. It didn't matter. She still wouldn't use it. She'd
already had enough heartache to deal with.

"Are you sure about the job?"

"This is one of the few things I am sure about."

"Okay. But promise me you'll quit if it gets to be too
much for you."

"I promise."

"I have your promise and I plan to hold you to it."

Charlotte got enough assignments to keep her busy. She
was making Atlanta her home and adjusting to her new life
there. She had brought her medical records with her, and
Janet's doctor, Dr. Harris, was now taking care of her pregnancy. The weather did its best to make Charlotte feel welcome, too.

May had come, bringing with it the renewal that people

wait for as they get through winter. The heavy snowstorm she had been caught in had been posted in the record books and stored in the backs of minds to be brought out, years from now, and shared with other 'I remember when' stories. In Atlanta, it had been an ice storm. Whichever it was, for most people, this past winter would be remembered as gone and good riddance.

For Charlotte, that snowfall of months ago was so fresh in her mind, it may as well have been last week. She had a precious reminder growing inside her. She also had other reminders almost every day.

Tyler was no longer locked away in his mountain retreat. He was everywhere, but not so she could touch him. Even if he wanted her to. Which she knew he didn't. Which he never would.

Tyler popped up in the news every day like a regular segment of the broadcasts as he set new attendance records in New York. Charlotte was thankful that Janet had been so persuasive about her moving to Atlanta. Philadelphia was too close to New York. The pain of losing Tyler couldn't be greater if she were home, but she would have more pain. Philadelphia was so close to New York that there was bound to be even more news.

She pulled into a shopping center parking lot. The mimosa trees waved in the warm May breeze, inviting her to enjoy their shade, but that wasn't why she parked under a delicate branch and turned off the motor. She left the radio on and sat even though she knew Janet was waiting at home. What was playing on the radio made her drive into the lot as if drawn by a magnet.

She wanted to turn the radio off, but she couldn't. The music escaping from it was too beautiful. Music filled the car and hovered over her, drifting down from time to time to touch her before soaring up again. Tyler's new album was the feature on the public radio program.

Charlotte had heard bits of some of the numbers several

times, but this was the first time she had heard the whole album played from beginning to end. She had seen bits of his concerts during television news and she had managed to keep from falling apart like she had in New York when Tyler's picture flashed onto the television screens in that store window.

She had even watched his fifteen-minute interview on the weekly Entertainers In The News program and she hadn't crumbled under the memories. That had been hard, but she was still in one piece after it was over. This radio program was different.

The number playing now was one she had heard several times before and not on the radio. To have a radio send her the music would have been bad enough. This was worse. The song was the one Tyler had worked on before they'd gone out to measure the snow. When he came out of his studio, he had apologized for leaving her then, as he did each time he went in there to work. She had waited patiently for him each time.

She blinked the memory away and smiled. Smiling was something she was learning to do again.

She had taught Tyler to make snow angels. He had taught her to care too much.

They had made snow families and a walled city before they went inside. Later that evening, they had made something more valuable. They had made love. Sweet love. Love that had filled her soul as he had her body. Love that was still inside her, taking up so much space, there wasn't room for much else. Except for her baby. Her baby was part of that love, even if Tyler would never know it.

He had lost the bet about the snow, but she had never made him pay. Now he never would.

She wondered if he remembered the bet. She wondered if he remembered how they had felt like they couldn't get close enough to each other. She sighed.

He probably didn't remember. It hadn't mattered to him

like it had to her. She had just happened to have been conveniently there for him. Later, after she had learned to care too much, he had pushed away everything about their time together like so much trash. He had gotten rid of all of her time with him except what happened after Jake gave her the purse, and Tyler had looked at her name on her license. No matter what happened or how much time passed, he'd never forget how the woman he loved as Cleo became Charlotte Thompson, a woman he hated. He'd never want to know about a baby conceived with her.

Charlotte listened to part of the interview with Tyler that followed the music. She heard the question about him working in isolation. She knew his isolation included her, and isolation wasn't the right word for what had been between them. She turned off the radio. She couldn't stand the misery his words were causing her. She didn't want to hear his answer.

She sat for a while as silence filled the space the music had left when it disappeared.

She was glad when a woman with two little children got out of a car that pulled into the slot next to hers. Giggling sounds from the children and a "Hold my hand" from the mother reached through the window and nudged Charlotte. The sounds helped her back to where she was and away from where she wanted to be.

The three took their family sounds with them as they walked toward the stores, leaving the early afternoon quiet behind with Charlotte still sitting in her car.

She took much-needed time in the quiet to gather the pieces of her that had been splintered by the music and by Tyler's voice. She put them back together as best she could. She didn't turn the radio back on. It had already done too much damage.

She stilled her hands trembling against the steering wheel, slowed her heart rhythm to what was necessary to keep her body going and her baby healthy, swallowed the tears trying to fall, and drove home.

Tyler was put away where he couldn't bother her for a while. Probably a short while. Janet didn't have to know he had visited through the radio. She didn't understand why Charlotte followed his tour through the media and Charlotte couldn't explain it to her. She didn't understand it herself.

She read every entertainment section and kept track of Tyler as the newspapers did their job. She knew when Tyler added a new number and how the concert-goers reacted to it. They loved each song, but not as much as Charlotte still loved him. She knew each time the dates were extended. The papers were very thorough in their reporting and, as though fulfilling an assignment, she cut out each mention of Tyler and pasted it carefully into the scrapbook she was making. "For the baby," she told herself each time she fastened the next clipping in place. But she knew it was for her, too.

Whenever she added a new clipping, she read through the old ones and thought of how different things would be if she was making the book for Tyler. What if he would be coming home to her? Or what if she was getting ready to join him? She sighed. No matter how hard she tried, she hadn't learned to stay away from 'what if.' She'd keep trying. All the way home, she tried.

"Look what I have." Charlotte forced a smile to stay on her face later when she burst into the shop. Her voice mixed with the tinkling of the bell hanging over the door. She hoped Janet would think the trembling in her words was from the excitement of her news. "Sis, where are you?"

"Right here." Janet's face barely showed above the carton she carried from the storeroom in back.

"Let me give you a hand." Charlotte tucked the envelope she had been waving into her purse and took the other end of the box. "Don't you know better than to try to carry something like this?"

"I was managing nicely. It's not heavy, just awkward."

"Like us soon enough," Charlotte added. Laughter drifted from both of them as they set the box on a low table behind a counter.

"You won't get awkward or heavy. Look at you. Except for your thicker waist, nobody would know you're pregnant. As for me"—Janet put her hand to her own middle—"I look like I've swallowed a beach ball. My middle feels like it, too."

"I'm only in my fourth month," Charlotte reminded her. "You had two months' head start."

"Dr. Harris never told *me* my priority should be to gain weight. She told me to remember that the second person I'm eating for is an unborn infant." Janet touched the top of the box. "This shipment will wait. Why did you call me?"

"To show you this." Charlotte pulled out the envelope. "My first paycheck. It's the end of my probation period with the paper, too." She waved the check as if it were a victory flag. "They want me to write on a regular basis. I'll be doing stories with a local flavor. Happy stuff." Like before, she almost added. But it wasn't like before. Nothing would ever be like before Tyler. She touched her middle.

"I'm not surprised. I always said your talent with words is too good to stay hidden for long."

"You're my sister. You have to say things like that."

"But in this case it's true."

"Thank you." Charlotte straightened figurines on the shelf near her. "How was your day?"

"Things are slow now, but an hour ago you would have thought I was having a clearance sale of bargains of the century. I was mobbed." She let out a heavy sigh. "Now I'm beat. Let's have a cup of tea to celebrate your first paycheck, your regular job, and a booming day of business for Why Not Whatnots? I'll also use it as an excuse to get off my feet."

As they sat at the tiny table near the back door, Charlotte told Janet about her next story and what section of the city it would take her to.

Janet's eyes sparkled as she told about some of her sales that day.

"One woman bought one of each of Flora's figurines. She didn't even blink when she saw the total on the credit slip, just asked me to let her know when the next one in the series is available. You can believe I'll do that before I un-pack the box." Janet laughed. "That's my kind of customer."

"Maybe you can get Flora to put a rush on her work." Charlotte giggled.

"I thought about that." Janet laughed again before her face softened into a smile. "Another woman spent about an hour looking around. It was a rare moment when no other cus-tomer was in the shop. She kept going back to that window." Janet pointed to the side. "Finally, she bought one of those tiny babies in a crib. She just found out she's pregnant after trying for five years. She's going to give the figurine to her husband as a way of telling him." Janet's eyes brightened and she blinked. "I gave her a big discount. She's my kind of customer, too."

Tyler's music kept playing in Charlotte's head. Several times, she had to work at adding a comment that made sense to the conversation. She didn't need Janet's concern to damp-en her day.

At five o'clock, Janet locked the door and they went home. Charlotte put Tyler and his music away as she had to do so often. It was hard as it always was, but she did it. During the drive, she made her mind stay on her job. She was feeling better than she had in a long time. She hoped the relaxed feeling stayed for a while. She needed it.

"Are you going to make your salad dressing for dinner?" Janet asked as she unlocked the door.

"There's still some in the refrigerator."

"Not anymore. I finished it last night when I got up."

"You had salad for a snack last night?"

"It beats pickles and ice cream."

"I won't argue about that." Charlotte hung her jacket in the hall closet. "I'm going up to change. Be back down in a few minutes and yes, I'll make the dressing."

Fifteen minutes later, Janet appeared at Charlotte's bedroom door.

"What's keeping you? What's left of the salad is naked and ready for its dressing." She frowned. "What is it? What's the matter?" She rushed over to where Charlotte sat on the bed holding the phone. "Sis, you don't look so good. You look almost as bad as you did when . . ." She took the phone from Charlotte's hand. "This has to do with Tyler, doesn't it?"

"There was a message on your machine for me. I have to go to New York. I have to be in court Monday morning for the trial. They just located me. They said they tried to reach me by mail, but their letters were returned. I don't know how they found me here. I guess they can find anyone when they want to." She looked at Janet. "I know you reminded me and Miss Mary reminded me, too, but I must not have sent the mail-forwarding form to the post office." She blinked hard. "I don't know how I could forget something as important as that."

"I guess you had other things on your mind." Janet's words were gentle. She patted Charlotte's hand. "Don't worry, we'll be there. We have plenty of time. We'll catch a flight Sunday afternoon."

"We? You can't go with me."

"You don't think I'm going to let you go through this thing alone, do you?"

"What about the shop?"

"Loretta can handle things here for a few days."

"But you told me you don't feel comfortable leaving somebody else in charge of the shop."

"So I exaggerated a little."

Charlotte stared at her.

"Okay, so maybe I lied to get you here. Fingers crossed and all that. You need to be with family now."

Charlotte didn't argue. She didn't know how she would have stood being alone and with Tyler so near but out of reach.

"Loretta is great," Janet went on. "Really, she is." Janet shook her head. "But even if she wasn't, there is no way I would not be there with you on Monday. I'd never let you face the trial alone."

"They didn't say how long I'll have to be there."

"It doesn't matter. I'll be with you the whole time."

"Do they put pregnant women in prison?" Charlotte stared ahead, not seeing Janet or anything. "They do, don't they? I remember reading about one woman last year. What happens to the baby if the mother still has time left to serve after it's born?"

"Charlotte, come on. Calm down. This is a civil case, remember. No one goes to prison in a civil case. They just go broke." Janet smiled. "You're already there, so you don't have anything to worry about." She let her smile go. "Besides, I keep telling you, when they hear your story, they'll realize you shouldn't have been charged in the first place." She patted her shoulder. "Don't worry. Everything will be all right." She held Charlotte's hand in her own. "Now go ahead and change into you salad dressing-making clothes. I'll go make our hotel and airline reservations." She took a few steps away, but turned back. "Really, everything will be okay. I promise you."

Charlotte watched her go. She wished she was as sure as Janet was about things ending up all right. She wished Janet had a way to keep her promise.

Tyler. She'd see Tyler. He had to be there. It was his lawsuit. He filled her mind as he did too often. She had moved from her old home, but she hadn't been able to leave him behind. She sighed. My mind should realize it's no use dragging out those old images. Nothing good can come from it. My memory should be busy storing up new pictures from my life here instead of hanging on to the old ones from the snow-covered mountains. She shook her head, but Tyler still lingered in the front of her memory.

Charlotte tingled as she remembered his hands caressing her for the first time. He had started with her face. He'd touched her as if he was afraid she would break. She could still feel the way his fingers burned a trail though they barely touched her. They had glided over her cheeks, slowing down to trace around her lips as if to make a pattern. Then his fingers had returned to her lips and brushed across them. When she had parted them, he had lowered his head. His lips took the place of his fingers. That was better. Oh, so much better.

Charlotte squeezed her eyes shut so she could see him more clearly. So she could see them together much better. His mouth had learned more about her than she had known about herself. He had taught her things no one had ever shown her before. He had made her feel things she had never felt before.

After her lesson with him, after she had learned how to be one with him, they had lain together as if they belonged that way. As if it would be that way for them forever. Tyler had tucked her close to him as if to protect her from anything or anyone meaning to harm her.

Charlotte blinked. She hadn't known that he was the one who would hurt her, that he was the one she would need protection from. But it was all right. He hadn't known then, either.

Her fingers went to her lips and slid across them the way Tyler's lips had done.

An ache grew in her and spread, following the same path it always did when she thought of him. She wondered when the ache would disappear.

She took off her suit and pulled on a shirt and jeans. She was glad for the elastic in the waistline of the pants. Even so, she wouldn't be able to wear them much longer. She'd have to take Janet up on her offer and "go shopping" in the clothes closet they called Janet's Fashions Shop. Janet couldn't wear the things hanging there, but they were right for Charlotte's growing new size.

She went downstairs, determined to worry about clothes later. That was an easy one, but she had decided to handle one worry at a time. That was the only way she could get through things, especially now. One worry at a time.

"We're all set," Janet told her when Charlotte reached the kitchen. "Our flight leaves here Sunday morning at eleven. I thought if we get to New York early we'll have time to relax and rest up before Monday. I made reservations at a hotel close to the courthouse. That way finding a cab won't give us something else to worry about."

"I guess it's a good idea to get there early, but I don't think I'll be doing much relaxing." Charlotte took in a deep breath and let it out slowly. "Resting is out of the question for me, too."

"Charlotte . . ."

"I know." Charlotte raised her hands to stop Janet's words. "Don't worry. It won't help."

"That's right. Now all you have to do is believe that." She handed Charlotte the olive oil. "Hurry up. I'm ready to eat my salad. Or the rest of it."

"Aren't you going to wait for Jim?"

"Nope." She took a piece of tomato from the salad bowl

and bit into it. "He knows I always start without him." She pulled out a cucumber slice next and bit into that. "If he doesn't hurry, I'll be a member of the clean plate club by the time he gets home."

"Janet." Charlotte shook her head from side to side.

"I'm eating for two, remember?" She finished the cucumber.

"And one of them is an unborn child, remember?"

"All right, Dr. Harris. Look at it this way: I could be eating something a lot worse than salad." A radish slice was the next to go. "I could be enjoying something chocolate, filled with chocolate, and smothered in chocolate syrup. With chocolate ice cream on the side, of course."

"Not that you're a chocoholic or anything." Charlotte handed Janet the shaker with the dressing. "You better take this while there is still something left to put it on."

"Thank you. If you're trying to make me feel guilty, it won't work." Janet piled salad onto a plate and drenched it.

Charlotte looked into the bowl. "I'll cut up some more veggies. Jim and I might like some salad, too."

"Thank you again."

"I don't have anything to wear." Dinner was over and Charlotte and Janet were in Charlotte's room. She stood sideways and looked at herself in the freestanding long mirror. Janet sat on the bed. "I can't wear this," Charlotte said. "I could barely get it zipped and buttoned."

"That's the way it's supposed to be when you're four months pregnant. The baby has to be somewhere, and we know where yours decided to settle in for the duration. Come with me. I think I have just the thing." She pulled on Charlotte's arm to make sure she followed.

Once in Janet's bedroom, she pulled a navy blue dress with a matching jacket from her closet.

"Try this on."

Charlotte took off the skirt she had put on a few minutes before and slipped the dress over her head. She stood sideways, looking in the mirror.

"I think this might work. What do you think?"

"It's you. I think it's perfect. No waist." She looked at Charlotte's middle. "You'll have to wear the jacket, too, though."

"I hope the courtroom is cool enough for the jacket."

"It will be. The judges have to wear those heavy robes. You know they'll have the temperature comfortable for them. Now, let's find something else, too. I'm sure we'll have to be there more than one day."

"Do you think so? How long do you think?" She blinked and took a deep breath. She released the questions she had been holding ever since the phone call. "Janet, do you think he'll be there? Tyler, I mean. He has to come, doesn't he? He can't just send his attorney, can he? I wish he could. Maybe he will. Do you think he will? I'm sure he doesn't want to see me any more than I want to see him." Her frowned deepened. She didn't want to see him, did she?

"Janet, this has to work," she continued. "The clothes, I mean. I don't want him to know I'm pregnant."

"The clothes will work, but I still think you should let him know. He should pay your expenses now and support for the baby after it's born."

"I don't want anything from him. He doesn't want anything to do with me. He wouldn't feel anything for the baby. I don't want him doing anything for me out of a feeling of obligation. I can take care of myself and the baby alone."

"You won't be taking care of the baby alone. I keep telling you that." Janet's words touched Charlotte. "Jim and I will be here to help."

"I don't know if I'll still be here."

"Of course you'll still be here. You have a job. You've settled in. We can even make the downstairs into an apartment. You won't even know we're up here unless you want to. When they get older, our kids can play together. Why would you want to go anywhere else?"

"Janet. . . ."

"I know I promised not to nag if you decide to leave after a few months, but the few months aren't up yet so don't go making up your mind. Just think about staying, sis. If you want to, you can even get a place of your own, though I don't know why you'd want to do that. At least think about staying, okay?"

"Okay, I'll think about it."

"Promise?"

"I promise."

"No fingers crossed?" Janet looked at Charlotte's hands.

"Look who has the nerve to check for crossed fingers." Charlotte smiled. "No fingers crossed." She picked up the green flowered dress Janet had put on the bed. It was straight and had a matching jacket, too. She went back to her room hoping the dress would fit as well as the other one did. She needed all of her concentration to get past seeing Tyler. She couldn't afford to worry about her clothes.

A short while later, she had tried everything on and was satisfied. She looked at the third outfit Janet had insisted she take with the other two. She looked at the third dress with a flared skirt. She hoped she wouldn't be there long enough to need three dresses.

She cradled her stomach. Another size, another step closer. She put the blue dress on again and looked closely at her image in the mirror. If a person didn't know she was pregnant, they couldn't tell. She patted her stomach. If they touched her, though, they would know. But no one would touch her. She thought of Tyler's strong, gentle hands. She looked in the mirror one last time before she turned away.

The dress didn't have the room in the waist it was supposed to have. She put the boxy jacket on. She definitely needed to wear the jacket. She touched her middle. She had to keep from doing that. It was a giveaway. Only pregnant women touched their middles like that. She stopped her hands before they settled there again.

She took off the dress and turned off the light even though she didn't expect to sleep anytime soon. She wished Monday was here. She wished Monday evening was here and she was through with court and didn't have to go back again.

This time when her hands stole toward her middle, she let them settle over the precious bundle growing there.

Eighteen

Charlotte always slept uneasily in a strange bed, especially in a hotel, but that wasn't the reason for her restless night that left her as tired as she had been when she went to bed the night before. They'd had a routine flight, she'd had no complaints about the hotel, and they'd arrived early enough to relax as Janet had planned, but Charlotte had been right when she said she hadn't expected to relax and get some rest. They may as well have waited until Monday morning to come.

Please let it be over fast, she pleaded as she had more times than she could remember since she had gotten the phone call. *Please let it be over so I can try to forget about this whole thing.* She frowned. Almost everything. She turned over yet again in what she hoped was a quiet way.

"You can stop trying to keep from waking me up, little sister. I'm already awake. I heard you when you went into the bathroom." Janet stretched. "That was a long time ago. Have you been awake since then? Are you all right? I mean as all right as you can be."

"Yes." Charlotte sat up in her bed. "I'm sorry I woke you."

"It's time to get up anyway." Janet sat up. "I'll bet you didn't get a whole lot of sleep."

"That's true. I feel like I just got into bed."

"Something would be wrong with you if you weren't worried. But you don't have a reason to be. I keep telling you that. Everything will turn out fine." She got out of bed. "Since we're awake, let's hurry and get dressed. I want to taste for myself whether or not the breakfast buffet is as great as they say it is."

Charlotte smiled and shook her head. "Janet . . ."

"What?" Janet grabbed her clothes. "Breakfast is the most important meal of the day. You know that. Stop wasting time." Charlotte watched her go into the bathroom. She would have to watch Janet eat. Her own worry had swallowed any appetite she might have had for anything except the end of the day.

The last time she was in New York, a store window had thrown images of Tyler at her. His music had marched around and between the images. The combination had almost knocked her down. This time, she would have to face only one. But it was the real one. She squeezed her eyes closed. *If I can just get through this.*

She pulled on the blue dress and took one final look in the mirror. She had to remember not to stand sideways to him after she got there. She took a deep breath. She wished she was coming back instead of on her way out. Why couldn't they be on their way to the airport? She pulled on the jacket as Janet returned. They left the room with Janet hurrying ahead to the dining room.

"We're going to be late." Charlotte looked at Janet's empty plate. She had been watching her eat enough for both of them. Charlotte looked at her own still full plate. Maybe she'd feel like eating when the hearing was over. She looked at her watch. "Come on. Hurry up."

"We are not going to be late." Janet looked at her own watch. "We only have two blocks to go, and forty-five minutes to get there. You have a quirky sense of time. If you're not an hour early, you think you're late." She followed Charlotte, running to keep up.

"Don't you know it's not nice to make a pregnant lady run?" Janet caught up with her.

"Save your energy for walking." Charlotte moved faster and Janet managed to keep up. They didn't stop until they came to the building standing guard on the corner. Police officers stood in little clumps as if waiting for her. Charlotte hesitated. Then she took a deep breath and made her shaking legs take her past the first group of uniforms.

"It's a civil case, Charlotte. Only a civil case. " Janet's whisper wrapped over her like a protective blanket. "These officers are not waiting for you." She took Charlotte's arm and led her into the building.

Janet looked at the long line funneling through an archway that belonged at an airport. She turned to the woman in uniform.

"Are you sure that won't harm our . . . my baby?" That was the same question she had asked at the airport.

"Yes, ma'am. It's harmless. It only detects metal." That was the same answer she had gotten there, too.

"I don't know . . ." Janet stood in front of the doorway without a door or walls. "Isn't there some other way to do this? This isn't stronger than the one at airports, is it?" Janet ignored the restless movements behind her.

"Ma'am, can I talk to you?" The female officer motioned Janet from the line. People who had been standing behind them rushed through.

Janet grabbed Charlotte's arm and pulled her to the side with her.

"I know how you feel, ma'am. That question is asked all the time. They've studied that very thing. I swear, the machine won't harm you or your baby. It's completely safe." She looked at Janet. "Are you a witness?"

"No, I'm here to give moral support to my sister." Janet looked at Charlotte. "What do you think?"

"I think the officer knows what she's talking about. We'd better get upstairs and find the right courtroom."

"Which room are you looking for?"

Janet told her the room number.

"It's Judge Harold Jenkins's courtroom," she added.

Charlotte felt like her mouth was full of dry bread. She tried to swallow as the officer told them how to find the room.

The hall outside the bank of elevators was crowded like somebody was giving out prizes upstairs. Charlotte looked at her watch after all of the elevators had come, filled up and gone, leaving her and Janet still waiting with dozens of others.

"I told you we're going to be late."

"We will not be late. Relax." She looked at Charlotte. "At least try to relax."

After waiting for two more trips, they squeezed into one of the elevators. The ride to the tenth floor was too short. Any length of time would have been too short. Or too long. When the doors slammed open, Janet wrapped her arm around Charlotte's and turned her to the left when she would have gone to the right.

Charlotte was glad Janet was with her, and not just because Janet could concentrate on finding the right room.

Janet read the plain thick white numbers posted on the wall outside each room. As they walked, Charlotte looked toward the large windows ahead at the end of the hall, but she wasn't seeing anything out of them.

"It's the next one, little sister." Janet stopped between numbers. Her words tiptoed out. "Are you ready?"

"I'll never be ready for this. Do you think he'll be there? Are you sure you can't tell that . . ." She leaned toward her. "Are you sure this dress is all right?" She pulled at her jacket.

"I'm going to have you start writing your questions down, like you threatened to make me do." Janet smiled.

Charlotte didn't have a smile to show.

"Number one: He will probably be there, but we won't care

if he is. Okay? Number two: I can't tell. No one can. Okay? And number three: The dress is fine. It's you. Okay? Okay?"

"Okay." Since the next room wasn't going to disappear, Charlotte let her feet take her to the uniformed man standing outside the closed door.

"May I help you, miss?"

Charlotte wanted to tell him that no one could help her. Instead she told him her name.

He pulled a finger down the paper fastened to his clipboard.

"Okay. Go right in." Charlotte saw him make a checkmark.

"Go on, little sister." Janet gave her shoulders a final squeeze then eased her into the room.

Charlotte stepped inside the room, but stopped. Janet bumped into her back, but Charlotte didn't notice. She was too busy noticing something more important. Somebody more important.

Tyler was sitting at a long table with another man. The other man was reading from the yellow legal pad on the desk in front of him. Tyler didn't have any papers in front of him. He was staring at the bare table. His hair curled over his collar like it had over her fingers when she . . .

"Go on, Charlotte." Janet's whisper poked her. "You can do this." She patted her shoulder. "I'll be as close as they let me get. You'll be okay." She kissed her on the cheek and smiled encouragement.

Charlotte closed her eyes. She took a deep breath and hoped Janet was right. She needed for her to be right.

She pulled her stare from the only other one in the room who mattered. She looked at the people sitting over to the side in seats on a platform that belonged in an auditorium. They didn't look any happier to be here than she was. She glanced at the other table. It was crowded with people dressed like a flock of crows. Charlotte trudged down the aisle. She was glad she wasn't the only one wearing a jacket.

Janet followed close behind.

"I don't know where to sit." Charlotte stopped. "I must belong at that table, but there's no room for me." She whispered to Janet, but everybody turned and looked at her as if she had shouted at a funeral.

A woman wearing a gray jacket that was a twin to the one the man outside the door wore came over to her. Charlotte made her gaze stay on the woman and not on the other table, where she didn't belong.

"Is there a problem, ma'am?"

Of course there was a problem. Wasn't this room, this whole building, for people with problems?

"I don't know where to sit."

"Let me check my list to make sure you belong here."

Charlotte said her name. She took a deep breath. Does this woman think I'd be here if I didn't have to be?

Satisfied that Charlotte was in the right room, the officer pointed to the crowded table. Charlotte walked toward it.

"Charlotte . . ." Tyler spilled the word, but was cut off.

"All rise. The Honorable Judge Harold Jenkins presiding," the woman who'd helped Charlotte called out. She gave the case number as if anybody would dare make a mistake and be in the wrong courtroom.

Charlotte hurried to the front of the room. She would not look at the person who had called to her.

"Please be seated."

Charlotte stood beside the full table.

"What are you doing here?" A woman at the table asked. Charlotte had seen her at the newspaper offices. Her eyes hadn't been narrow then. How could she see through those slits?

Charlotte looked at her former editor, who looked no friendlier now than she had the last time. She looked like she wanted to chase Charlotte away. Did everyone think she had a choice in this? Although she didn't want to look, Charlotte saw Tyler lean his head to the man sitting beside him. Tyler looked angry. She knew that look too well. He had given one like it to her the day her paradise had disappeared. It had still been in place the day after that.

"Your Honor." The man with Tyler stood. "May I address the court?"

"What is it, Counsel?"

"May it please the court, it appears there is a mix-up, Your Honor. Charlotte Thompson's name has been stricken from the list of defendants. Her name should no longer appear on the slate."

Charlotte looked at him, but not at Tyler.

"Are you Charlotte Thompson?" The judge's question grabbed her attention.

Charlotte nodded slightly. Then she found her voice.

"Yes, sir."

"Counsel will approach the bench."

Tyler's lawyer took some papers and went up to the judge. He handed them to the officer, who gave them to Judge Jenkins, who did not look pleased at all.

Charlotte looked at Janet, who smiled courage at her. She could feel Tyler's gaze on her, but she would not turn his way.

"Why wasn't the court informed of this change?" The judge looked at the crowded table. "Are you aware of this change?"

The woman with the narrow, mean eyes stood.

"Yes, Your Honor, we are."

The judge swung his glare back at the man standing in front of him.

"Don't you think it would have been nice if someone had seen fit to notify the court about this?"

"But your Honor, we did. We . . ."

The judge's glare cut off the rest of his words. Charlotte saw the lawyer swallow hard. Then he let "Yes, Sir" squeeze out.

"Good answer." Judge Jenkins looked at the other table.

"I will see counsels in my chambers. All of you. Now." He stood.

"All rise," the woman said again.

"Miss Thompson, you may have a seat over there." The judge pointed to a bench at the back of the room. "I don't know how long this will take."

Charlotte wished he had pointed to where Janet was. She watched the judge lead the group of paper-carrying people to a room at the side. She turned and took the long way to the bench, following the path that wouldn't take her past Tyler Fleming.

"Charlotte . . ." Tyler's voice reached to her again.

"Mr. Fleming." Charlotte saw the officer glare at him. "You cannot have contact at this time with anyone involved with the case."

Janet started to move back to where Charlotte was.

"I'm sorry, ma'am, you can't go back there until Judge Jenkins tells us what's going on."

Janet stood a moment longer, then she sat back in the chair.

Charlotte sat staring at the floor, hoping a supply of strength was hiding there, but not expecting to find it.

Nothing interrupted the silence except muffled sounds in the hall from people passing by.

The judge returned after what seemed to be hours, trailed by everyone who had gone to his chamber with him.

"All rise" was followed by "Be seated" before Charlotte had a chance to stand.

"Miss Thompson. The charges against you have been dropped. Were you aware of that?"

"No, sir."

"Your Honor, we tried to notify . . ."

The judge's glare made Tyler's lawyer swallow the rest of his words again. The judge looked back at Charlotte.

"The charges have been dropped against you, but counsel has informed the court that you may be called as a witness for the prosecution. You're excused for the day, but let the court officer know where you can be reached. You'll be notified when you are to appear."

"Yes, sir," Charlotte answered, though she didn't understand what was going on.

"It will probably be two days at the most. You're excused."

"Charlotte, wait."

"Counsel, control your client. Doesn't he know not to make contact with a witness?"

"Yes, sir. He knows."

"Then explain to him about contempt of court charges."

"Yes, sir."

Charlotte's glance caught two heads bent together, one covered with hair that would be soft to her touch. She closed her eyes and took a deep breath. Then she opened them and hurried to the door before anybody could change the rules of the court.

She didn't want to talk to Tyler. She didn't want to hear his reason for dropping her name from the case. It didn't matter. Nothing mattered but getting out of the room as fast as she could. She was glad Janet was beside her. She didn't have to wait for her in the small room any longer. A last glance as she slipped out the door told her that Tyler and his attorney were still talking. She was glad he didn't look back and catch her with a glance.

Tyler had trouble keeping his angry words close when he wanted to let them fly. He didn't belong here, stuck at this table. Why wouldn't they let him talk to her? Didn't they know it was necessary for him? Tyler couldn't make Jerry understand, either. If Tyler only had a chance, he could make the judge understand that his talking to Charlotte was more important than anything else. If Jerry hadn't convinced Tyler that if he was in jail for contempt, it would be longer before he could see Charlotte. If Jerry hadn't drummed that into his head, Tyler would have gone after her, rules of the court be damned.

He had tried to follow the opening arguments, but his mind had been filled with Charlotte. It still was.

He needed to hold her. He needed her in his arms. He needed to feel her heartbeat close to his. Being able to only see her was like a sip of water to a man dying of thirst. He had to find a way.

She had looked so frail standing there all alone. She looked as if she had wanted everything to disappear. He sighed. She probably did. Especially him. He had made her like that.

He was glad he'd had Jerry with him to make sense of the court proceedings. It was the first thing he had to be glad about in a long time.

"Tyler? Hey man, are you ready?" Let's go."

"What? Oh sure, Jer, I'm ready." Tyler looked around. They were the only ones left in the courtroom. Had he stood when the court officer had ordered them to? He must have. He was still in this room instead of locked away in a jail cell.

He followed Jerry down the hall and into an elevator. He looked for Charlotte among the people in the hall just as he had looked when they went to lunch, and again when they came back. He hadn't found her then, so he didn't expect to find her now.

"Okay, man, give it to me." Tyler turned to Jerry when they reached the street.

"Give you what?"

"The name of her hotel. Her phone number. Something. You know I have to talk to her."

"Tyler, didn't you hear the judge? You can't talk to her."

"I don't care about the damn case. Let it drop."

"The case is out of our hands now. It's before the court and only the judge can dismiss it."

"Jer. . . ."

"Tyler, even if I was willing to, I couldn't give you the information. I don't have it."

"What do you mean, you don't have it? You have to have it. She's your witness. Don't you have to talk to her before she testifies?"

"If I hadn't been busy trying to keep you from talking your butt into jail, I might have thought to get it from the officer. I can talk to her tomorrow. We probably won't get to her before tomorrow afternoon, anyway."

"Tomorrow is a long way off. We've got the rest of today."

"Tyler, we can't do anything about the situation today. Accept that." He looked at Tyler. "Why don't we walk around a while and stretch our legs? We've been cooped up in that room all day."

Tyler glared at him. "Make some calls. Do something."

"Man, you have to get rid of that pressure pent up inside you before you explode. You look like you're a second away from losing it."

Still, Tyler glared. He didn't care that Jerry was right. Jerry took his arm.

"Tyler, come on. You didn't eat any lunch. Let's go get something, if only a cup of coffee. Decaf for you, though." He tugged. "You've waited this long, you can wait until tomorrow."

Tyler let his feet take him with Jerry. Maybe tomorrow would have to do. Maybe by then he would have figured out the right words that would make her at least listen to him. Maybe. *Please let me find the magic words. Maybe I can figure out how to reach her tonight.*

He walked with Jerry to the restaurant on the corner in the next block, but he knew the food wouldn't taste any different than the newspapers waiting in the box on the corner.

"You got through that all right. And your name has been dropped as a defendant. Isn't that something to be happy about?"

Charlotte looked at Janet who was waiting for a 'yes'

from her. She didn't want to hurt Janet's feelings. Besides, she didn't have the energy to argue. She didn't have energy left for anything except facing tomorrow.

"Hey, little sister. You managed a lot today," Janet went on. "You saw Tyler and survived. He called to you and you ignored him. You can do the same tomorrow. Today had to be harder than tomorrow will be. Tomorrow night, we'll probably be back home."

Charlotte stared out the window of their room. Why had Tyler tried to reach her that second time? Didn't he hear the judge tell him to leave her alone? She sighed. Tomorrow morning, she had to face him all over again.

Charlotte could never really ignore Tyler. She could only pretend to do so. Today pretending had been enough. Would it still be enough tomorrow?

Why had he called to her? Why had he changed his mind about believing her? She had tried so hard so many times to convince him before she had left his house. He hadn't believed her then and it had been close to their times together. Why now?

She twisted her hands in her lap. Maybe he still didn't believe her. His attorney probably convinced him that she didn't have anything for them to take, and it would be better for his case if they used her testimony for their side so he could get to the newspaper.

She swallowed hard. They were right about one thing. She didn't have anything left to lose. Tyler had seen to that.

She shook her head and cradled her stomach with both hands.

That was wrong. She did have one thing left to lose, but it wasn't anything Tyler wanted and she wouldn't lose it.

"Should we go down to eat, or do you want room service?" Janet talked about food as if Charlotte could eat it.

"Whatever you want, Janet."

"Okay. Let's go . . ."

"No. I changed my mind. Let's eat up here." She couldn't

take the chance of running into Tyler in a restaurant. Her strength supply was close to empty.

"You're sure? Don't you want to stretch your legs? It's so beautiful out."

"I'm sure. Let's eat up here."

"What do you want to eat?" Janet held the menu.

"Whatever you order will be fine." She wouldn't be able to eat anything, anyway.

Janet looked at Charlotte. "Okay, sis, I'll take care of it." She picked up the phone.

About an hour later, Janet placed her napkin beside her empty plate.

"You know, Charlotte, the object of a meal is to eat the food, not rearrange it on your plate."

"I know. I just don't have an appetite." Her face softened in what was trying to be a smile. "Why don't you help yourself to mine and call it your baby's dinner?"

"I think I will, thank you, on one condition. You have to eat by Mom's rules. You have to eat at least one bite of each thing on your plate." Janet smiled. "Of course, remember, Mom's rules don't include dessert. You can leave that for me. Okay?"

"Okay." Charlotte took exactly one bite of baked chicken. She followed that with a forkful of rice and one of sauteed mixed vegetables. Then she held her plate out to Janet.

"Charlotte. . . ."

"I took one bite of everything." She looked away and back. "I really can't eat any more."

"You need to eat."

"I know. I will when this is all over. Here. Enjoy."

"If you're sure . . ."

"I'm sure."

Janet took the plate and put it on top of her own empty

one. She ate as if it had been half a day since her last meal. Then she touched the dessert plate.

"Are you sure you don't want dessert? I think we can waive the rule about 'no dinner, no dessert.' " She lifted a forkful of chocolate cake, oozing chocolate filling and covered with an inch of chocolate icing. "Look at this. I've tasted something like this before. It's worth the calories."

"I'm sure. Enjoy both pieces." Charlotte looked at her watch. Too many hours before tomorrow morning.

"Tyler, you don't know when to give up," he said to himself. Who was that woman with Charlotte? They must be registered under the other woman's name.

He had called every hotel listed in the phone book, but Charlotte wasn't registered at any of them. The patience he thought he had was gone. He had used it waiting for Charlotte's old neighbor to come through.

Maybe the neighbor had given Charlotte his number and she'd refused to call him. He shook his head. No. That couldn't be. He'd counted too much on her calling him. He wanted it too much. He needed to talk to her too much for her not to call him. He sighed as heavy as his problems made him feel. He'd have to wait until tomorrow to see her. She had to let him talk to her then. She just had to. All he had to do was find the right words to make her listen.

"What about this dress?" Charlotte looked at herself sideways in the dresser mirror the next morning, just as she had in the mirror in her room. "Does it look all right? Can you tell?"

"Here we go again." Janet shook her head. "Yes, it still looks great, and no, I still can't tell by looking at you that you're pregnant. Nobody can." She picked up her purse.

"Are you sure?"

"Charlotte, unless you want to be late, we need to leave now. You look fine."

"I wish it was afternoon. Then this would be over." Charlotte sighed. How could she forget that wishing doesn't work? She picked up her handbag and followed Janet out. The door clicked softly behind them.

"Thank you for your testimony, Miss Thompson." Tyler's lawyer turned his back to Charlotte and looked at the judge. "Your Honor, I'm finished with this witness."

"Counselor?" The judge looked at the table still crowded today as if there wasn't a room full of empty seats available.

"Your Honor, may we meet with you and counsel in your chambers?"

"Yes" had barely been spoken by the judge when Tyler's attorney and the others marched past Charlotte. Now what? Why didn't Judge Jenkins let her go back to her seat? Why did he leave her here, where, if she looked up, Tyler was all she would see? She stared at the floor and refused to look at her watch. Not much longer. Please don't let them be much longer.

As if answering her prayer, the door opened and the judge led everyone back into the courtroom. He looked at Charlotte.

"Miss Thompson, you may step down. The court will not need you again."

Charlotte started toward Janet and stopped. She looked at the court officer. When a nod greeted her, she rushed to her sister, sitting in the back.

"Ladies and gentlemen of the jury, a settlement has been reached in this case. The court wishes to thank you for your services. Without your participation, the justice system in our country wouldn't work. Please follow the officer to the jury room. I'll be in shortly to answer any questions you may have."

Charlotte didn't wait for them to leave. She pulled Janet this time.

"Charlotte." Her name was as soft as a tear, but she heard it. She didn't want to, but she stopped. She wouldn't turn around, though.

"Charlotte, please." The voice was closer. If she turned, she would be able to see the golden flecks in those eyes. Were the eyes warm as at first sight or as cold as they had been the last time she'd looked into them? She didn't want to find out.

"She doesn't want to talk to you." Janet's voice stood guard. "Why don't you leave her alone? Haven't you hurt her enough?" Janet moved closer to Charlotte and held her arm.

"I have to talk to you, Charlotte. I know I don't deserve it, but please give me a chance to talk to you."

"Leave her alone. Haven't you done enough?"

"It's all right, Janet." Charlotte closed her eyes and breathed deeply. Then she turned to face Tyler for the last time.

"Charlotte. Please let me . . ."

"Tyler, I don't want to hear anything you have to say. I don't know what game you're playing. Since you reached a settlement, I assume they told you the same thing I told you at your house. You took their word as truth, but you didn't believe me. Well, it's too late. I don't want to hear anything you have to say. I won't let you hurt me again. I don't want to ever see you again. It's too late." She blinked hard. "I'm sorry I ever met you." She wiped at the tears sliding down her face.

Then she turned and went with Janet to the elevators that would take her to the next part of her life. A part where Tyler would never be allowed in.

Nineteen

Charlotte watched children jumping rope double Dutch-style and smiled. She and Janet had spent many hours doing the same thing when they were kids. "Perfecting our routine" and "getting it together," they had called it. One year, they were determined to enter the annual double Dutch contest and bring home a trophy. They had argued for days about whether the trophy would go on the hall table or on the bedroom dresser.

"I want it on our dresser so I can see it every night before I go to sleep and the first thing when I wake up," Janet had argued.

"No. I want it on the table in the hall so I can see it whenever I come home and I'm in a sad mood," she had said. "It will make me feel happy."

After weeks of hearing the argument that made neither one change her mind, their mother had convinced them that the best place for any trophy was on the mantel over the fireplace in the living room.

"That way everybody can sit and look at it," she had said. "That is, if you win," she had added. "Even if you don't win, look at the fun you've had making up your routines and practicing. No matter what happens, I'm proud of you for the way you stuck to it like you did."

Charlotte's smile widened. Of course they didn't win. But after the competition, Mom had handed them a trophy of her own. "To the Best Daughters in the World," it had read. "Fantastic Job."

Charlotte left the girls still jumping rope and her smile left her as she walked away. It would be nice to have a trophy waiting in the hall when she got home, so she could see it when she was in a sad mood. Like now. Like every day since she had left Tyler after the snowstorm.

Should she have called Tyler when Miss Mary tried to give her the number? Should she have let him talk to her outside the courtroom? She shook her head. There was no use thinking about it. It was too late. Much too late. Tyler had pushed her out of his mind by now.

Charlotte had read about the settlement after she and Janet had come home from New York the next day. It hadn't taken long for the story to hit the newspapers. Not everybody who sued that newspaper for libel won, but he had. The article didn't say how much the settlement was for, but it did say that Tyler would use the money to set up scholarships for inner-city music students.

He had told her how his mother had struggled to pay for his own music lessons. How like him to ease the way for others. She breathed deeply. Where was he now? Was he still presenting new numbers or had he finished his tour? Neither the papers nor the news programs gave much news about his concerts anymore. It was as if they lost interest after the settlement. She hadn't realized how much she had come to depend on learning about him from the news until it stopped. How could anyone lose interest in Tyler?

How much longer would he be in New York? Has he found somebody else? The last question slipped out unexpectedly. She sat on a bench in one of the little pocket gardens scattered throughout the complex. He'd find somebody else. Maybe he already had. He had found her, hadn't he? It was June, but he didn't need a snowstorm to bring him somebody he could share his life with. He'd take his new someone to his mountain home. Would he make snow angels with that woman next year?

She rested her head in her hands. No. He couldn't. That was something for Tyler to share only with her.

A cardinal hopped on a branch near her, trying to sing her sadness away. It didn't work.

If Tyler cared, he would have tried again to see her. If he really loved her, he wouldn't have taken no for an answer. He had told her how he stuck with a difficult musical passage until he got it right. Wasn't she as important as a musical passage?

She sighed. No, she wasn't even on his list at all. His music was always the most important thing to him. It always would be. She frowned. Unless he had met somebody who could push music down into second place.

"I'd feel the same about you if we were in a skyscraper apartment building in the middle of Manhattan in June," he had said that last day, before Jake came, when Tyler's love was still alive. But he had been talking to Cleo then, not Charlotte. He never would have said that if he had known she was Charlotte Thompson. He never would have loved her and she never would have learned to love him back.

Still, her body tingled as it remembered lying with him that day when their love was still alive.

She spent the rest of the walk home trying to forget Tyler, as she did every time he came to her. No matter how often it happened, it didn't get any easier with time.

She was still struggling with the memory when she reached the wide steps leading up to the porch.

The bright red-, pink-, and blue-blossomed cushions covering the white wicker furniture tried to cheer her, but they couldn't. She slumped onto a chair off to the side, not noticing the bright greeting.

The brilliant June sunlight playing over the shining oak floor planks didn't make Charlotte feel playful at all. She stared at the dancing pattern as leaves from the live oak beside the porch moved the radiance around as if trying to spread its light mood. It might as well have given up and gone to find someone who would appreciate it. The door opened and Charlotte heard it, but she didn't turn toward it.

"Charlotte, I'm glad you're back. Come on with me." Janet stood in front of her. "The day is too beautiful to waste just sitting here."

"I haven't been sitting here. I just got back from my walk. I don't feel like coming with you, Janet."

"That's what you said yesterday. And the day before that. And the day . . ."

"I know, but you go on without me."

"You've said that every day, too, for more days than I can count." Janet went to Charlotte and lifted her chin. She looked into her sister's eyes.

Charlotte knew Janet saw the pain still as fresh as when they left Tyler standing in the hall outside the courtroom. Charlotte had been trying since they got back, but she didn't know how to make the hurt go away. She was afraid she'd never find out and would be stuck with it for the rest of her life. She blinked. Could she stand that? She listened patiently to Janet, although she knew what she was going to say. She had heard it so many times, she could have recited the words herself, but knowing the words and learning from them were two very different things.

"You haven't been anywhere but to the doctor in the last month and a half. You know this is not good for you."

"I know it's not good for me, but that's not true. I have been somewhere. I . . ."

"Walks around the neighborhood do not qualify as going somewhere, little sister, and you know that, too. How long do you intend to go on like this? Charlotte, you have to stop doing this to yourself. You have to get on with your life."

"Janet, I appreciate your concern, I really do, but I can't go shopping with you."

"Just like you can't eat a decent meal." Janet touched Charlotte's shoulder. Then she straightened up and pressed her hands against her own back. "You have to think of your baby." She crossed her arms. "Those are your words. I'm only giving them back to you because you seem to have forgotten them."

"I know. I am thinking of him. He's the only reason I've been able to eat anything at all. And I have gotten better. Last night I joined your clean plate club."

"Yeah, and then this morning it was back to toast and tea. That's an all right breakfast for someone who's sick, but not for someone eating for two. Even though one of the two is an unborn baby."

"I'll eat a full, nutritious lunch later. I promise. With no crossed fingers. See?" She smiled a smile she didn't feel and took her feet off the wicker footstool. "Look, you go by yourself today, and I'll go with you the next time. I promise that, too." She held out her hands. "Still no crossed fingers."

"Are you sure? Why wait until next time? Come with me now. I promise not to take too long. I've finally decided on the crib I want for Junior." She patted her large middle. "Jim said no canopy. 'No son of mine is going to sleep in a bed with a frilly canopy,' he said when I told him about it. As if the baby will know the difference. This morning I found a strange-looking bag in the back of the storage closet. That man bought a football, a basketball and an electric train set. I can't believe he . . ."

Charlotte didn't hear the rest. Tyler would never buy anything for his son. He wouldn't know about him. Would he buy things if he knew? Would he want to know? Was it fair not to tell him? She didn't have answers, so she listened to Janet go on and was happy that Janet had Jim to share the baby with her.

"New fathers are something else. But I haven't figured out what yet. Anyway, the crib I'm getting is made so a canopy can be fitted to it later. When we have our daughter." She molded her hands around her middle. "I can't believe what I'm saying. I'm as big as a blimp with this baby. If I couldn't walk around, I wouldn't be sure my feet are still where they should be, and already I'm talking about having the next one. Maybe I should ask Dr. Harris to examine my head when I go see her next week. What do you think?"

"About what?"

"Charlotte, you're going to have to stop leaving your body behind when you go off like that. I might think you're still with me." Janet stared at her. "It's not important. Are you sure you won't come? You might see something you like."

"I'm sure. I have a lot of time to get what I need." She frowned. *What I can get from the store. What I really need, I can't have. Not ever again, and it's really my fault this time.* She blinked. "Next time I'll come. I'm just not ready to go anywhere right now. You go have fun. Don't buy everything you see. One crib that's it."

"I'll try hard not to load up on teeny-tiny things for tiny people, but you know I always see a cute outfit whenever I go shopping, and I just can't resist it." She looked at her. "Are you really sure you won't come with me? It will do you good to get out of the complex."

"Yes." She nodded a little. "Maybe I'll feel like going to the shop with you when you go later. Don't worry about me, big sister, I'm okay." She gave a smile she wasn't feeling, but that was okay. It was for Janet, not for herself. "You go on." Janet gave her a hard look before she shrugged and went down the steps.

Charlotte watched her go. She sighed and put her feet back up on the footstool. What excuse could she use this afternoon for not going? How long would this mood last? How could she make herself snap out of it?

She knew Janet was right. She knew she should go out.

She shouldn't spend every day here. No matter how many walks she took, even she couldn't consider it 'going out.' This rut she was stuck in wasn't good for the baby. She had to make herself think and do what was best for the baby.

She rubbed her rounded middle. "I promise, little man, I'll do better." She sighed. "I just can't today. I'll try harder tomorrow. Okay?" The baby shifted as if in answer.

She closed her eyes. Will he look like Tyler? Will he have that thick hair and those knowing eyes.? Will he have Tyler's love of music? He had to. As strong as it was, that talent had to show up in her baby. Their baby. Should she tell him? She shut her eyes. Will he grow to be as tall as his father?

She remembered how her head had fit under Tyler's chin when he held her close, as if he wanted to keep her there forever. That was before he changed his mind. Still, she tingled at the memory.

Did I do the right thing at the courthouse? Was it fair to push his words away before he'd had a chance to say them?

Every day, this question came to her at least once. Sometimes she sent it away. Today she let it stay. *Should I have let him at least explain?*

He had seemed sorry. He had seemed more than sorry. The hurt in his eyes had looked as real as hers had felt when he hadn't let her explain to him. It had looked as real as hers still felt.

She closed her eyes but she couldn't shut him out. By not listening to him, was she being any more fair than he had been to her? She had been angry that he hadn't believed her, but had believed somebody else. Had he? Was that how it had been? His lawyer said her name had been dropped. When? She wouldn't even let Tyler talk to her that day. She sighed.

What difference did it make to go over and over it in

her head? It was too late, now. She'd sent him away. She'd never see him again. She still loved him. She always would. But he was gone because she thought that was what she wanted. Tyler. *Was what I did right?*

Tyler looked at his love slumped in the chair. He wanted to run to her and hold her. She looked like she was in such misery. He had caused it. He wished he could take it all back. He wished he could take away all the hurt he had caused her. He couldn't see her eyes, but he knew that what he had planted there so deep had to still be there.

He smiled as her hand moved to her hair. She still hadn't tamed that curl. He clinched his fingers. It should be his hand smoothing it back. He should be kissing her forehead after he brushed the curl back. He should be kissing her. An open book lay on her lap, but she wasn't reading. He blinked.

I remember another time she sat like that. I went to her then, and she was glad to see me. That was before our love had grown enough for me to hold her and learn her body, but even then, I knew that time was coming. I knew I would get to hold her close and give her my love. I knew we were destined to be one. I taught her to make love. She taught me to love again. And then I shoved her away. I threw our love away. How will she feel about me being here? Does she still hate me?

His arms ached to hold her and feel her close. *Please don't let my memories of holding her be all I'll ever have.* He took a deep breath, swallowed hard, and went up the steps.

"Charlotte?"

"Tyler? What are you doing here?" Charlotte jumped, then eased the book higher up on her lap.

He followed the movement as she quickly placed the book over her middle, but she wasn't quick enough. He took a deep breath. Was this part of the reason why she wouldn't see him?

"How . . ." She tried to think of the next words, but they lost their way while she looked at him. She tried again. "How did you find me?" She wasn't imagining him. Tyler stood in front of her, too solid not to be real.

She let her gaze stay on his face as she stored up a new image to go with the many old ones. He looked more tired than she remembered. His schedule must be grueling. This new look of his couldn't have anything to do with her, could it? She tried to listen for a chance to send him away. It couldn't work out. Too much had happened between them to be forgotten. She couldn't let him get close enough to hurt her again. She searched inside herself for the strength to send him away again.

"I've been looking for you since. . . ." He stopped. Pain left his eyes and spread out over his face. "I've been looking for you since you left the courthouse. When I couldn't find you, I hired a private detective, who found your sister's shop. I just left there. The clerk wouldn't give me this address, but the woman in the shop next door recognized me. It was the first time in a long while that being recognized mattered. I gave her an autograph and she gave me this address. I would have given her everything I have if that was what it took to find you." He blinked. "She was happy to help Tyler Fleming find his cousins."

"Cousins? You told her you were looking for your cousins? I guess I'm not the only one who lies."

"You didn't lie to me."

"You only believe that because the people from the paper told you I was telling the truth." She looked away from him. She couldn't let him see the love still inside her.

"During the tour, I've been in touch with my attorney. I decided to drop your name from the suit long before we talked with them. I did it before I left the house after the storm." He stared at the past. "The house is so full of

memories of you. I haven't been back since then. I don't
know if I can go back without you." His gaze held hers as
if they were fastened together. *Like before, a long time before. Back when love was enough.* "I'm a slow learner, but
I do learn." He wanted to call her 'Sweetheart,' but he didn't
have that right. Not yet. Maybe not ever.

"It took until the day after you left my house for me to
think you told the truth." He blinked and a brightness appeared in his eyes. "I didn't need anybody else to tell me
what I knew in my heart." His soft words reached to her.
They sounded as if they had come from a place deep inside
him.

She heard him take a step closer. Still she couldn't look
at him.

"Please, Charlotte, let me talk to you."

"I told you at the courthouse that I don't want to hear
anything you have to say." Charlotte hoped her words were
stronger than they sounded. It wouldn't work out. She would
only be hurt again. She couldn't trust him. She was still
trying to get over the hurt from the last time. She couldn't
take any more of it. She looked out to the yard. "What are
you doing here, anyway? You're supposed to be going to
Chicago."

She pulled the book closer. She did want him to go away,
didn't she? She could live with her love for him but without
him, couldn't she? Couldn't she?

He sat in the chair across from her as if he never heard
her last words trying to make him leave. He acted as if
her words about Chicago were more important that any others she had said. He grabbed 'Chicago' like a drowning man
would snatch a life preserver. And that was what it was for
him. A life preserver.

"You've kept up with my tour?" Tyler's hope shoved his
despair aside. "Why, Charlotte? If you don't care about me,
why have you kept up with my tour?"

She didn't have an answer. Her words and the truth were

tangled up inside her and she couldn't separate them. She glanced at him. He leaned toward her and rested his elbows on his knees the way she remembered. She saw his hands tighten. Then his voice came out as strong as in her memories.

"I couldn't go to Chicago or anywhere else because I had to find you. I love you more than I thought possible. I can't leave you alone like you told me to because you're the part of me that's been missing for so long."

Charlotte made the mistake of looking at his face. His eyes looked old. Her heart twisted at the pain filling his eyes. Pain she had put there.

"I know I hurt you terribly. I'd give anything to undo the pain I caused you. I know I don't deserve it, but please give me a chance to show you how much I love you. I know it will take time, until you can trust me again, but I'll wait as long as you say, if you'll just tell me I have a chance. I'll spend the rest of my life proving my love and earning your trust."

Charlotte felt two damp lines racing down her cheeks. Blinking didn't stop them. She looked out at the yard. Then she looked at the porch floor. She looked anywhere but at this man begging her with his words, with his eyes, twisting her feelings loose from where they were hiding deep inside her and setting them free.

"If you . . ." Tyler stopped his words. The glass-topped wicker table rattled when he touched it. "I don't want to hurt you any more than I already have, so I'll leave."

Charlotte heard him take in a deep breath. Then his words, weaker and huskier, went on.

"If you decide you'll . . ." He stopped his words again before he let them go on. "If you'll let me see you again, here's a list of dates and phone numbers where I'll be. Please at least think about it. I hope you'll. . . ." He stopped yet again. "Please, Charlotte. Call me. Give me a chance."

Charlotte stared inside herself. *Is this what I want? Am*

*I so afraid of being hurt again that I'll let him go? Do I
want him to go away and leave me alone? Do I never want
to see him again?* Her life without him stretched empty before her. *Can I bear to live without his touch? How will I
fill this spot in my heart owned by him?*

"I guess that's all I can say." Tyler stood as if something
was trying to pull him back into the chair. "I won't bother
you any more, Cleo." He stood beside his chair for long
minutes before he turned to the steps.

"There is no Cleo." Charlotte stood. She wiped at her
eyes. "There never was."

"Yes, there was a Cleo." He turned to her, but he didn't
move closer. He let his gaze hold her for now, afraid that
if he moved to her he would unravel the threads trying to
fasten them together again. "That flesh-and-blood woman I
held in my arms was real. It was no imaginary woman I
made love with." He put his love into the words he sent
to her and hoped she would see it. She looked as if she
did. He went on.

"It wasn't a figment of my imagination that I awakened
with the delights and pleasures a man and a woman can
give each other. It was a woman I joined with the way only
a man and a woman can. Cleo or Charlotte, you're the same
person. You're the woman who entered my heart and took
it with you when I drove you away."

He dared to go toward her then. He moved slowly when
what he wanted more than anything at this moment was to
run to her. He had to give her the chance to move back
from him, if that was what she wanted. It would shred his
insides, but if that was what she wanted, he would make
himself accept it. He wouldn't cause her any more pain.

"Tyler, I . . ." She had to look at him. His words
wouldn't let her do anything else. "Tyler." Charlotte wiped
her eyes again, but that didn't stop more tears from coming.

"Don't. Please don't cry." He let himself go to her. "I
didn't mean to make you cry again." He wrapped his hands

around her shoulders. They had found their way home. "I swore I'd never hurt you again, and now look what I've done." He let a finger brush away a tear. His hand stayed on her face.

To Charlotte, his hands on her felt as right as they had the first time he had touched her. She looked into his eyes and was lost in the love shining there for her. She belonged with him.

She took a step to him and allowed his hands to pull her in closer. She shut her eyes and found her place in his arms, the place she had lost and never expected to find again. She put her head against his chest and heard the beat she thought was gone from her forever. His aftershave greeted her like a friend lost for too long.

His hands caressed her back. Her hands found his chest, glad to be home. Glad was the wrong word for how she felt. It wasn't powerful enough. No word could be. She lifted her face to him and his lips met hers. She was complete again.

"You don't know how many times I dreamed about this." Tyler brushed his lips across her forehead.

"Yes I do." Charlotte brushed her hands along the sides of his face. "I've had the same dreams." She felt a smile cover her face. It was the first real smile since she had left him.

"This is better than any dream. Don't you agree?" His lips traced a path down to her neck.

"Yes." Charlotte almost forgot the question.

"Let's make sure we don't have to depend on dreams." He kissed the side of her neck. "Okay?"

"Yes, Tyler." His mouth was making its way back to hers. She'd agree to anything right now, as long as he was there.

He eased her away from him, but held both of her hands.

"I can't lose you again. I couldn't take the hurt, although I know that's all I deserve. I want you with me for the rest of my life. I want to fall asleep with you in my arms every night and wake up with you beside me each morning."

He stared into her soft brown eyes that had captured him the first time he saw them. Love shone back at him. Was trust there, too? He took a deep breath. He, who never had trouble with words, was having a hard time finding the right ones now.

"Charlotte?"

"Yes?"

He swallowed hard.

"Don't say 'yes' until you hear the question." He hesitated. "But I still want you to answer 'yes.' I *need* for you to answer 'yes.' " He stared at her. "Okay?"

"What are you talking about?" Charlotte smiled.

"I want . . ." He shook his head. "That sounds selfish. As if I'm putting my wants ahead of yours. I don't want to do that. Not ever." He frowned. "I need . . ." He shook his head again. "That sounds selfish, too, doesn't it?"

"Tyler, what are you trying to say?" Charlotte slowly rubbed her hands up and down his arms.

"Marry me." He let out a deep breath. "Please marry me, Charlotte."

"I . . ." She pulled back. This was a big step.

"If you can't say yes, please don't say no. At least say you'll think about it. I know it's an important decision and you didn't expect me to show up here, let alone propose to you, but please don't . . ."

"Yes."

"What?"

Charlotte looked up into his face. He looked like he was steeling himself in case her answer was 'no.' She loved him even more then, if that was possible.

"I said yes, I will marry you, Tyler Fleming."

She brushed her hand down the side of his face and traced a finger along his jaw.

"Oh, Charlotte." Tyler pulled her against him and wrapped

her close to him, where she belonged. "You don't know how afraid I was that you'd send me away. I know that's all I deserve after the way I treated you, but I hoped you would forgive me."

"Tyler, let's not talk about that ever again. It's over."

"I think we need to discuss it and clear things up once and for all. But not now." His face relaxed into a smile. His voice wasn't as tense. "Now we have better things to discuss. When will you marry me? Can we get married today?"

"Tyler, what happened to the taking time and waiting?"

"It disappeared when you said 'yes.' Besides, we have our baby to think of. I want our baby to have two parents who love him. I want to share every new moment of your pregnancy with you. I don't want to ever leave you."

"It's going to take a bit longer than today before we get married. There is a waiting period, you know."

"We could fly to . . ."

"We won't fly anywhere." She caressed his face. "I won't change my mind, Tyler. I love you as much as you love me. I have from the start." She brought his hand to her mouth and kissed it. "And you will leave me because you have to share your music with others. That's why it was given to you."

"But . . ." Charlotte placed a finger gently against his lips.

"Shh, darling. We'll discuss that later, too." She lowered his hand and laced his fingers through hers. She led him to the glider. "Let's sit over here and you tell me your plans. The ones that aren't based on getting married today." Their hands were still connected as they sat down.

"All right, but my plans all involve you." Tyler squeezed her hand. "Are you well?" He let his hand ease to her middle.

"Yes." She held his hand in place. "Tyler, the baby isn't the reason you asked me to marry you, is it? Did you notice at the trial?"

"I planned to ask you to marry me ever since I realized I love you. But you were gone and I couldn't find you. The case was the only hope I had of ever seeing you again. That's the only reason I agreed to let my lawyer list you as a witness. I'm so sorry I put you through that."

He closed his eyes but not before Charlotte saw the mountain of pain piled there. She squeezed his hand and held it tightly as he went on.

"The only thing I noticed in the courtroom was how sad you looked. I was the one who made you feel that way. I didn't know about the baby until I saw you today." He turned her face to his. "But I'm happy about it. I can't tell you how happy it makes me. I hope you are, too. Maybe it will be a beautiful miniature of you." He kissed her.

"I was afraid the baby was all I would ever have of you." She kissed him. "But, no, it's not going to be a miniature me. Our baby is going to be a handsome Tyler, like his father." Charlotte sighed. "I'm afraid I'm going to wake up and find this is all a dream. I couldn't stand that. I couldn't stand the hurt of losing you again."

"This is no dream. I intend to spend the rest of my life proving how real my love for you is and trying to make up for the hurt I caused you in the past."

"I'll do the same. I . . ."

But Charlotte's last words were swallowed by Tyler's lips on hers, sealing their love and tying them together for the rest of their lives in a living dream of love.

Coming in August from Arabesque Books . . .

__THE BUSINESS OF LOVE by Angela Winters
1-58314-150-2   **$5.99US/$7.99CAN**

The heir to a hotel chain, Maya Woodson is determined to make her plan to go public a success—even is she *is* at odds with handsome Trajan Matthews, the investment expert who's overseeing the deal. But when a crime endangers the chain's future—and their careers—Maya and Trajan must discover what they cherish most . . . if they are to find a love-filled future.

__FIRST LOVE by Cheryl Faye
1-58314-117-0   **$5.99US/$7.99CAN**

When shy Lena Caldwell and Quincy Taylor strike up a friendship, it isn't long before a sweetly sensual fire is sparked. But as their attraction grows, Quincy's past mistakes inject doubt into their newfound romance and the two must confront their insecurities to find a love worth fighting for.

__SOULFUL SERENADE by Linda Hudson-Smith
1-58314-140-5   **$5.99US/$7.99CAN**

Hillary Houston has it all—personality, looks, talent, and now, sexy engineer Brandon Blair. But when Hillary is offered the chance to become a recording superstar, Brandon's threatened with the possibility of losing the woman of his dreams . . . unless he can find a way to keep her forever.

__ADMISSION OF LOVE by Niobia Bryant
1-58314-164-2   **$5.99US/$7.99CAN**

When supermodel Chloe Bolton settles down in her mother's rural South Carolina town, she is at instant odds with handsome, reserved Devon Jamison. But amid hidden hurt and unexpected romantic rivals, Devon and Chloe begin to discover what they both really desire—to gain the dream they want most and have always waited for . . .

Call toll free **1-888-345-BOOK** to order by phone or use this coupon to order by mail. *ALL BOOKS AVAILABLE AUGUST 1, 2000.*

Name _____

Address _____

City_____ State _____ Zip _____

Please send me the books I have checked above.

I am enclosing $_____
Plus postage and handling* $_____
Sales tax (in NY, TN, and DC) $_____
Total amount enclosed $_____

*Add $2.50 for the first book and $.50 for each additional book.

Send check or money order (no cash or CODs) to: **Arabesque Books, Dept. C.O., 850 Third Avenue, 16th Floor, New York, NY 10022**

Prices and numbers subject to change without notice.

All orders subject to availability.

Visit our website at **www.arabesquebooks.com**